THE SONG OF LOVE

Book of Love, Book Four

Meara Platt

Dragonblade Publishing, Inc. is an imprint of Kathryn Le Veque Novels, Inc.
P.O. Box 7968
La Verne CA 91750
ceo@dragonbladepublishing.com

Produced in the United States of America

First Edition November 2019
Print Edition

ARE YOU SIGNED UP FOR DRAGONBLADE'S BLOG?

You'll get the latest news and information on exclusive giveaways, exclusive excerpts, coming releases, sales, free books, cover reveals and more.

Check out our complete list of authors, too!

No spam, no junk. That's a promise!

Sign Up Here

www.dragonbladepublishing.com

Dearest Reader;

Thank you for your support of a small press. At Dragonblade Publishing, we strive to bring you the highest quality Historical Romance from the some of the best authors in the business. Without your support, there is no 'us', so we sincerely hope you adore these stories and find some new favorite authors along the way.

Happy Reading!

CEO, Dragonblade Publishing

Additional Dragonblade books by Author Meara Platt

The Book of Love Series
The Look of Love
The Touch of Love
The Taste of Love
The Song of Love
The Scent of Love
The Kiss of Love

Dark Gardens Series
Garden of Shadows
Garden of Light
Garden of Dragons
Garden of Destiny

The Farthingale Series
If You Wished For Me (A Novella)

*** Please visit Dragonblade's website for a full list of books and authors. Sign up for Dragonblade's blog for sneak peeks, interviews, and more: ***
www.dragonbladepublishing.com

To all whose hearts are filled
with the song of love

CHAPTER ONE

London, England
May 1820

ONE HOUR.
Romulus Brayden could not have been in his new townhouse on Chipping Way for more than an hour before the Chipping Way curse did him in. He'd heard about it. Had laughed it off. So, he had only himself to blame for being caught in his kitchen with the delectable Miss Violet Farthingale, both of them reeking of vinegar, and her gown unlaced.

"I can explain, Uncle John," Violet said as his neighbor, John Farthingale, and two of his brothers charged in on them while Violet sat on the lone kitchen stool, and Romulus knelt beside her, his hands too far up her legs to shrug off the appearance of impropriety.

"Blame it on the bees," Violet said with a huff as two more uninvited guests barged in. "Oh, good day, Lady Dayne. So nice to see you, Lady Withnall."

Lady Eloise Dayne resided at Number Five Chipping Way, and the Farthingales resided at Number Three. Romulus had just purchased the townhouse known as Number One, which was divided from the Farthingale home by a large, stone wall…obviously, not large enough.

Lady Dayne and the Farthingales had lived on this usually quiet street for years, but the ink was hardly dry on Romulus's new purchase. It was so new in fact, he had yet to have the elegant residence properly staffed or furnished. For this reason, he and Violet were found alone in his home.

Romulus knew he was done for. He removed his hands from Violet's legs and rose to stare down at the diminutive Lady Withnall, London's most prolific gossip, silently imploring her not to spread word of this completely innocent misunderstanding.

He supposed he ought to put on his shirt. Or help lace up Violet's gown now that they were gathering quite a crowd.

"What bees?" John Farthingale intoned, crossing his arms over his chest and looking at Romulus as though he wanted to kill him. He then turned his scowl on Violet, looking at her as though he was going to lock her in her bedchamber for the rest of her life.

Romulus moved to stand protectively beside Violet who appeared quite calm about this whole unhappy affair. His own heart was beating so hard and fast, it was about to burst. To make matters worse, he could not look at Violet in her state of undress without fireworks going off inside his body, and everyone but Violet seemed to know it.

"You see," she started, taking a deep breath that caused his eyes to bulge as they darted to the magnificent swell of her bosom. Her gown was unlaced—he could explain—exposing the creamy softness of her shoulders along with said magnificent swell of her bosom.

Avert your gaze, you arse.

But it was too late. He'd been caught looking by everyone presently standing in the kitchen. Again, everyone but Violet who took no notice of him as she pressed on with her explanation. "The children were playing with their slingshots in the garden, shooting rocks at the acorns in the oak tree. Well, they were pebbles, really. I was reading under the tree. You know, it was that book Poppy gave me."

Romulus glanced at the red-leather tome now innocently sitting on his kitchen table, the one Violet had used to smash his nose as she swung at a bee and then strike him in the jaw to swing at another bee. Her aim was execrable. He now sported a bruise to his jaw. Thankfully, his nose was not broken, although it had bled a little when that binding had caught his nostrils.

"I hadn't gotten very far into reading the book, a most interesting scientific exposition of–"

"Violet," Lady Dayne said gently, "you are getting off the topic."

"Oh, do forgive me. There's so much to get out all at once. Well, the children were shooting their pebbles, trying to knock off the acorns, but they hit the beehive instead. Oh, the bees were so angry."

She paused a moment to roll her eyes.

Who knew Violet had such beautiful eyes? Well, he supposed everyone did now that he'd crushed her spectacles beneath his boot after she'd accidentally knocked them to the ground while swatting at more bees.

Her eyes were violet.

Not just violet, but a vivid, sparkling violet.

Which explained why her parents had thought to name her...Violet.

"I was surrounded by the swarm, trying my best to avoid being stung." She stuck out her arms and craned her neck to expose its slender curve and the red welts covering her skin. "They got me everywhere. That's when Mr. Brayden came to my rescue. He covered me with his body and–"

"He did what?" her uncle Rupert said with a growl. He'd run in behind her Uncle John but had remained silent until now.

"He sheltered me and took the brunt of the bee stings." She turned to Romulus and smiled up at him. "You were brilliant. I cannot thank you enough for what you did. I was certain I was done for."

George Farthingale, Violet's other uncle, chuckled lightly. "I fear it is Mr. Brayden who is done for."

Romulus knew George fairly well. He was the doctor who had saved his brother's life. For this, Romulus would be eternally grateful to the man. Wasn't it George who had mentioned General Allworthy was selling his townhouse? Romulus had jumped at the chance to acquire it, for he'd just returned from his latest naval assignment and felt it was time to set down his own roots.

He'd be called into service again, no doubt.

The Royal Navy had no wish to lose him. He was a decorated sea captain. He was also four and twenty years of age and needed a place of his own.

"He tried to return me to our home, but the bees were a solid wall of anger amassed at our front gate." Violet turned to Lady Dayne. "We attempted to make a run for your home, but the bees blocked us there as well. Mr. Brayden picked me up and made a run for his house."

"He lifted you into his arms?" Lady Withnall asked.

Violet pursed her lips and nodded. "Well, yes. I stumbled, you see. So, he caught me up in his arms and carried me inside. Then we had to rush to close all the windows that he'd opened up only minutes before to air out his home." She glanced at Romulus again. "It does smell like General Allworthy's cigars."

"I know." He tried not to look at her lips, but they were quite extraordinary. Full and plump and heart-shaped. They were a deep, pinkish-red. The sort of color on a pair of lips that had been thoroughly kissed. Only no one had ever kissed Violet, that was quite obvious.

The girl had no experience with men.

Nor any understanding of them.

Which is why she must have been given that book by her sister. Violet had been rambling about it when he'd grabbed it out of her hands so she'd stop hitting him with it. The Book of Love it was called. She had only gotten a few chapters into it before the bees had struck, but she was already gushing about its scientific insights and muttering something about him making a perfect test frog.

What the hell was that about?

"The bee stings were beginning to burn. Mr. Brayden feared I would go into shock. So, he led me into his kitchen." She waved her hand to point out their surroundings. "He soaked a cloth with vinegar and began to rub it all over me."

Romulus groaned silently.

Could she not phrase that a little better? "I applied it to her arms and neck."

Violet nodded. "Then he had me roll down my stockings and–"

"He had you do what?" Her uncle John was still fuming.

"How else was he to get at my legs? He had his hands on them when you burst in. You know he did. He rubbed them down with vinegar. He did the same to my shoulders. I had to return the favor. I simply had to, Uncle John. He was going into shock. His eyes were bulging and his breaths became quite strained."

Lord help me.

She was describing his arousal.

And everyone but Violet knew it.

"I've read that bee stings can kill. I insisted he remove his shirt so I could apply the vinegar to his neck, shoulders, and back. That's what we were doing to each other when you all came in. I'm sorry if I alarmed you. I suppose I was shrieking quite a bit when the bees first attacked me. Is that what you heard? And brought all of you running in here? Were you following the sound of my screams? You needn't have worried. Mr. Brayden came to my rescue, and thanks to him, I am as you see me now."

Romulus ran a hand across the nape of his neck.

The girl certainly had a way with words.

And a lovely, lilting voice as she spoke. Not the cloying, feigned sweetness so often used by debutantes who sought to gain his notice.

No, Violet's voice was cheerful and pleasant as she blithely led him to the gallows. "Mr. Farthingale, if you will allow me an hour to wash and dress, I shall call upon you at your home."

John nodded. "We will await you in my study. Do you wish me to send word to your brother? I think he ought to join us."

"Yes, why not? I ought to tell him immediately anyway."

"Who is your brother?" Violet asked, still clutching her gown to her bosom to keep it from sliding off her body, for it remained unlaced and the sleeves were hanging precariously off her cream-soft shoulders.

"James is the Earl of Exmoor," he replied, trying to keep from choking up, for the difficulties his brother had experienced after coming home from Waterloo still tore at his heart. He would have given anything to spare his brother the pain he'd suffered.

Her gaze softened. "Oh, yes. Aunt Sophie told me about him. But what must you tell him so urgently?"

Romulus stared at her for the longest moment before clearing his throat and emitting a pained groan. "That I am about to be married."

CHAPTER TWO

"**Y**OU ARE TO be wed? Congratulations." Violet's eyes suddenly rounded in horror as the import of his words sank in. "Wait…you can't possibly mean…are you mad? Why in blazes would you wish to marry me?"

Violet realized the answer to her question the moment she'd asked it. Romulus Brayden did not wish to marry her or have anything to do with her. He was offering in order to preserve her reputation. "No! It is out of the question."

Everyone was staring at her.

"No," she repeated to make certain everyone had heard her refusal the first time.

Of course, they had. She could tell by their frowns and glowers.

Mr. Brayden's intense stare practically bore a hole through her. Oh, goodness! His eyes! A dark, smoldering green. The sort of eyes that would make a girl tingle with just a glance. She looked away, but still felt the heat of his gaze upon her.

"No?" Several voices said at once, or perhaps everyone was tossing the word back at her in disbelief.

Mr. Brayden knelt beside her. "Miss Farthingale, do you not understand? Your answer cannot be a rejection of my offer."

The man was big and muscled. In truth, he was daunting. It wasn't his fault he had an imposing presence. His shoulders were broad and the bulges of muscle and sinew in his upper arms appeared to be sculpted out of hardest marble. There was no mistaking he was nicely formed. Exquisitely formed, to be sure.

"Please, Miss Farthingale." There was a tenderness in his regard that simply melted her insides. He was quite handsome. Built like a warrior, taut and lean, and those glorious bulges rippled whenever he moved.

She cast him a reassuring smile. "Surely, you must realize I am turning you down for your sake. To accept your offer would be punishing you for your good deed. How is this fair?"

He raked a hand through the waves of his dark gold hair.

Goodness, even his hair was perfect. Mostly the color of honey, but with a few lighter blond strands shot throughout, no doubt the effect of exposure to the sun and salty sea air. His face was lightly tanned and had a few lines etched on it, just enough to give him character but not enough to make him look weathered.

He reached for her hand, the one not clutching her gown to hold it up. "I don't suppose this bargain is fair to either of us, but it must be done."

"That is nonsense. Everyone here understands the innocent reason for our...um, state of disarray. No harm occurred, and you did nothing untoward. Why can it not remain a secret among all of us?" She glanced at the five elders who were still frowning down at her. "It isn't a scandal unless word gets out."

She trusted her uncles and knew Lady Dayne would take this to her grave. But Eloise's diminutive companion was going to be a problem.

A big one.

Oh, dear.

"Lady Withnall...*please.*" She licked her lips, for they suddenly felt as cracked and dry as her throat. "Please don't ruin Mr. Brayden's life by leg-shackling him to me."

Lady Withnall pounded twice on the stone floor with her walking cane. "I'll strike a bargain with the pair of you."

"Anything," Violet said, eager for the chance to wriggle out of this embarrassing situation. Mostly, she was thinking of Mr. Brayden's future and his happiness.

His hand tightened on hers.

She glanced down, realizing he still held it. Their fingers were now entwined, and she was surprised by how natural and right it felt. She'd forgotten they were still holding on to each other. She smiled at him once more. "Whatever it is, we'll do it. Isn't that right, Mr. Brayden? For my part, I'll do anything to save you from having to marry me."

She turned back to Lady Withnall and took a calming breath in anticipation of the terms she would demand. "What must I do to fulfill your bargain?"

"Violet, my dear girl," she said, her hawk eyes darting between her and Mr. Brayden. "You shall have one week to work it out between the two of you."

Violet frowned. "I don't understand. It is worked out. As a gentleman, Mr. Brayden felt obligated to propose to me. I have refused him, thereby releasing him from said obligation. All is back to normal. We shall put this incident completely out of our minds and move on as though it never happened."

She wiggled her nose, for one of those bees had stung the tip, and she felt a light burning sensation where the unsightly bump was forming. "We'll have to give it a few days for these horrid welts to disappear. Once they do, we shall go on with our lives."

The little harridan tapped her cane to the floor once again. "But it did happen. No. We shall meet again in one week. At that time, I shall expect you to convince me that you can never love this man."

Violet turned to look at him.

Blessed saints, he was handsome.

She took a deep breath and let it out slowly.

He really ought to put on a shirt to cover that golden-tanned chest of his. It was quite impossible for her to concentrate. Indeed, she was feeling quite giddy. Perhaps she'd inhaled too much vinegar. Yes, that was the more likely explanation for these heady sensations. "Lady Withnall, look at him. I doubt any young lady is capable of resisting him."

She noticed the twitch of his lips and the amused arch of his eyebrow. Well, he was gloriously built. She wasn't going to deny the obvious. Just as obvious was the fact that he was honorable. He'd rescued her and had not hesitated in proposing to her to preserve her reputation. "It isn't me I'm concerned about."

"I haven't finished my terms, Violet. For you see, Mr. Brayden must also convince me that he can never fall in love with you."

"What? Really, this is too absurd." If her hand wasn't occupied holding up her gown, she would have done something quite unladylike. Lady Withnall, despite her age and diminutive size, deserved a good poke in the nose.

"So, I suggest the pair of you waste no time in getting to know each other. I shall come to visit Mr. Brayden at the end of the week. I think a tea party is in order, Mr. Brayden. Invite the Farthingales, for I'll tell you now, this incident will be an open secret." She turned to John Farthingale. "You'll tell Sophie," she said, referring to his wife. "She will tell your daughters. They'll tell their husbands."

Lady Withnall was right.

Violet was already planning to write to her sister, Poppy, asking for urgent advice. Farthingales did not keep secrets among the family. Were the Braydens as loose-lipped? If so, they were in trouble.

How large was his family?

Within days, over thirty people would know. Trusted family members, of course. But still, too many to keep this unfortunate encounter a secret.

Violet sighed. "So, we must spend each day together, and at the end of those seven days, must prove to you we are not a good match?

Is that all?"

"Yes, my dear. That is all...except..."

Mr. Brayden groaned. "Here it comes," he whispered in her ear.

"He must not kiss you."

Violet jumped to her feet. "That will never do. He must kiss me." In the next moment, she realized what she'd just blurted. She felt her cheeks suffuse with heat. Good heavens, why had she said such a thing? "I mean...once. He must kiss me, but only once." She glanced in dismay at the book Poppy had given her to read. It was all about love. She'd gotten only a few chapters into it. However, she'd read enough to know this particular experiment was too important to overlook.

Romulus Brayden simply *had* to kiss her.

She heard his light groan as he rose to stand beside her. He towered over her, really. Were all the Brayden men this big? And handsome?

He trained his attention on Lady Withnall, too busy hurling daggers at the woman to pay Violet any notice. "Ahem...Mr. Brayden."

"What?" He tore his gaze away from Lady Withnall and settled a stormy frown on her. But his expression immediately softened as Violet returned his stare.

She cast him a gentle smile. "I expect I'm going to like your kiss."

His lips twitched again.

Her uncles groaned, and she heard muttered whispers of *murder if he tries it.*

She ignored their ridiculous and misplaced protectiveness. "But I have no experience kissing men. I don't think you will enjoy mine nearly as much as I shall enjoy yours."

Her uncles renewed their whispers of *death if he tries it,* so she frowned at them before returning her attention to Mr. Brayden. "My point is, I believe we are safe. You'll be able to honestly state that you did not like it, and we shall never suit."

His amusement faded. "No one's ever kissed you?"

"Well, my parents have. My cousins." She motioned to her uncles. "My family has. But they don't count. I've never been kissed romantically. So, you see, you're—"

"Lady Withnall, you are pure evil," Mr. Brayden said to the tiny woman who barely reached to his navel.

Violet's eyes rounded in surprise. "Mr. Brayden! That is very rude of you." He wasn't wrong, merely rude. This woman had them trapped in a vise and was squeezing them unfairly. It was extortion, if one wanted to put a name to it. "I understand how you feel. But—"

"No, Miss Farthingale. You have no idea."

Now he was being rude to her.

He groaned and turned to don his shirt that was damp and reeked of vinegar. He didn't care and just stuck his head and arms through it and then turned away a moment to tuck it into his pants.

Oh, thank goodness. If she'd had to look at his magnificent chest a moment longer, she would have given in and accepted his proposal. She'd never seen such perfection.

A young lady could enjoy herself...

Which reminded her, she had to lace up her gown and cover her own shoulders. "Lady Dayne..."

Eloise understood her dilemma. "Gentlemen, leave us now. We'll escort Violet home in a moment."

Mr. Brayden turned to her as though he wished to say something more, then shook his head and grabbed his jacket and cravat. "I'll see you later, Miss Farthingale."

He'd already *seen* more than enough.

She knew he meant nothing by it, but her cheeks heated once again. "Yes...um...yes." *Well, that was clever.*

She watched the men stride out of the kitchen, then adjusted her gown so that Eloise could lace it up for her. Lady Withnall did not take her eyes off her for a moment. "You are being most unfair to Mr.

Brayden," Violet said, returning Lady Withnall's stare. "Won't you reconsider?"

She simply tapped her cane again and sauntered off.

"Oh, Eloise. What am I to do? Can you not speak to your friend? Talk sense into her."

"I wish I could, my dear. But there is no talking to her when she gets that look about her. Perhaps she'll mellow in a few days and listen to reason."

Violet emitted a breath of relief. "That would be wonderful. Do you think so?"

"No, my dear. Unfortunately, she seems quite set in her decision."

Violet slumped her shoulders. "This is terrible. What am I to do?"

Eloise cast her a grandmotherly smile. "He is handsome, you must admit. Why don't you take the week to get to know him?"

"I don't have much choice in the matter, do I?" She glanced at the red leather tome perched on the kitchen table. "I will not allow Lady Withnall to interfere with the course of my life, but Mr. Brayden may prove useful in educating me about men. One can read about them, but it isn't quite the same thing as first-hand knowledge, is it?"

Eloise's eyes rounded in obvious alarm. "Violet, you do not know what you are saying."

What had she said that was so shocking? "I am quite aware of the importance of maintaining my reputation. It is Lady Withnall who seems determined to shred it, not me." She picked up the book and held it up to Eloise. "My sister claims it is a brilliant scientific explanation of the course of true love. She suggests I test its theories on someone safe. Who better than Mr. Brayden?"

Eloise shook her head. "Oh, dear me."

"We're thrown together for the rest of this week anyway. It is obvious he's a gentleman. So, where's the harm in seeing how he responds to some of these ideas? I plan nothing wicked or immoral, I assure you."

Yet Eloise appeared unconvinced, her kind eyes wide and filled with amused concern. "Violet, I think I had better chaperone the two of you."

"I'm sure it isn't necessary. I doubt we'll be left alone long enough for matters to get out of hand. My family will make certain of it."

"Well, don't try anything on him before you talk to me about it first. Goodness, you Farthingale girls are never dull. No, indeed. The London theaters are nothing to the entertainment you've provided. Better than any Covent Garden comedy."

Violet felt none of Lady Dayne's cheer. "It is more of a tragedy. Why would your friend insist on taking the choice away from us? It is our lives and happiness at stake. If word leaks out, that will be the end of my debut season. No man will come near me except for the dishonorable ones, and I'll have nothing to do with them. More important, Mr. Brayden will insist on marrying me. It isn't fair to him."

Eloise finished lacing her up and turned her so that they faced each other. "Violet, have you not noticed?"

She tipped her head in confusion. "Not noticed what?"

"Mr. Brayden has not uttered a word of complaint about his *punishment*. He has gone along with Lady Withnall's demands without a fuss. Indeed, it seems to me he does not seem to mind nearly as much as you do."

Violet was surprised by the remark. "What are you suggesting? That he wants to marry me?"

"Yes, and why not? You are a lovely girl."

"How could he tell beneath all the bee stings?" She shook her head and glanced down at the book in her hands. "We don't know each other at all. I could not have made a less favorable impression. But if Lady Withnall will not relent and matters come to a head, then I had better read The Book of Love cover to cover. If we are trapped in an unwanted marriage, we'll need to come to an understanding."

"Oh, my dear. I hope you find much more than that."

14

She sighed. "I hope so, too. Poppy insists this book holds the secret to making a man fall in love."

Eloise patted her lightly on the hand. "Do you believe it does?"

Violet sighed again. "No, but I lose nothing by testing out its lessons on Mr. Brayden. I think I had better attend to it immediately. I wouldn't feel so badly if he loved me. But Eloise, you know far more about men than I do."

"Yes, my dear. I suppose I do."

"Is it possible for him to fall in love with me in only one week?"

CHAPTER THREE

V IOLET HAD BEEN sent by her parents to reside with her Uncle John and Aunt Sophie on Chipping Way during her come-out season. They had generously agreed to sponsor her, and she now felt terrible all their efforts would go to waste if scandal broke out. Not that Farthingales were strangers to scandal. Had any of John and Sophie's daughters enjoyed a traditional courtship?

The answer to that was a resounding no.

Her cousin Lily had been abducted and the Royal Society gone up in flames quite spectacularly during her courtship. Still, her husband Ewan Cameron and his dog Jasper, managed to fall in love with her when lesser men...and dogs...might have run away as fast as their legs would carry them.

"Aunt Sophie, once Mr. Brayden and his brother arrive, how long do you think they will be huddled in Uncle John's study?" Violet had just come downstairs to join her aunt in the parlor while they awaited the arrival of Romulus Brayden and his brother.

James Brayden happened to be the Earl of Exmoor.

Perfect, not even through her first season and she'd already made an enemy of an earl. She deserved his anger, but hoped he would not direct it at her aunt and uncle as well. They were entirely innocent in this sad affair.

Hoping to make herself presentable, she had tried her best to wash the stench of vinegar off her body, using an oatmeal soap known for its soothing properties on the skin as well as for its mild scent. Afterward, she had donned a fresh gown, a pale lavender silk that was perhaps too formal for a quiet afternoon's entertaining, but this was no ordinary afternoon.

Despite having been offered a seat on one of the delicate, blue silk-covered settees, she chose to remain standing by the doorway, her ears straining to hear the sound of Mr. Brayden's voice at the front door. Or should she think of him as Captain Brayden? Perhaps Commander Brayden since she knew he had command of one of the ships in the Royal Navy fleet.

This was the problem. He was quite accomplished despite his relatively young age.

She had been sheltered all of her life and was not accomplished in anything.

There was nothing in the least remarkable about her, other than her singing voice. But that accounted for very little. She wasn't the only debutante who could warble like a nightingale. And what practical use was it? Most men did not care if their wives could sing.

Indeed, while women seemed to enjoy evening musicales, most men detested them and would strain for any reason to beg out of attending. She knew this first hand from the Farthingale men who constantly came up with excuses *not* to sit for hours listening to the dulcet tones of their daughters or nieces.

"Do sit down, Violet. Fretting will not make Mr. Brayden arrive any sooner," her elderly, and very crusty Aunt Hortensia grumbled as she entered the parlor and settled her ample frame in one of the matching blue chairs beside the settee. No doubt, Hortensia wanted to be perfectly positioned to watch the explosion of fireworks when the Braydens arrived. "Nor will it make your predicament disappear."

"I know." Still, she remained standing by the door, trying to ignore her aunt's disapproving gaze.

Hortensia meant well, but she sometimes had such a sour disposition, it was not at all pleasant to be around her. Violet loved her, of course. But did everyone have to pass comment on her situation? It was unnecessary and not in the least helpful.

She did not need Hortensia's prophecies of doom and gloom just now and was considering how to politely tell her to mind her own business when the Braydens arrived.

Violet clasped her hands and took a deep breath, forgetting her aunt for the moment since the intractable family elder was firmly planted in her wing chair. All Hortensia lacked was a box of marzipan or chocolates to munch on while the fireworks went off around her.

Violet expected a running commentary from her, too. Farthingales were known for their meddling. It is what they did best.

To her surprise, Lord Exmoor had brought along his wife, so that Mr. Brayden arrived with both of them. Well, perhaps not so surprising. Lord Exmoor, being the ever dutiful and protective brother, must have asked his wife to join them in order to find out more about this interloper who had tricked Romulus into marriage.

Lady Exmoor was several years older than Violet, but hardly matronly. Indeed, she looked young, and upon quick inspection, Violet decided she was beautiful in a warm, approachable way. She had a sparkling smile and obviously knew the Farthingale family quite well.

She and Aunt Sophie greeted each other as longtime friends, kissing each other on the cheek and exchanging "Good afternoon, Sophie," for they were both named Sophie, to add to Violet's confusion.

Lady Exmoor greeted Hortensia more formally because her prickly manner required it. Only then did she turn to Violet and cast her a warm, welcoming smile. "There seems never to be a dull moment on Chipping Way or in the Farthingale household. And now you and Romulus have collided. I wish I had been there to see it."

Violet sighed. "They are hanging him out to dry because of his good deed. It isn't fair."

"Life is never fair," Hortensia intoned before anyone had the chance to utter a more cheerful response.

Violet held her comments while the Farthingale butler, Pruitt, rolled in the tea cart and set out the pot, cups, and cakes. Those lovely looking cakes had been elegantly placed on display on a tiered plate.

When Pruitt left, Lady Exmoor took a seat beside Violet on the settee and gave her hand a comforting pat. "Romulus is no milksop. He'll fight for himself, assuming he really wishes to. He is a naval captain, after all, and no stranger to fierce battles. He's been fighting the savage pirates who prowl off the coast of Cornwall and Wales for several years now. Made quite a name for himself. James," she said, referring to her husband the earl, "is very proud of him."

Violet glanced at the study door. The men had been in there only a few minutes.

Lady Exmoor followed her gaze. "They're discussing the betrothal terms. I'm sure there is a lot to review. I doubt they will come out to join us any time soon. Another hour, I should think. What do you suppose, Sophie?"

Aunt Sophie tried to appear calm, but Violet knew she was also fretting, for her gaze was constantly darting to the study door, and she was nibbling her lip. "Oh, yes. At least one hour."

Lady Exmoor seemed far more relaxed. Indeed, she was still smiling.

Hortensia was frowning, but she always frowned, so that was no indication of anything.

"James and Romulus are honorable to the point of making one want to scream," Lady Exmoor remarked, casually sipping her tea. "There will be little argument, for they won't quibble about anything. You will be well provided for, Violet. Whatever your uncle demands, they'll accede to it."

Violet's heart sank, for not only had she trapped Mr. Brayden in an unwanted marriage, but her family was going to bleed him dry. "Lady

Exmoor, this does not make me feel better."

"I knew I'd like you. You are worried for Romulus and wish to protect him. Have you seen the size of him? He is quite capable of protecting himself." She laughed lightly. "Of course, you've taken notice of him. He's quite handsome, isn't he?"

Violet grimaced but nodded. "Yes, very."

"Ah, an honest answer. I fear it is so rare these days to find that trait among those in Society, especially when the season is at its height. Mothers will lie, cheat, and steal to trap a worthy bachelor. What is the expression? All is fair in love and war. But it should not be so. No man wants to marry a woman he cannot trust. Lies and trickery are never acceptable. He will value your honesty."

Violet stared down at her plate, wishing she could go back to sleep and pretend this day had never happened. "I don't know about that. I'm sure he feels he's been tricked. It was never my intention. I only meant to save myself from the bees."

"I know, my dear. Romulus was quite clear on that point. He does not blame you at all." She patted Violet's hand again. "I look forward to getting to know you. I'm sure we shall become fast friends."

"Thank you, Lady Exmoor." She sincerely meant it, for the woman was kind and amiable. Despite her gentle appearance, she obviously had the spine to hold her ground when dealing with her husband.

Violet admired her for that.

She'd noticed James Brayden, Earl of Exmoor, when they'd all walked in. He was as big as Romulus. But he was not nearly as handsome, for his face was badly scarred. At first glance, Violet had thought him quite frightening. However, she quickly looked beyond those scars and saw how much he loved his wife and the goodness inside of him. "I hope we do become friends, whether or not I marry your brother-in-law."

Hortensia sighed. "Resign yourself to it, Violet. You and Mr. Brayden shall marry. The sooner you accept it, the easier it will go for you."

Aunt Sophie frowned. "I hate to agree with Hortensia in this matter. If Lady Withnall spreads gossip about what she saw, you will never recover from it. I'll do my best to make her see reason. We Farthingales marry for love, and it isn't fair to deprive you of the chance."

"Thank you, Aunt Sophie." She stared at the ginger cake set on her plate but had no appetite for it just now.

Her aunt nodded. "Meanwhile, clear your head of these worries and simply take the time to get to know Romulus. Perhaps your hearts will lead you to each other. This would be the happiest outcome. I shall remain ever optimistic. After all, look at the chaos my daughters caused during their debut seasons, and they came out of it all right."

Violet was heartened by that. Lily's courtship wasn't the only one botched, and yet she and Ewan were now blissfully happy. Her cousin Rose had abducted her best friend's brother who later had the good sense to marry her. Laurel met her husband when she practically trampled him to death with her beast of a horse. Fortunately, Graelem had merely suffered a broken leg. Daffodil had almost killed her husband by shooting off an elephant gun. That was most frightening of all, for no one wanted a dead duke on their doorstep. Hard to explain that one away. Daisy had saved her husband from certain death when he'd almost sailed into a trap laid by Napoleon's spies.

Bees were nothing.

Violet sighed and raised the teacup to her lips. "Lady Exmoor, what else can you tell me about your brother-in-law?"

"What does it matter, Violet? He took off your clothes," Hortensia interjected before Lady Exmoor had the chance to respond. "No matter who or what he is, you are marrying him."

Violet choked on her tea, but covered it up with a small cough and a dab of her lips with her table linen. "He unlaced my gown, that is all. It is not the same thing as taking it off. As for marrying him, that remains to be seen."

She was doomed if her own family insisted on overlooking the innocent facts.

Lady Exmoor took a sip of her tea before responding to Violet's question. "Well, as you have no doubt guessed, Romulus is honest, fiercely loyal, and quite protective. All these Brayden men are."

Hortensia sniffed the air. "What is that odd scent?"

Violet groaned softly, realizing she still reeked of pickling brine. "Do you mean the oatmeal soap I scrubbed myself with? Or the lingering scent of vinegar? Mr. Brayden claimed it was an antidote to the venom from the bee stings. The welts are still all over my face, neck, and limbs, but the venom is no longer burning me. I didn't think to ask him how he is feeling. I hope he is not suffering from his stings."

"He hasn't complained," Lady Exmoor assured her. "He was more concerned about you."

The men came out of the study a short while later. They were five men in all. The two Braydens and her three uncles, John, George, and Rupert. She called them uncles, but they were really her father's cousins. Still, in this large family, it was easier to simply refer to the older men as uncles and the women as aunts.

If one attempted to delve deeper into the family connections, it would all be too confusing.

John Farthingale was the eldest, and this was his home. He was the patriarch, but everyone knew his wife Sophie was the heart and soul of the family and their comfortable home. George was a renowned doctor. He'd taken her aside before she'd gone upstairs to wash and dress in order to examine her and make certain the bee stings were nothing more serious. For some people, even one sting could be deadly. She'd suffered at least twenty, and Mr. Brayden probably more.

Rupert was the negotiator of the family, responsible for their contracts and finding new materials, the Italian velvets, muslins, satins, exotic sarcenet silks, to introduce into the family's thriving mercantile business. It was likely he led these betrothal negotiations.

Romulus marched straight toward her and offered his arm. "Take a walk in the garden with me, Violet. We'll stay in sight of the house, if you are concerned."

She readily accepted, eager to be away from all these prying eyes. "Do you think the bees have gone?"

He ran a hand through his hair. "I think so. We should be safe enough. With their hive knocked down, they've probably moved off to find another garden and another tree in which to rebuild their honeycomb."

She nodded. "I'm eager to hear what went on in the study. Will you tell me what you gentlemen discussed?"

"Yes, I don't want the financial arrangements to be kept from you."

Once Violet had grabbed her shawl, Romulus led her outdoors to a wooden bench beside the stone wall that separated their homes. She sat while Romulus remained standing next to her with his foot on the bench. He propped an arm on his bended knee and leaned toward her. "We are betrothed now," he said, stating it as a matter of fact. "The contracts will be drawn up in the next few days, and your uncle and I shall sign them at the end of the week."

She tucked her shawl around her shoulders as a soft, May breeze blew cool air through the garden. The sun was shining, and a few birds were chirping in the trees, but thankfully, Violet heard no buzzing. It was as Mr. Brayden had said, the bee swarm had flown off to make a new hive. "Hopefully, Lady Withnall will change her mind before then."

His expression turned grim. "She won't."

"Nevertheless, we ought to keep our betrothal as quiet as possible on the chance she does. What would she gain by telling the world what she saw?"

He shrugged. "The satisfaction of striking terror in the hearts of all in the *ton* who have sinned. I suppose that would be just about everyone. Not even the best people are always saints."

"Well, nobody knows me in London other than my family. I am not a wealthy heiress and my father is no one important. The news will be met with a big yawn."

He arched an eyebrow. "We shall see what happens by the end of the week. For now, I intend to see this through."

He had that implacable look again, so she nodded. "Mr. Brayden, what are your thoughts on our next step? Since we are obliged to see each other anyway, I was hoping we might spend some time testing out the advice in The Book of Love. But we don't have to if you're opposed to the idea."

"Not at all. It could be useful." He cast her a wry smile. "I've never been in love before. I'd be curious to know what it entails."

She nodded, relieved he was being so reasonable. "Poppy, she's my sister and now married to the Earl of Welles, insisted I read it before I started my round of balls and soirees. She and her friends, Olivia and Penelope, claim it is magical." She shook her head and laughed. "We'll certainly need a bit of magic to get ourselves out of this fix."

Although the way Romulus was looking at her just now, he did not seem to be in any particular hurry to extricate himself from their betrothal. There was something utterly devastating about his gaze, a mix of tender and steaming. She quite liked the way he was looking at her.

This man would melt her insides if she weren't careful.

He made her feel beautiful, but she couldn't possibly be. Not with bright pink welts on her nose, chin, and all along her neck and shoulders. And her scent. Good grief! Even though she'd rubbed herself down with oatmeal soap, she had been unable to completely rid herself of the vinegar odor.

She was hardly alluring.

He had welts all over his body, but his clothes now covered those. He did not seem to have any on his face. It was unmarred and strikingly handsome.

"Mr. Brayden–"

"Romulus will do."

"Romulus...um, forgive me. Really? That sounds quite intimate. Would you prefer if I call you Captain Brayden? Or Commander Brayden?"

His smile was also devastating. "Romulus, now that we are betrothed. I know you are not pleased by the idea. Think of it as merely being friendly, for I hope that is what we shall be. Friends, at the very least. Save Captain Brayden or Mr. Brayden for when we are in company. As for me, I prefer the informality. Violet is a pretty name. It suits you."

She laughed. "My eyes. I know. My parents dressed me in violet clothes, decorated my bedchamber in shades of violet. All my life, everywhere I've turned, there was something violet."

"Ah, then I shall hold off on my suggestion."

She tipped her head, curious as to what he meant.

"I was going to offer to redecorate one of the bedchambers in my house to suit your tastes. I had thought to have it done in shades of purple, but I see now you would prefer something completely different for your quarters."

"My quarters?" Was he suggesting they would not share a bedchamber if they married? "Mr. Brayden–"

"Romulus."

She sighed. "Romulus, this may sound quite forward..."

"You may tell me whatever is on your mind. Why are you frowning?"

"I did not realize I was." She clasped her hands together, hoping to appear composed, but her blush probably gave her away. Her face tended to turn a bright, strawberry red when she was embarrassed…which she was now. "I hadn't thought about sleeping arrangements if we were to marry."

"I'm sure there's lots we ought to be thinking about. We'll have the week to figure it all out."

"I don't need a week for this. You see, Farthingales make love matches…"

"And?" He arched an eyebrow, appearing quite wicked and taking unnecessary delight in her discomfort. "Violet, you will cut off the circulation in your fingers if you grip them any tighter."

She looked up at him in dismay. "The thing of it is…it doesn't seem right…that is, what is the advantage to having separate sleeping quarters near each other? Is there any?"

"Oh, I see. You prefer privacy. I can set you up at the opposite end of the hall, if that is what you wish. I just thought…never mind."

Her heart sank. She wasn't getting her point across at all. "What if I wish for other arrangements?"

His eyes rounded and then his gaze turned wary. "Do you mean you would not wish us to reside under the same roof?"

"Oh, no. I should hope we do live together."

"But not near each other and not at separate ends of the hall? I'm not certain I understand your question. Do you wish to be close or far?"

"Close."

He nodded. "Our rooms will adjoin, if you like. You won't need to walk into the hall to enter my chamber. I won't put a lock on the door between our rooms. You may enter whenever you wish. Or if you prefer a lock, I can have one put in."

She shook her head. "But that is the problem. The chamber is yours."

He ran a hand through his hair, now looking more confused than ever. "And you will have yours. As I said, right next to mine, if you wish. Or at the opposite end of the hall. The choice is yours. And you may decorate it any color you choose."

She took a deep breath. "Is there any reason why we cannot share a bedchamber?"

His entire body tensed, and he appeared to have stopped breathing. "Share?"

"Yes." She thought she was being clear on this point, but he was frowning and shaking his head as though still confused. "This is done in my family," she continued, realizing it was best simply to make the demand. The worst he could do was refuse. "Farthingale husbands and wives share sleeping quarters...they share a bed."

She thought she heard him choking.

He cast her such a puzzled look, she couldn't tell whether he was about to burst out laughing or give her a blistering lecture. "Are you saying you wish to share my bed?"

How many times had she mentioned the word 'share' already? Did she have to hit him over the head with the suggestion? And how had they gotten on this intimate conversation? Oh, she supposed she'd brought it up. As Lady Exmoor said, better to be honest. "Yes. *Share.* Unless you'd rather not." She looked up at him. "I don't know about such matters. I just thought... Well, because this is what my family does. This is how they've always..." Her voice trailed off. She wasn't going to say it aloud. What would he think of her if she just blurted that she wanted to sleep with him?

"Violet..." Now he was laughing at her.

She rose. "Obviously, I should not have brought it up."

He took hold of her hand and would not release it when she tried to walk to the house. More like run back inside, if he would let her. "You mistake me," he said, obviously holding back a burst of laughter. "I think it is an excellent idea."

"You do?" It was her turn to be wary, for she feared he was about to mock her.

"I'm glad you raised it. We shall do as you suggest." He nodded.

"It is settled. No separate bedchambers. You'll share my bed."

"Oh, thank you."

"Sweet mercy, you don't have to thank me." Was he sweating? It wasn't all that warm. Although she was starting to feel a little uncomfortable under the intensity of his gaze. She eased her hand out of his grasp and hugged her shawl a little tighter about her shoulders as a hot shiver coursed through her. It made little sense. One shivered when one was cold.

Apparently, not always.

She could use a fan about now.

Her insides felt quite hot.

The burning look in his eyes was setting her on fire. "Any other demands, Violet?"

CHAPTER FOUR

"I DON'T KNOW, Mr. Brayden…er, Romulus. I might have other demands. Not really demands, merely requests. Must I list them right away? There may be more, but I'm new to this betrothal business. I hadn't expected to be dealing with it so soon."

Romulus knew he wasn't being fair, but there was something wonderful about Violet, and he just liked being in her company and hearing her talk. She was being far more reasonable than he deserved. Yes, he'd come to her rescue, his first thought being to pull her out of harm's way from that swarm of bees. But his second, third, and fourth thoughts once he'd gotten her into his kitchen and started unlacing her gown?

Lord help him! All he could think then was how fast could he get the gown off her exquisite body and begin exploring every delectable inch of her with his hands, lips, and…yes, he was going straight to hell for this…with his tongue.

He wanted to touch and taste her everywhere.

He wanted to hear her soft, breathy, responsive moans.

Lady Withnall knew exactly what he'd been thinking, and the harridan was not going to let him get away with his sinfully evil desires without making him pay for it. So, while everyone else was willing to sweep his bad behavior under the rug and breathe a sigh of relief for avoiding the close call, the old, gossiping bat was determined to air it out for all the world to see just how lecherous and depraved he truly was.

But he wasn't, or rather, he had never been before. This wasn't at all in his nature. Perhaps it was all those bee stings that had made him daft. Perhaps it was just Violet. There was an undefinably appealing quality about her. He couldn't explain what it was, only that she stirred him as no other woman ever had.

She was soft to the touch and spectacular to look at, but the same could be said of other *ton* beauties. Even her voice did odd things to him, as though she spoke to something deep within his soul.

How silly that sounded, but he would not deny her sultry lilt affected him. He was like one of those hapless heroes in myth, lured toward the rocky shoals by her siren call.

Gad, even her innocence was alluring.

Not to mention her perfect breasts or the perfect way they'd been heaving as he'd unlaced her.

No, he wouldn't mention it.

He would blot it from his memory…if only he could.

"I'll have to ask Aunt Sophie about what else I might need. Not that sleeping with you is a…" *Oh, heavens.* "…need." Her sigh came out more as a groan. "What terms did you agree upon with my uncle?"

"Financial terms only," he said, nudging her back down on the bench and settling beside her even though he knew it was a mistake, for everything about this girl set him on fire. "We did not think to discuss sleeping arrangements."

"Oh, thank goodness." She was blushing again.

He wanted to kiss her, but Lady Withnall would have his hide if he did it now. "We agreed upon your allowance and your inheritance rights should anything happen to me."

She fidgeted with her shawl as she gazed up at him, obviously feeling uncomfortable and blaming herself for their predicament. "It sounds awfully mercenary. I am truly sorry. You know I wish this had never happened."

"I know. It isn't your fault." He stretched his legs in front of him. Although it was a long bench, it suddenly seemed small for the two of them. He was big, and she was this delicious morsel seated beside him and unknowingly shooting flames through his body. "Your uncle is right to worry about your future. I have no doubt James will always look after you if something were to happen to me, but you are my responsibility now, and I do not intend to leave you penniless."

"You hardly need worry about that. My family will never abandon me."

He was not pleased by her desire to impose on him as little as possible. He'd been caught behaving badly, fair and square. He thought he'd feel angry or frustrated, but couldn't seem to rouse even a dollop of indignation.

He was beginning to think of himself as fortunate. He'd known Violet only a few hours, but he liked her very much already. Not just her body that had him convulsed in a shark-like frenzy every time he looked at her. But if he thought of the entirety of *her*, she was amiable, caring, and probably quite intelligent, in addition to being beautiful.

He already knew she was nothing like the spoiled, pampered diamonds of the *ton* who were often paraded in front of him at those mind-numbing balls and supper parties. Nothing warmed a man's heart more than knowing he'd been thoroughly investigated and the woman being introduced to him already knew the size of his purse and how much gold he had in his teeth.

Violet was quite possibly the one, true diamond among these supposed gems.

"I see no reason to make myself an obligation to you," she said, interrupting his musings. "I am quite capable of remaining independent. You need not fear, I shall not be left destitute if you fail to provide for me. If we must marry, I have no intention of becoming a clinging vine."

But she would sleep in his bed?

Allow him to claim his husbandly rights?

He sighed and ran a hand through his hair once more. "Neither of us is used to this betrothal business. I did not mean to insult you or your family. I just wanted you to know that I will not shirk in my duty to you. I will take care of you, no matter what your family chooses to provide for you."

She frowned.

"Violet, why are you not happy about this?"

"I don't know exactly," she admitted. "You're offering me everything. I don't wish to seem ungrateful, but I can't help feel that it is all to my advantage."

"I gain from it, too. A beautiful, caring wife. I could do a lot worse for myself."

"But don't you think something is missing?"

He leaned back and extended his arms across the back of the bench. "What do you feel is missing?"

"I haven't worked it out yet. This marriage business doesn't sit well with me. Perhaps I'll understand it better once I've finished reading The Book of Love."

"Ah, yes. That book." He closed his eyes and leaned his face toward the sun. Just what he needed, some ancient, dead author's advice on how to satisfy one's wife. *Blessed saints.* Was this book about the erotic acts of sex?

His eyes shot open, and he stared at Violet.

She returned his gaze. Smiling. Unruffled.

No, this book could not be about *that.* Could it?

The girl would not be looking at him with the innocent calm of a churchyard angel if it were. And Lord help him if it was all about the naked positions he could get into with Violet. He'd be dead by Sunday, his heart exploded and his male parts shriveled from wear.

No, the book had to be about finding romantic happiness with one's wife. Or one's husband, for her part. He wanted to dismiss those ridiculous notions of abiding love and contentment out of hand. But in truth, it was exactly what he needed, wasn't it? "Let's go over the book tomorrow. How about we meet right here after lunch?"

"All right. But I could meet you earlier if you prefer."

"No, I'll be interviewing staff and supervising some furniture deliveries tomorrow morning. Oh, and I owe you a new pair of spectacles since I crushed yours under my boot."

"I'll get the spectacles." She chuckled lightly. "It isn't a rush. My eyesight isn't all that bad I use them mostly to chase men away."

He regarded her with some surprise. "Why would you want to do that? Aren't you here to find yourself a husband?"

She nodded. "But I'd rather do it at my own pace. I was looking forward to spending this first year as…" She cleared her throat. "As an impossibly hopeless wallflower."

He laughed. "Violet, a man would have to be as dead as a door-knocker to overlook your beauty. You can't hide it. Even if you tried, it wouldn't work. If I may be honest with you, men don't always look at a girl's face first. Your body is not something you can easily hide from a man's discerning eye."

He worried that he might have been too crude and insulting, but her eyes lit up. "That is amazing! This is exactly what the author of The Book of Love suggests. Did you know that a man's brain functions differently than a woman's brain?"

Romulus grinned at her. "No, I did not. But it doesn't surprise me. How are they different?"

Her eyes were sparkling, and her smile was entrancing. Lord, he could wake up to Violet each morning once they were married. Did that little termagant, Phoebe Withnall, know this when she gave them a week to sort themselves out? He'd wanted to throttle her two hours ago, but it could be that he ought to be kissing her in gratitude.

Of course, he'd much rather be kissing Violet's rosebud lips. He shook out of the thought and concentrated on Violet's words as she began to explain the difference between men and women. Bless those differences.

Bless her lightly heaving, perfect chest.

"A man's brain functions on two levels, the low brain and the high." She glanced up at him, looking rather pleased with herself.

Ah, yes. Low brain function. When it came to Violet, his thoughts were surprisingly dug deep in that low ditch. But he schooled his expression, allowing nothing more than the arch of his eyebrow. "What does that mean?"

Her cheeks now had a soft pink stain on them. "The author suggests that a man first assesses a woman's body to determine whether or not she's healthy enough to bear his offspring. This is an important part of his low brain function. But I think I ought to leave the rest of the explanation for tomorrow when we discuss the book in greater detail. I'm sure we'll find it very helpful."

"It sounds intriguing. Even a little horrifying."

"It is quite scientific." She nodded with enthusiasm. "You mentioned you were going to interview staff tomorrow. May I help?"

"Yes, if you'd like."

She emitted a light breath. "Yes, I would. Very much."

He smiled, actually looking forward to her company as he went about this task. "The first scheduled appointment is for ten o'clock in the morning. Is that too early for you?"

"Not at all. I'm usually up with the sunrise. These late town hours are not for me. I'll be ready and will come over at ten."

"Bring your maid with you."

"Oh, do you wish for her opinion as well?"

He chuckled. "No, I wish for a chaperone for you. I don't think Lady Dayne will be up and about that early. We're in enough of a mess as it is. If Lady Withnall, that old gossip, suddenly grows a heart and decides to keep our bee escapade a secret, I don't wish us to create another scandal that will be impossible to overlook."

"Of course. I should have thought of that. I can ask my Aunt Sophie to join us. She has lots of experience in matters of staffing one's household. There is constant turnover in the house, although it is mostly nannies. Our cook, Mrs. Mayhew, has been with my aunt and uncle forever. Her brother, Abner Mayhew, is our coachman, and her son, Amos, is our groom. He is very good with horses. By the way, so is my cousin Laurel. Let me know if you need a horse. She'll help you choose the finest."

"I will. Thank you."

She smiled, nodded, and continued. "Pruitt is our butler. He's also been with the family forever. Since before I was born. I could also ask the Mayhews and Pruitt if they have friends or family in service they might recommend."

"That would be helpful. I much prefer their references than those of some lofty toff who knows nothing about what it takes to keep his household running smoothly. Leave it to a servant to understand their duties best or to sense whether an applicant will be suitable or not. Trust is most important to me. Discretion, loyalty, competence."

"And a cheerful attitude."

He nodded. "If you say so."

"I do. There is nothing more depressing than a dour countenance. Although I would allow it in a head butler. He must appear a little daunting. Pruitt is perfect in this way, fearsome on the outside, but on the inside, he is the soul of kindness."

"Then I shall look for someone like Pruitt when I choose my head butler." He rather liked the idea of Violet helping him out. After all, this would be her home as well. He wasn't merely indulging her to be kind.

But she was nibbling her lip.

Something was still troubling her.

He couldn't figure out what it was, so he simply decided to ask her.

Yes, he supposed the direct approach was best. Her happiness mattered to him…well, it would matter once he got to know her better. For now, he wanted her to understand that he would respect her contribution to their soon-to-be household. "Why are you fretting, Violet?"

"Am I? Yes, I must be. It isn't important."

Other young ladies might enjoy being pampered or treated like brainless fribbles who needed a strong man to protect them, but Romulus sensed that she was not one of them. "You can confide anything in me. I hope you know that."

"I do. Lady Exmoor warned you had a protective nature. Apparently, all the Brayden men do."

He grinned. "We are a military family, raised from birth to go out in the world and slay dragons. I'll try not to be too overbearing."

The Brayden women were not traditional either. They were true partners to their husbands in every way. Not a single porcelain doll to be kept on a display shelf among them. "Violet, you haven't asked me details of the financial arrangements of our betrothal."

"Oh, yes. I forgot."

He was pleased by the notion. "You are not mercenary by nature."

"I've never had to worry about my future. We Farthingales look after each other. But I suppose I ought to know what has been decided." She nodded. "Go ahead. Tell me."

"Since I am not a nobleman, I do not have to worry about entailed properties. So, everything I have will be yours. My townhouse will pass to you outright along with twenty thousand pounds. The rest will be placed in trust for your benefit and that of our children, but managed by my cousin Finn. He's brilliant when it comes to matters of finance."

She shook her head and laughed. "That's absurd. You don't even know me. What of your own family?"

"My brother is a rich man. He doesn't require my wealth. If he should die without male issue, then I will inherit his title and estates. Those will not be yours, but will pass to our eldest son from our marriage. Of course, as I said, assuming James has no sons of his own."

"And then assuming we have sons." She was nibbling her lip again. "I hadn't considered that you might be the next Earl of Exmoor."

He gave a mirthless laugh. "Then you are the only debutante in London who has not given it thought. James and Sophie have been husband and wife almost five years now and have produced no children. I would be overjoyed for them if it happened. They haven't said anything to me, nor have I asked, but it is quite possible they can't."

"My aunt adores Lady Exmoor. So do I, although I don't know her nearly so well. Nor do I know your brother, but it is obvious he adores his wife."

"He does." Romulus hoped to keep the pain from his voice, but he did not think he could. Yet, he already trusted Violet enough to reveal his anguish and know she would treat him gently. "I never saw a man more miserable than James when he returned home after Waterloo. He used to be the *ton's* golden boy. So handsome, it was as though the sun shone down from the heavens whenever he entered a room."

She placed a hand on his arm. "You must have adored him, too."

He nodded. "He is my big brother. I worshiped him."

"I feel the same about my sister, Poppy. She's my best friend. I'm close with my cousins, too." She laughed softly. "People jest about the Chipping Way curse, as though my cousins were these awful monsters who trapped unmarried men, but nothing could be farther from the truth. Your brother was your hero, I understand how badly you must have felt when he was injured."

"He was treated so unfairly when he returned home from the war. Women used to fawn all over him. But those scars on his face changed everything. Suddenly, he was no longer that magnificent Roman god everyone adored. Those very women now thought of him as a beast, no matter that he had sacrificed everything for those ungrateful, pampered peahens. He married Sophie because of a promise made to a dying friend, but she has been his salvation. She saw beyond his scars immediately."

He cast Violet a grim smile. "I don't wish to say more about him. I've said too much already. His health suffered greatly during the war. Your uncle George saved his damaged leg. For that, my entire family is forever in his debt. George is a brilliant doctor. But the fact remains, James has no children and may never have any."

On impulse, Violet entwined her fingers with his. "I am truly sorry."

He nodded. "He's made provision for Sophie. She'll never have a moment's worry. As I said, Finn is the family's King Midas. Seems everything he touches turns to gold."

"Still, if what you say is true, then you've been quite generous with me."

"Yet, it troubles you?"

"Yes," she admitted. "It all feels too easy. I don't resent it, but I am not comfortable with it. In truth, I'm not comfortable with you. With us. What do we have in common? What will bind us to each other if we are forced to marry? To be precise, what is there about me to hold your interest?"

He shook his head in surprise. "Violet, you're beautiful."

"Is that all? Beauty fades over time. What then?"

CHAPTER FIVE

A LIGHT MIST fell the following morning as Romulus stood by his front gate awaiting the wagons bringing his sparse furnishings to his new home. In truth, he had woefully little. So little, he'd been sleeping at his brother's home for the past few days. It was better than sleeping on the dusty floor in front of one of the sooty hearths.

That he'd been here yesterday when the bees attacked Violet was a coincidence. He'd only gone to the house to complete an inventory of the kitchen and then start on the other rooms when he'd heard her screams and run to help.

It was also a remarkable coincidence that General Allworthy had left a stock of herbs, spices, and bottles of assorted pickling brines including vinegar in his pantry.

He watched the men unload the wagons. A bed, armoire, and bureau for his bedchamber. A desk and leather chair for his study. General Allworthy had left behind many things, including bookshelves in the library, and an elegant buffet, table, and chairs in the dining room.

The dining table was of mahogany wood. The cushioned chairs were covered in a colorful bird pattern. The massive buffet was also of mahogany wood and took up the entire west wall. They were all in pristine condition since the old curmudgeon rarely entertained. This was the most presentable room in the house.

As a distant bell chimed ten o'clock, Romulus glanced toward the

Farthingale house. A moment later, Violet tore through the front gate. She darted between raindrops that were falling more steadily now, and had nothing more to protect her than a paisley shawl held over her head while she raced to his house.

"Violet," he said with a laugh, catching her by the waist as she was about to run straight into him. She would have bounced off his chest and landed on her nicely shaped derriere in one of the newly formed rain puddles if he hadn't grabbed her. "Do you never simply walk?"

"No," she said, smiling up at him. "Am I late?"

"Right on time." He glanced over her head. "Where is your chaperone?"

"I shall have two chaperones this morning, Aunt Sophie and Mrs. Mayhew. They'll be along in a moment. Did you know Lady Dayne is hosting a supper party this evening? I'm sure you've been invited."

He nodded. "I have."

"So have I. She has assured me that she will take over chaperone duties tomorrow. What a relief, she isn't nearly as snoopy as my family. But for now, it is Aunt Sophie and Mrs. Mayhew shouldering the duty. We noticed the wagons pull up in front of your house and thought the workers might like some tea and currant scones. I came ahead to see what else you might need."

"Other than a replenished stock of vinegar?"

She laughed.

He held out his arm to her. "Come inside. I suppose we're safe enough with all these men traipsing in and out."

As he led her in, he realized his new home was in desperate need of a woman's touch. The men were now carrying the unloaded furniture inside, and he had no idea where to place the pieces. Nor had he thought to have the house properly cleaned from top to bottom before moving in. His sister-in-law had suggested it, even offered to help, but he'd forgotten all about it and now it was too late.

Violet walked in ahead of him.

Once inside, she wrapped her shawl around her waist and casually brushed back her hair. It was fashioned in a loose bun, but stray wisps had escaped the pins and were now curling around her ears.

Romulus could not resist tucking back a few of those loose curls. His knuckles grazed her cheek, immediately causing Violet to blush, but she did not draw away. He traced his thumb along that same cheek to wipe a raindrop off it. She smiled up at him, and his heart beat faster.

She was so pretty.

Stars shone in her eyes.

He cleared his throat and turned away to direct the workmen in placing the furniture in the appropriate rooms. Violet modified some of his suggestions, muttering something about the flow of a room and seating arrangements. At times, he stood back and watched her go about her business. He was going to make a fool of himself over this girl if he studied her much longer. But how could he stop staring?

She wasn't merely beautiful. She was fascinating in a warm, appealing way. He doubted he would ever tire of looking at her lovely face or not be drawn in by her expressive eyes. "Violet, have you been in General Allworthy's home before?"

"Other than yesterday's spectacular visit?" She had a sweetly wicked grin.

He laughed. "Yes, other than yesterday. You only saw the kitchen and that hardly counts."

"I've never been inside. May I wander around now?"

"Of course. Anywhere you please." This would be her home by next week if Lady Withnall chose not to keep silent about his oafish hands all over the delicious girl.

"Do you think he has a music room? Aunt Hortensia claims he did once. There may be a pianoforte hiding in here somewhere."

"There is, but it's covered in a dusty sheet. Do you play?" He groaned inwardly. He liked Violet, he truly did. But if he had to listen to one more *accomplished* debutante bang on the keys and sing like a sick cat, he was going to do himself in.

"My cousin Dillie is the one who plays best. I play adequately. I'm much better at singing. Shall I sing for you?"

Bloody hell.

He ran a hand across the back of his neck. "Well, perhaps another time. The workmen are here, and I'll be interviewing the household staff shortly. The first of them will be arriving at any moment."

"Romulus Brayden, are you cringing at the thought?" She shook her head and emitted a merry trill of laughter. "You look like you'd rather walk through fire than hear me sing. I promise you, I'm not that bad."

"I'm sure you have the voice of an angel."

"In fact, I do. But no matter. You needn't listen to me. I'll go find the piano and tinker with it until the interviewees arrive. You can stick your fingers in your ears if my howling bothers you, although I'll do my best to be quiet." She glanced at the front door. "I wonder what's keeping Aunt Sophie and Mrs. Mayhew?"

With a shrug, she went off in the direction he'd pointed to find the music room.

He hoped he hadn't been too rough on Violet, but it was only ten o'clock in the morning, and he really did not need a soprano shrieking out high notes at this early hour. He preferred to have a few drinks in him first to numb him from the noise, and he tried never to drink before late afternoon.

"Ye're a lucky man, m'lord," the foreman said after placing his bed and bureau in the master bedchamber. Romulus had gone upstairs with the man to direct the other workmen. The strains of a slightly out of tune piano carried into his bedchamber. Violet had obviously found the instrument and was testing it out.

"Lucky?"

"Yer wife, m'lord. She's a beautiful lass. Lovely smile."

Romulus nodded. "She's a good egg." He groaned inwardly. Violet would club him if she heard herself described as that. A good egg. One described one's addled but well-meaning grandfather as that. Violet, if she was an egg at all, was a magnificent, amply endowed, bewitching egg. "Yes, she's lovely."

He did not bother to correct the man about his marital status, for it was too complicated to explain. It was no one's business anyway. Moreover, it felt to him as though Violet belonged here.

Violet's voice drifted up to them and caught his attention.

The workmen also stopped to listen.

Blessed saints. She'd told him she had a nice voice. She wasn't jesting. Angel. Nightingale. Magnificent. Those words rattled around in his head. He didn't even need to imbibe strong spirits to tolerate it.

He went downstairs and stood in the doorway, his arms folded across his chest while he watched her play a country lilt and quietly sing along to it. She sang softly, not realizing her voice carried throughout the house, no doubt because of a design quirk of the room.

He imagined this chamber back in the day, packed with guests seated in their chairs as the performers made their way to the front of the room and sang their arias or played their harps or violins.

Violet stopped suddenly and turned to him, her cheeks a cherry red. "How long have you been standing there?"

"A while."

"You should have stopped me. I didn't mean to disturb you."

He unfolded his arms and crossed to her side. "You didn't. The workmen enjoyed hearing you sing."

"They heard me? Upstairs?"

"Yes. You weren't too loud. It's the way the sound carries in the room. There is a science to it. Your voice carried everywhere."

"Oh, dear."

"It was splendid, Violet. Truly."

She shook her head and rose. "I think I hear Aunt Sophie and Mrs.

Mayhew. I'll show them to the kitchen. We'll take inventory of all you need. Of course, call me if you'd like me to sit in on any of your interviews. Aunt Sophie will likely be more helpful. Oh, and I almost forgot…Mrs. Mayhew said her nieces were maids in the Duke of Danforth's residence. But he passed away last week and it seems his nephew will be bringing in his own staff. So, I thought you might like to interview them as well. The older niece, Cora, would make a good housekeeper. She's clever and diligent."

"Have you met them?"

"Yes, they served as the children's nannies for a short time in Aunt Sophie's home. That was the season several of the nannies quit all at once, then another nanny got sick, and another eloped. Cora and Mary stepped in and did an admirable job of watching over the young ones. Aunt Sophie would have kept them on, but she and Uncle John do not stay in town year-round. They return to their home in Coniston for summers and Christmas. The nieces were quickly hired by the duke's housekeeper, so all worked out well."

"Thank you, Violet. I'll gladly meet them. Let Mrs. Mayhew know."

She seemed pleased.

He shook his head and walked out with her to meet Sophie Far-thingale and her cook, Mrs. Mayhew, as they entered his home.

By noontime, his furniture was in place, he'd hired a butler and two footmen, and expected to hire the Mayhew nieces as housekeeper and maid by tomorrow. Their interviews were a mere formality. Once the elder Mayhew niece accepted to come on as his housekeeper, he'd leave the rest of the staffing to her.

He'd also leave the matter of cleaning the house to her.

As for properly furnishing the rest of the house, he'd ask Violet and the two Sophies to help him out.

He went into the kitchen to forage for food.

Violet, her aunt, and their cook were in there still making lists of all he lacked. They looked at him as though he was an interloper. "I'm hungry," he explained. "Are we all out of the currant scones you brought over earlier, Mrs. Mayhew?"

"Dear me, yes. Those were eaten by the workmen within minutes of my arrival."

Violet cast a pleading look at her aunt, who cast her a nod in return.

"Mr. Brayden," Violet said, smiling warmly, "please join us for lunch. You have nothing decent here. We can't allow you to starve. It wouldn't be neighborly."

"I'm hardly in danger of that, but thank you. I'd like that." He walked to the Farthingale home with the three ladies and was immediately made to feel comfortable amid the horde seated around their enormous dining table.

Violet's aunt did not run a household, she ran a chaotic, undisciplined regiment.

Her aunt must have sensed what he was thinking, for she laughed softly and shook her head. "It is a bit much, isn't it? I thought we would quiet down once our daughters were married and out of the house, but they keep coming over to visit, often bring their husbands and children along. We are never alone."

Violet joined in on the conversation. "Then there's the rest of the family who think nothing of visiting for months at a time. I was sent here for my debut season, which I've managed to botch, I suppose. My Oxfordshire cousins will arrive shortly. You'll like Honey and Belle. They are next to be herded like cattle to the marriage mart."

He tried to follow the names and relations, but men were never good at this sort of thing. The Farthingale women, as beautiful as they were, just became a big jumble in his head. Violet stood out, of course.

Her spectacular eyes.

Her body that would have him panting like a dog if he weren't careful. He'd seen more of her than any man who wasn't her husband ought to have seen. The hint of her bosom. Her long, shapely legs.

"Romulus," Violet said, cutting into his wayward thoughts. What was wrong with him? And what was it about Violet that turned him mindless? "I'd like to introduce you to a few more of my cousins."

Lord, more names to remember.

Most of the men were at their offices, so he was surrounded by women and children. He responded politely when introduced to Violet's cousins, Daffodil and Daisy. "Call me Dillie, everyone does," one of the pretty, dark-haired, blue-eyed, young women said, smiling at him. "I detest the name Daffodil. But I think my parents were caught by surprise when I popped out right after Lily. I don't think they were expecting twins and had to scramble for another flower name. Do you know my husband, the Duke of Edgeware?"

"Everyone does." *Blessed saints.* She was Edgeware's wife? He was the duke who was never going to marry. She was the girl who'd saved his sorry life twice. No wonder the man had fallen in love with her. Dillie was beautiful. More than that, there was a warmth and vitality to her that could not be overlooked.

"Daisy's husband is Lady Dayne's grandson, Gabriel," Violet remarked.

"I know of him as well." Romulus took a closer look at Violet's two cousins. They looked remarkably like Violet, but Violet... Lord, she did something to him. Her cousins were beautiful, for certain. But there was so much more to them than merely their fine looks. "A pleasure to meet you, Daisy."

He meant it, too. Gabriel Dayne had been awarded an earldom for his bravery during the war. His work had saved thousands of British lives, but Daisy had saved Gabriel and broken up a spy ring in the process. Indeed, these Farthingale women were extraordinary.

The meal was delicious, for Mrs. Mayhew's kitchen staff was well trained.

Everyone chattered around the table, all talking at once and mostly tossing questions at him, but he did not mind. Half the time, the conversation moved on before he had time to respond, and he particularly enjoyed the children's questions. "Are you bigger than a house? Are you bigger than an elephant?"

No. And no.

"Are you a gladiator?" a young cousin by the name of Charles asked.

"I'm a sailor."

The boy's eyes grew so wide, they bulged from their sockets. "On a sailing ship? A real ship?"

"Yes, I'm captain. My frigate is being repaired right now. Our mizzenmast was damaged during our battle with the dastardly pirate, Red-Eye McFlynn."

"Pirates!" The children sat rapt as he told them of the battle. He embellished a little, of course. He did not swing on the rigging, sword in hand, to leap onto the pirate ship. Nor did he engage in a sword fight with McFlynn. But there was hand-to-hand combat, and he did knock out the bastard when he'd tried to stick a dirk into Romulus's gut.

By the time the meal was over, Romulus was eager for quiet.

But he'd promised to read The Book of Love with Violet, and he was not about to renege. In any event, Violet was quiet by nature. She'd hardly said two words throughout their meal. Not that anyone gave her the chance.

He looked forward to a little time alone with her.

They'd be in full sight of anyone who cared to observe them from the house.

The rain had stopped, and the sun was now breaking through the clouds to shine down on the Farthingale garden. The air was warm and humid, but Romulus was used to the sea air, so this moisture bothered him little.

He waited for Violet on the bench near the dividing wall, taking a moment to scan for the angry bees. They were definitely gone. He only saw one or two hovering by the bed of flowers along with several butterflies. One of them was a magnificent purple color.

He thought of Violet.

She walked toward him moments later with the red book in hand. Her steps were light and naturally graceful, almost flitting like that of a delicate butterfly. He smiled at her and rose to greet her. "Is supper like this as well?"

"Oh, no. The children don't join us for supper. But I rather enjoy having them about during the day. Did you see the excitement in their eyes when you spoke of your pirate battles? I was enthralled as well. I had no idea you faced such dangers daily."

He shrugged. "We patrol along the Irish Sea and St. George's Channel mostly. Sometimes the Atlantic Ocean, but it is too vast to properly patrol. The pirates easily avoid us out on the high seas. We are more effective keeping close to land, catching them in sight of a port or smuggler's cove. We engage them in battle when we find them, but most of the time, they manage to evade us. McFlynn was my toughest assignment. He controlled a pirate fleet of ten ships. They sailed together, like a wolf pack on the prowl."

She settled on the bench, now holding the book on her lap. "You were alone against ten?"

He sat beside her. "No, we sailed in our own naval pack. We were six, but first-class frigates. Their ten vessels were no match for us." He glanced at the book. "I've been talking about myself too long. Let's talk about love now."

Her cheeks turned bright pink.

He'd spoken lightly, his manner teasing. But he was eager to learn as much as he could about falling in love. How did one go about it? Was it something that just happened?

How was it different from lust?

Of course, he knew it was different. He had seen the way his brother behaved toward his wife, and the way his married cousins behaved toward their wives. Cow-eyed, besotted, ready to do anything to make them happy.

He didn't like to think he would allow any woman to walk all over him like that. However, being with Violet did not feel like a duty or obligation, nor did he mind any of her demands. Not that she'd been demanding at all. It bothered him that she was requiring so little of him.

Perhaps this is why he enjoyed her company. She wasn't meek, but she was soft and gentle. She stirred his protective instincts in a way no other woman ever had. In truth, she could ask things of him, and he would comply without fuss or hesitation.

Well, he'd practically undressed her in his kitchen.

He owed her some recompense for that.

He still wanted to undress her.

How did this innocent girl rouse such sinful thoughts in him?

"When my sister gave me this book, she warned it might not make sense at first. She made me promise to read it in its entirety."

"And share it with me?"

Violet nodded. "I don't see why not. Poppy shared it with her husband before they were married, so I think it is perfectly fine for me to share it with you now. After all, we only have one week before Lady Withnall lowers her verbal axe on us. With so little time to get this right, isn't it important for us to work together?"

"I agree. Let's start. Where do we begin?"

CHAPTER SIX

V IOLET OPENED TO the first chapter and began to read. "Love does not come from the heart but from the brain. It is the brain that sends signals throughout the body, telling you what to feel. Therefore, to stimulate a man's arousal–"

"What?" Romulus placed a hand over the page to stop her from reading further. "Is it a book about sex acts? Forget it."

"Don't you dare take it from me." Violet frowned at him. "It isn't about that at all. It's scientific."

"It's indecent." And he did not need a book to tell him just how indecent his thoughts about Violet were. Nor—Lord help him—did he need Violet to read to him in explicit detail just how many positions the male and female bodies could contort into when coupling.

"How can you make that claim when you haven't read it? Please let me finish the paragraph. You promised. Will you prove yourself a liar and say you didn't?"

"I did promise. But you misled me. There is nothing scientific about arousing a man."

"See, you are already leaping to false conclusions. This is what the book is all about. Listening. Hearing. Seeing the truth, not what you imagine it to be. Will you let me continue?"

Against his better judgement, he removed his hand.

She took up where she'd left off. "Therefore, to stimulate a man's arousal response, one must arouse his sense receptacles in a pleasing way. By touch, taste, sight, smell, and hearing. This author explains how we must properly use the five senses to find true love." She glanced up at him. "I will admit, I did not make a good first impression."

He laughed and shook his head. "I don't suppose I did either."

"You were brave and heroic. I was ghastly. I could not have appealed to your senses in any way. For touch, I crashed into you while running from the bees. As for the sense of hearing, I was shrieking at the top of my lungs, so I must have shattered your eardrums. Are they still recovering?"

He grinned back. "My hearing is only now starting to return."

"The sense of smell, you doused that ghastly vinegar all over me. I think I still reek of it. I must smell like something pickled, even though I've been scrubbing my skin with oatmeal soap ever since. That leaves the senses of taste and sight." She sighed. "I was aiming at the bees, but I kept hitting you with this book, so I don't know how you managed to get a good look at me while your hands were in front of your face to protect yourself."

"I looked my fill later in the kitchen." Whatever irritation he'd felt toward her had simply melted away as he'd unlaced her gown. *Touch.* Her skin, as he'd run his hands over her body and slid them along her spectacular legs, was silky soft. *Sight.* The sight of her breasts as the gown slipped low. He'd only seen the swell of those mounds, nothing more. It was enough to tip him over the edge.

Scent. There was a rose-petal sweetness to her skin. Perhaps it was the oatmeal soap. He couldn't tell. All he knew was that Violet did not pour odious perfume all over herself. Her scent was pure and natural, like a garden in spring. *Hearing.* Her voice was a mix of innocent and sultry, and hearing her sing was like listening to an angel chorus.

That left *taste.*

Yes, he wanted to taste every inch of her. A gentleman might start with her lips, but he was no gentleman when it came to Violet. He was a lusting hound. He'd start with her breasts and work his way down from there. Taste her, breathe in the scent of her arousal. Hear her soft sighs and passionate moans.

"...which is why we ought to leave the kiss for last." She stared at him. "Romulus, have you been listening to a word I've said?"

"Of course. Kiss. Last." Over his dead body. He was going to kiss this girl before the day was through. And it would be more than one kiss, to hell with Lady Withnall's edict.

"Poppy says the sense of taste is the most dangerous. That's why we must leave it for last. We're only going to test the one kiss anyway. It will have more meaning once we get to know each other better. This is the beauty of the book. It shows the reader how to connect with the mate of their heart, how to look at that person and see them for who they truly are."

She flipped forward a few pages. "What I find most fascinating is the book's discussion about the male brain."

Romulus was intrigued. "Go on."

"The male brain functions on two levels, the low and the high. The female brain functions only at the higher level."

He leaned back and stretched his arm across the top of the bench. "Who wrote this book? A woman?"

"I'm sure it was a man." She rolled her eyes at him. "His description of the workings of the male brain is too perfectly detailed to have been done by one of our sex. Most of us don't understand men."

"We don't understand women either."

She snorted. "You just want us in your bed."

"Violet!"

"It's true, isn't it? This is why the book is so important. I am not passing judgment, merely explaining how your brain works."

"I know how it works." He stifled the wrenching groan threatening to spill from his lips. Yes, if he could take Violet up to his bedchamber right now, he would.

"I don't think you truly understand. You only think you do. But this is also about how the female brain works, so we will both be helped by reading this book. The author claims that a man's lower brain function is designed purely for successful mating."

Romulus lolled his head back. "Oh, Lord. Do your aunt and uncle know what this book is about?"

"It is about love, Romulus. There is nothing lewd about it. According to this book, men look for beautiful women. They may define beauty differently, but there is one thing they all agree upon. The woman must appear to be a successful vessel for their seed or they will immediately dismiss her in their minds—too old, too young, too frail, too sickly. So, all men will first look for cues that a woman can provide him healthy offspring." She glanced up at him. "See, it is a scientific analysis."

He snorted. "Right."

She sighed but pressed on. "At this first inspection, the color of her hair and eyes is not as important as the shape and symmetry of her body."

Violet paused in her reading to look up at him again. "Do you understand what the author is suggesting?"

Romulus nodded. "It means men look at a woman's breasts first."

"Yes, that's it exactly." She cleared her throat. "Were you looking at mine when we were in your kitchen and you were rubbing vinegar all over me?"

"I'd rather not answer that." But of course, he was. Gaping. Gawking. Staring. Couldn't take his eyes off her heaving chest.

"I'll take that as a yes. If the male likes the look of the female's bosom, he will then move on to inspecting the rest of her. Did you inspect the rest of me?"

He groaned.

"I'll take that as a yes as well. You should not feel badly about it. You can't help yourself. This is your lower brain function at work, the one that is designed purely for successful mating."

"Got it. May we move on to the higher brain function now?"

She nodded. "This is where the truly important connections are made. Your low brain will accept hundreds of women, because its purpose is only to seek out healthy females. At that point, your high brain takes over. That part of your brain is more complex, for it must select the best woman for you among these hundreds. It will sort out the peahens, the manipulators, the ill-tempered, and so on."

This was the oddest conversation he'd ever had in his entire life, but Violet was serious about this nonsense, so he sat back and let her take the lead.

"Your high brain is seeking the one woman who will produce the finest heirs to secure your bloodline."

He grunted. "Women are not fields of wheat to plough, fertilize, and harvest."

"Indeed, not. This author does not suggest that is all men do. As I said, finding the right mother for your children in addition to her being the right wife for you is quite complex. And it is of vital importance to our sex that we find the right man for ourselves. We need that male to remain faithful to us in order to protect us and our young. Otherwise, if left alone and exposed to all manner of predators, we might be eaten by wolves."

"Eaten by wolves? In London?"

She frowned at him. "Are you purposely being dense? When a female has just given birth to her young, she is at her most vulnerable. She needs to know her husband will remain by her side, will provide for her and their children. Life is difficult enough for a woman on her own, but with young children? She cannot leave them to fend for themselves from dawn to dusk. But how is she to feed them, clothe them, provide shelter for them if she cannot go out and work?"

"Violet–"

"Perhaps at the dawn of civilization we were worried about real wolves and bears and other animal predators. But our present-day wolf can be anything that puts the woman and her children in peril. This is why the female brain also assesses each male who passes before her. Will he protect me and my children? Will he provide for us? Will he love us? So, when a woman sets her cap for a duke, no matter how unremarkable he may be, she isn't being greedy. What she is really doing is securing her future by the only means available to her since she is not permitted to work. And if she had to work, where could she go? She can't command a ship or stand for Parliament or teach at Oxford, no matter how intelligent she may be."

She frowned at him and continued. "What are her choices? To run a lady's shop, or be a governess or companion. There's little else available to her. So why not aim for the duke? And why not assess him for his ability to protect her and her children? A duke, by his mere title, is deemed desirable."

"Violet, I'm sorry. It was callous of me to make fun of the book. It is quite a frank assessment of the lot women face in life. Few choices are open to them. But to hear you talking about men that way...yes, I suppose we do look at a woman first and think about her in a lustful way. But we are also civilized enough *not* to act upon such urges."

She appeared to accept his apology. "I know. I never meant to admonish you, but this is an important lesson I've learned from this book. We each carry our burdens and have to figure out how to best accomplish our goals. Discussing the masculine urge to mate must have sounded odd, especially coming from me."

"Very," he admitted.

"I'm almost finished reading the book. I can lend it to you if you prefer to read it on your own. These opening chapters are the most controversial ones. The rest of this book is about forming the unique bonds of love that unite our hearts and not merely our bodies."

She paused, as though waiting for him to contradict her, then pressed on when he did not. "My goal is to become special to you, but

I don't know if I can accomplish it in a mere week. The author says I don't have to be regarded as beautiful by everyone, just you. You are the only man whose opinion matters. You are the one who must look at me and think that I am beautiful. Not just my features, but all of me. The way I look, my scent, the sound of my voice, and so on. This is the importance of our five senses and why we must learn to use them properly."

Romulus had never once thought of marriage in this way. Yet, it made perfect sense. When Sophie looked at James, she saw beyond his scars. She loved him for his wit, intelligence, and honor. She saw him as handsome.

He turned to Violet.

Lord, was it possible she was the one for him? Time would tell, he supposed. "What do you see when you look at me, Violet?"

She blushed again. "Obviously, a handsome man."

He arched an eyebrow. "That's a good start."

"One who may know lots about ships but nothing about setting up a household," she teased. "You like your independence. That's why buying General Allworthy's house was so important to you. The details of how to properly furnish it and keep it up are secondary to you, but you'll soon have the staff to attend to that part."

"I don't expect to be independent for long."

She nodded. "Lady Withnall. If I could bind and gag her, toss her in a travel trunk, and ship her off to the wilds of Mongolia, I would."

"Why, Violet. I believe you would." He smiled in approval.

"This is what infuriates me the most, to have our independence stolen from us. That is, you are truly independent. I'm not. But I am not willing to give up the right to choose my own husband."

"What is it you wish for in a husband?" Romulus wanted to kick himself for not thinking to ask her this question before. He'd been thinking mostly of himself. Yes, he'd wanted to protect Violet but hadn't given thought to her wishes beyond that.

"Kindness, intelligence. Someone who can make me laugh, although obviously not a witless fool. Someone who will accept me for who I am and encourage me to be the best person I can be."

"Ah, and here I hoped you'd be a mere appendage." He took the book from her hands and set it beside him on the bench. "I'm jesting, of course. Violet, you need never fear that I won't appreciate you or respect you."

"How can you be sure? You cringed at the mere mention of my singing. It is something I love to do."

He winced. "And once I'd heard you, it wasn't nearly as bad as I'd feared. It was lovely."

"But not something you'd care to listen to at all hours of the day."

He tensed. "Do you sing all day?"

She shook her head. "No, but there are times when I wish to. I give you fair warning, there will be musicales in our home, should we marry." She stared at him. "See, you're already feeling shackled. How will we ever work this out?"

"We will, Violet. I'm sure there are things I will do that you won't like. Not that I don't like your singing. In fact, you have a lovely voice. It's the thought of everyone else singing in my house that I detest."

"Detest?"

"Well, perhaps that's rather harsh. But a man likes to come home to peace and quiet."

She frowned. "So, our children will be shut up as well?"

"No, of course not. I'll want to see them." How had this discussion suddenly descended into a brewing fight? "Violet, don't leap to conclusions about me. The Braydens are a large and boisterous family. You Farthingales aren't the only tightly knit clan. And Braydens mostly produce boys. So many boys, in fact, that we became known as the wildebeests, because when we were younger, we surely were wild as beasts. There are eight of us who are fairly close in age. Do you know what a house full of growing boys is like? Especially boys the size of

Braydens?"

Her frowned eased. "No, we are mostly girls in this family."

"A very different thing. We didn't just walk to the table and take our seats. We were a thundering herd, stampeding to grab our share of food before one of the other wildebeests claimed it for his own. I am used to noise. I am used to having lots of family about. Frankly, I don't know how my parents or my aunts and uncles put up with us. I don't know how my sister, Gabrielle, survived trampling."

Now Violet was smiling.

He breathed a sigh of relief. "We'll work it out, whatever our differences."

She said nothing for the longest moment, which prompted him to ask, "What are you thinking?"

"That you managed to climb out of the hole you dug for yourself," she teased. "That was well said. But you surprise me."

"How so?"

"You seem more invested in this marriage idea than I am."

Gad, was it true? He wanted *in* while she wanted *out*?

The possibility had never occurred to him. He was wealthy in his own right. Nothing like his brother, but still quite well off. He was smart. He wouldn't have been given command of one of the finest vessels in the Royal Navy fleet if he wasn't. Women found him handsome. He'd never had to work hard to get any female he wanted into his bed.

Wealthy. Smart. Handsome.

But Violet hadn't listed wealthy or handsome as a consideration when describing her ideal husband.

So what? He had other good qualities. Faithfulness, for one.

There would be no more chasing women now that he was quietly betrothed to Violet. Nor would he chase skirts after they were married. Violet would be the only one to share his bed. The Brayden men were always true to their wives.

He ran a hand across the nape of his neck in dismay. What if Violet decided she didn't like him once they were married? What if she decided not to share his bed?

He wanted a wife…well, not just yet. But he would marry Violet to protect her even if she seemed reluctant to protect herself.

He never considered marriage merely as a means to breed heirs.

He wanted to share a life with Violet. All of it, the good times and bad. Children, even when they were messy and noisy. Intimacy, because he wanted her body. Laughter and tenderness, because he wanted her heart.

He stared at the red leather book. "Violet, let's try this again. Tell me what you hope for in a husband. This time, I'll really listen."

She glanced up at him, her beautiful eyes filled with hurt. "Do you mean you weren't listening before?"

CHAPTER SEVEN

A s Violet prepared for the dinner party at Lady Dayne's neighboring townhouse, she was starting to worry this book her sister had claimed was magical, was in fact, more of a harbinger of doom.

It saddened her to come to this conclusion, for she liked Romulus Brayden very much. But the more they found out about each other, the more incompatible they seemed. The physical part was not the problem. Goodness, he was big and handsome, and if one were to make a list of the qualities a woman would want to find in a man in order to protect her children from being eaten by wolves, Romulus had all those qualities.

He was strong and would be fiercely protective of his offspring.

But would he care for her?

She did not need to rush into marriage, unless Lady Withnall flapped her big mouth and thoroughly ruined her. But otherwise, she wasn't destitute or desperate.

Were she to have children, and her husband could not protect them, she had her parents, a wonderful sister who was married to a kind and generous earl, and a horde of welcoming relatives to help her. She would be fine, even assuming said husband took all her wealth and left her with nothing.

Perhaps she was overly fretting about Romulus. This was only their first full day of knowing each other. Yesterday hardly counted, it had all gone by in a blur.

Tomorrow would be better.

She studied herself in the mirror, disappointed the welts from the bee stings were still noticeable, especially the one on the tip of her nose. These sting marks dotted her arms, neck, and chest as well. "Oh, Miss Violet, I'm sure no one will notice the spots," her maid said. "But this powder might help hide them."

"No, Emily. It's all right." The powder would wear off quickly, and then she'd simply look blotchy as well as dotted with red spots. Her gown, a lovely tea-rose silk that draped perfectly over her body, did little to hide them.

She grabbed a matching shawl to toss over her shoulders if people began to stare. "Well, perhaps a little powder on my nose."

Romulus was already at Lady Dayne's home when Violet arrived. He was standing in the parlor beside his brother, both of them with a drink in hand. But he set his glass down on the tray of a passing servant and came over to her as soon as she'd been announced.

"You look lovely." He took her hand and bowed over it as any proper gentleman would. "I mean it, Violet."

He looked splendid, too. Quite daunting, for his shoulders were broad and his big body was quite magnificently outlined in his impeccably tailored formal attire. The black of his jacket brought out the gold of his hair and the jeweled green of his eyes.

"I'm all spotted," she said in a pained whisper.

He gave her hand a light squeeze. "No one can tell under the glow of candlelight. We all look orange, don't we?"

She laughed. "I look orange. You look golden. But thank you for attempting to make me feel better. Truly, Romulus. You look so handsome."

Before he had the chance to respond, they heard the *thuck, thuck, thuck* of Lady Withnall's walking stick against the polished wood floor as she entered the parlor and was announced. "Bloody hell," he muttered, tucking her arm in his to keep her protectively close, "the wicked witch has arrived."

Despite the din in the room, for it was packed with guests, Lady Withnall came straight toward them. "Yes, the wicked witch is here and not about to relent."

"*Bloody hell.* You heard that? You do have the ears of a bat." He frowned down at the diminutive dowager, making no attempt to apologize.

Oh, dear. Why was he antagonizing her? Violet emitted a nervous titter. "Good evening, Lady Withnall."

"Good evening, Violet. Care to add to Captain Brayden's comment?"

Violet's identical twin cousins, Dillie and Lily, often *eeped* when their nerves were on edge. Violet held back the urge to *eep* like a demented bird, but a few more high-pitched twitters escaped her lips. "Um…er… Lovely to see you, Lady Withnall."

"I'm sure it isn't, but I appreciate your lying to me anyway."

Romulus covered Violet's hand with his to calm her.

Lady Withnall noticed the gesture at once. "Protecting Violet? From me? Don't be a nodcock. I'm not going to bite her head off," she snapped. "But I ought to do worse to you."

He groaned. "You are the wickedest, old bat who ever lived. Relentless, too."

"And you are an insufferable dolt. Come, give me a kiss on the cheek and tell me you are happy to see me."

Romulus did so, and the two of them chuckled as though they were the best of friends sharing a jest.

Violet's gaze shot from one to the other.

Wait, what had she missed? Incredibly, Lady Withnall seemed not to have taken offense at the harsh remarks Romulus had tossed her way. Well, she must be used to hearing worse from her victims.

"How have the pair of you been getting along?" she asked, piercing

Romulus with her spear-like gaze. "Feeling leg-shackled yet, dear boy?"

He arched an eyebrow. "No shackles. Only a bit rushed."

Lady Withnall pounded her cane again. "You got what you deserved, and you know it."

Violet tipped her chin up, determined to come to his defense. "You aren't being fair to him. He–"

"No, my dear. As I said, he is getting exactly what he deserves. I hope so are you." With that, the old harridan walked away to strike fear in Lady Dayne's other guests.

Violet gasped. "What did she mean by that? Why would she say something so rude to me? What did I ever do to offend her?"

Romulus stared at Lady Withnall for a long moment, then turned to Violet with a smile tugging at the corners of his mouth. "She just complimented you...and me."

She followed his gaze. "She insulted us. Weren't you listening?"

He laughed and playfully tugged on her earlobe. "I was. You weren't. She likes us, Violet. She's giving us a hard time because she thinks we are perfectly suited for each other. This is her heavy-handed way of matchmaking. She also thinks I'm getting the better part of the bargain. She likes you best."

Violet shook her head. "You gleaned all that from trading insults with her?"

"I did."

She rolled her eyes. "Well then, we may as well toss The Book of Love aside since Lady Withnall obviously has all the answers."

She expected him to respond with a glib remark, but he regarded her in all seriousness. "If anything, I am more determined for us to read through it. I *heard* what she was saying."

"Because you *listened*."

He nodded. "And you did not. You are angry, so you assumed the worst in her. So did I until now."

"So, this torture she is putting us through is her desire to have us find love?"

"Yes, but is it torture for you? I don't mind it nearly as much as I thought I would. Of course, we hardly know each other." He frowned lightly. "To my shame, I probably would not have noticed you if you sat in the wallflower corner with your spectacles on and your hair done up in a tight bun. But those bees changed everything, didn't they?"

His expression eased, and he smiled at her. "I can't look at you without low brain thoughts swimming into my head."

She eased out of his grasp, for people were starting to notice he had not released her yet. "My high brain thanks you. It liked the way you held onto me to protect me."

"No wolves will ever eat you while I'm about."

"Then thank you again," she said with a laughing shake of her head. She was beginning to think perhaps Lady Withnall had the right of it, that she and Romulus might grow to like each other...perhaps love each other.

Those thoughts were dashed a moment later when a stunning woman simply marched up to Romulus and greeted him with startling familiarity.

"You wicked, wicked man," she purred like a predatory feline. "Have you grown tired of me already?"

She extended her elegant, gloved hand, and he dutifully bowed over it. "Lady Felicia, a pleasure to see you."

"I don't know. You seem quite attentive to this...creature."

Violet arched an eyebrow. She'd never been referred to as a creature before.

"Does she know how depraved you really are?" She cast Violet a dismissive glance. "Well? Aren't you going to introduce her to me, Rom?"

He did, but only after a telling moment of hesitation. "Lady Felicia is the widow of the Marquis of Herringdon." He cleared his throat and went on to explain. "We are old friends."

"We are childhood friends," Lady Felicia corrected, for she certainly wasn't old. "And have always been very *close* friends." She ran her hand lightly down Romulus's chest and then glanced lower. "The closest of friends, I should hope."

Violet was the first to admit she knew nothing about men. But she wasn't born yesterday. That glance followed by a lick of her lips was a not so subtle indication of their past relations. Indeed, it fairly screamed the intimacy of their past and likely current relations.

"I'm thinking of having a party this weekend at Herringdon Hall. Just a few friends...doing the usual...like old times."

Romulus glanced at Violet. "Sorry, I am not available this weekend."

"Rom, darling. Don't you dare grow boring, as I am afraid you shall if you insist on keeping such dull company." Lady Felicia positioned herself between them, effectively cutting Violet out of their conversation. "Do join me this weekend at Herringdon. You are always such a comfort to me."

"I shall leave you to catch up with each other." Violet had a dozen snide remarks on the tip of her tongue and ready to be hurled, but why engage the haughty woman? It would serve no purpose.

If Romulus wanted to continue his relations with the widow, that was his privilege. But it would not bode well for their current betrothal...secret betrothal. Indeed, she would never marry him if he thought so little of her as to continue to *comfort* Lady Felicia.

Romulus frowned at her.

Perhaps it was more of a look of frustration. Violet wasn't blind to their obvious past together, for Lady Felicia was quite proprietary about him. The widow's gloves surely hid some very sharp claws.

Violet was about to walk away, but Romulus took her gently by the arm. "Stay, Miss Farthingale. It is only harmless reminiscing."

She studied the woman, noting her golden hair and crystal, blue eyes shaped like those of a cat. This widow was used to getting her way in all things. Her beauty alone would have men tripping over their feet to indulge her every whim. She moved in the highest circles, and if the diamonds around her throat was any indication, she had been left quite wealthy by her husband after he'd cocked up his toes.

"I don't think so, Mr. Brayden. Seek me out later if you wish."

"I do wish it."

She ignored him and turned to walk away.

She heard Lady Felicia's lilting laughter behind her. "What a quaint, little bird. Not your usual sort, is she, Rom?"

"No, not at all."

Violet would not linger to hear the rest of his response.

The man who married Lady Felicia next, assuming she cared to marry, would live in unsurpassed luxury. But there was little else to recommend her. Oddly, although the woman was beautiful and rich, there was a hardness about her that detracted from her otherwise considerable assets.

Violet thought of the Book of Love when it spoke of beauty. The widow's features might appear beautiful at first glimpse, but there was an ugliness to her character that could not be overlooked. How could she be beautiful in any man's eyes when on the inside she was cold as ice?

What did Romulus think of this woman?

Violet realized how little she knew of him. Still, she had learned something of his character. He was protective by nature, but that was a far thing from being a fawning dolt. He was ruled by honor and kindness, not desperation and jealousy. He was not the sort to fall in doting rapture at any woman's feet. Was he?

Nor did he appear to be impressed by all Lady Felicia had to offer.

Quite the opposite, he looked as though he was irritated by the woman's flirtation.

She turned back to glance at him.

To her surprise, Romulus was looking at her as she retreated. If she didn't know better, she'd think he was casting her a pleading glance. Was he imploring her to return to his side? Did he not wish to be alone with the beautiful widow?

Violet wished she was more sophisticated and adept at handling such matters. In truth, she was confused. Romulus seemed to want her to remain by his side, but his words as she'd turned to walk off still stung.

Not your usual sort, is she, Rom?

No, not at all.

That's what he'd said in response to Lady Felicia's remark.

He had the choice of two women before him. One, namely herself, a reluctant debutante with a bee sting on her nose and ugly red welts all over her body. The other was perfection itself. And this perfect woman was rich, worldly, and hungry for him.

Violet could see Lady Felicia for what she was, cold and calculating. But would Romulus see her this way as well? Perhaps. But would he care?

She crossed the room to greet her cousin Daisy who had arrived with her husband, Gabriel. "I hear the Chipping Way curse is still going strong," he said with a rakish grin and a wicked sparkle in his eyes. "I'm sorry you were beset by bees, Violet. But this is how the blasted curse works. Something calamitous always happens to throw you and your intended together. How soon before the wedding is announced?"

She glanced at Romulus.

Lady Felicia was standing so close to him, she appeared to be atop him. "It won't be."

Gabriel and Daisy followed her gaze.

Gabriel sighed. "Don't be too hard on him. I know Lady Felicia's type. She is the one making all the advances."

Violet shook her head. "He doesn't seem to be objecting."

"It isn't easy for a man to step away under these circumstances. He isn't about to rebuff her now, for he knows Lady Felicia is not above causing a scene. He is handling her the only way he can at the moment, by remaining polite but cool to her advances. Ah, he keeps looking your way. See, that proves my point."

"He didn't want me to leave his side," she admitted. "But I had to. I'm not good at sophisticated banter with a cutting edge to it. And look at me...then look at her. She's elegant. I look like a measles case."

Daisy regarded her affectionately. "Oh, Violet. It is obvious she is jealous of you."

Violet laughed. "Thank you, Daisy. That is utter nonsense." She refused to pay any more attention to Romulus and his overly amorous widow.

The evening passed more pleasantly than expected, even though Romulus happened to be seated beside Lady Felicia at the dining table. Violet's place was immediately across from them, but next to the son of an old family friend. "Miss Farthingale, do you still sing?"

"Yes, I do." She was pleased Lord Jameson Forester had remembered this about her. "And your sister, Lord Forester? How is she faring?"

"Valerie is well. She sends her regards." He studied her a little too closely for comfort, no doubt noticing the spots and being too polite to comment on them. "She is Lady Rawley now, a viscountess. Unfortunately, she is not in a happy marriage."

"I'm so sorry."

"She and her husband live apart. Lord Rawley is a dull bird who prefers the life of a country squire. He spends most of his time trudging through his cornfields, and when he isn't doing that, he's duck hunting. His estate is in Cumbria. Valerie prefers London, of course. Who doesn't? She's found a house to let on the outskirts of Mayfair. Barely fashionable."

"I'm sure it's lovely."

"I suppose it will have to do for her. She would have liked a residence as fine as those on Chipping Way, but Lord Rawley is tightfisted and barely sends her enough pin money to last her through the month."

Violet was surprised when he proceeded to tell her precisely how much his sister received. Goodness, it seemed more than generous. But still crude to mention his sister's finances here and now. "I must disappoint you, Lord Forester. I prefer the countryside as well. It can be quite lovely, especially in summer when the air is mild and the foliage is lush and in bloom. Autumn is also quite splendid, especially when the leaves are changing colors and–"

He laughed. "I forgot what a little pigeon you are. I think I would enjoy the country quite well if I spent time up there with you. But I have something serious to discuss with you, Violet. May I call you that? We are good friends. I hope you won't take offense. And do call me Jameson."

She eyed him warily. Yes, they had been friends. She hadn't seen him or his sister in years. What was this serious matter he wished to discuss? Jameson always had one wild scheme or another rolling in his head. His father, the Marquis of Broughton, had hoped he would settle down over time. Was he still dreaming up wild schemes? "What's on your mind, Jameson?"

"My sister and I have decided to raise funds for St. Aubrey's Orphanage in Langdale. The buildings on the property are in a sad state and require urgent repairs. Father has made a generous donation, but it isn't nearly enough. We don't want the orphans to be turned out. Where would they go? I shudder to think, for where can they go but to the workhouses?"

"That would be awful." She knew of the orphanage. Everyone who spent time in the Lake District knew of it and admired the abbess who ran it. "How can I help?"

He cast her a beaming smile. "I was hoping you would offer. You see, we thought we'd hold a charity recital and we need an extraordinary singer. We thought of you immediately. It is the reason I arranged to be invited to this party."

The notion surprised her. "Why me? I'm not a professional."

"You are young, beautiful, and you've always had the voice of an angel. The men will flock to hear you sing."

"Men? You expect me to sing to a roomful of men?" It sounded indecent and she was sorry she'd offered to help him. "No, that is out of the question."

"You mistake me, Violet. It will be an elegant affair, with all the best Society in attendance. Lords and ladies. It's just that the men hold the purse strings, don't they? So, they'll be the ones making the large donations. A man will pay more if the singer is young and beautiful."

She supposed she ought to be flattered, but the discussion made her uncomfortable. "Surely, there must be professionals who will do a much better job than I would."

He took a sip of his wine, then frowned and studied the crystal glass as he set it down. "Most of these opera singers demand a fee. So do the stage actresses. But they are lower class. You are a gentlewoman and will elevate this event. Won't you do it for the children?"

Ugh, he knows just how to pull at my heartstrings.

She wasn't an utter ninny. Yes, she wanted to help children. But why this sudden compassion for the downtrodden and helpless from Jameson? This was out of character for him. "Send me more details and I'll discuss it with Uncle John and Aunt Sophie. I'm staying with them for the season. They're sponsoring my come-out."

He frowned. "They'll refuse. Why can't we keep this as our little secret?"

When he was younger, Jameson had a tendency to pout when he did not get his way. Too bad this had not changed. He looked like a petulant boy as he drained his glass and raised it to be refilled by one of the attending footmen.

"You forget, I'm a Farthingale. We don't keep secrets from each other. Yes, they will likely refuse. If so, I will write to the abbess and see if we can help in some other way."

His eyebrows shot up. "Why her? I'm the one putting this event together on behalf of the orphanage. All she has to do is receive the funds."

Although the desserts looked quite tempting, Violet had no appetite for them. She merely wished this dinner party to be over. Jameson was now sulking beside her, and Romulus appeared enraptured by Lady Felicia, his head tipped toward her as she engaged him in another intimate conversation.

When supper finally came to an end, she rose and joined the ladies in the parlor while the men remained at the dining table for drinks and smokes.

Lady Withnall intercepted her as she made her way to Aunt Sophie and Daisy. "Sit next to me, Violet."

It wasn't a request, but a command.

"That was not well done of you," the diminutive dragon said and tapped her cane on the floor twice to mark her disdain. *Thuck. Thuck.*

"I don't know what you mean?" In truth, she could not imagine what she had done to overset this woman.

"You allowed Lady Felicia to steal Romulus from you." She tapped her cane again. "And who was that blackguard you were speaking to all evening?"

Violet arched an eyebrow. "Do you mean my dinner partner, Lord Jameson Forester? His family and mine are long-time friends. And what did you expect me to do to Lady Felicia? Challenge her to a duel over Captain Brayden? She's known him for years. I've known him for a day." She rose abruptly. "Forgive me if I seem rude, Lady Withnall. But I have enough demands placed on me just now. I don't need more from you."

Oh, that did sound rude.

It wasn't the old gossip's fault Romulus had lavished his attention on Lady Felicia throughout supper. Nor was it her fault that Jameson had spent the entire meal urging her to sing to a roomful of men. "I'm sorry. I still feel like a duck out of water here."

She made her way into the garden, needing to be alone for a moment. The night was overcast, the clouds covering the moon and stars. The breeze was laden with moisture and carried the scent of lilacs, the heady fragrance filling the air.

She was alone no more than a moment before Jameson came up to her. "Violet, this is important to me. I need to know that you'll help."

"I told you I would think about it." She took a step back when he attempted to take her hand. "Go away, Jameson."

"You wound me to turn me away. Please don't spurn me, you bewitching creature."

She rolled her eyes. There was that word again. *Creature.* No one had ever called her that before, and now she'd heard it twice in one night. "Oh, for pity's sake. Do not insult me by pretending you have the slightest interest in me."

"I'm not pretending. You were always a pretty girl, but you've grown into a ravishingly beautiful woman. You are like a magnificent butterfly just sprung from its cocoon." He suddenly took her by the arms, his touch light enough, but entirely inappropriate.

She didn't struggle, for she didn't fear him. He wasn't a brute, just a pampered, idiot lord. "This *butterfly* would like you to let go of her. Nor will I sing for you if you continue your ridiculous behavior, so take your flattery elsewhere."

"I meant every word. If you won't help me with the charity, then indulge me by granting me a kiss." His grip tightened on her arms.

She sighed in exasperation. "Go back inside and leave me alone, Jameson. Don't insult me by attempting to steal a kiss. You are certainly *not* going to be the first man I kiss. So, let go of me before I do you bodily harm."

He laughed and held his hands up as he drew them away. "There. See. I can be a gentleman."

"I don't know about that," Romulus said, catching both of them off guard as he came up from behind. "Get out of here, Forester."

Jameson gave an extravagant bow and backed into Lady Dayne's parlor where the men had now joined the ladies.

Violet let out the breath she'd been holding. "Thank goodness he left without incident. The man was giving me a headache. I had no desire to use physical force on him, but I would have done so if he'd attempted to kiss me."

"Physical force? Against him? You aren't strong enough, Violet. He would have gotten his way." Romulus folded his arms across his chest. "Why are you out here alone?"

"To escape all of you." She mimicked his stance. "Why are you out here? Won't your precious Lady Felicia miss you?"

"No. She couldn't care less about me."

"Are we speaking of the same woman? Your *old* friend? She couldn't keep her hands off you."

"That was for your benefit. She was bored and this is how she amuses herself. What did Forester want? You seemed to be having an intense dinner conversation."

She arched an eyebrow. "I didn't think you'd noticed. Your eyes were on Lady Felicia and her scantily clad bosom the entire time." She groaned. "Oh, I sounded quite bitter and jealous, didn't I?"

He sighed. "We're both out of sorts. If Forester hadn't taken his hands off you, I would have hurt him, probably broken some part of him, and then tossed him into Lady Dayne's rose bushes."

"Jameson is harmless. You needn't have worried. Besides, I know how to defend myself."

"I don't know about that," he muttered.

"What? That he's harmless or that I can defend myself?"

"Both, I suppose. There's something about him I don't like. Perhaps it's that he was so attentive to you." He cast her a wry grin. "I can be bitter and jealous, too."

Her annoyance eased, and she laughed softly. "Good to know I'm not the only one out of sorts tonight."

"Are you busy tomorrow morning? Let's meet by the bench and go through more of that book."

"The Book of Love?"

He nodded. "I think we both need to learn how to trust each other."

"Agreed, but how do we build a lifetime's worth of trust in less than a week?"

CHAPTER EIGHT

THE DAY WAS once again overcast and breezy, but there was no sign of rain. Violet was up early, as was her routine, so after washing and dressing, she decided to write a letter to St. Aubrey's abbess, Sister Ursula, about the condition of the orphanage buildings and what needed to be done. She did not know if Sister Ursula's response would come in time. Still, she thought it important to let her know what was planned.

Although Jameson had been his usual, irritating self, he was trying to do a good deed and she wished to help him. Also, it was rather flattering of him to think of her singing talent as a means to raise funds for this charitable cause.

She walked downstairs and had just given the letter to Pruitt to post, when her aunt bustled into the entry hall. "Aunt Sophie, would you mind if I invited some friends of mine to tea tomorrow? Lord Jameson Forester and his sister, Lady Rawley."

Sophie smiled. "The Foresters? They are friends of your parents, are they not?"

Violet nodded. "Their father and mine are best of friends. I know Jameson and Valerie quite well, although I haven't seen them in a few years. The marquis relied on my parents to help him through the difficult months after his wife died. We saw a lot of him and his children back then."

"They are most welcome, my dear. Give me their direction and I'll send off an invitation at once."

She hugged her aunt. "Thank you, I don't know how we would all get along without you."

Her aunt laughed. "I think you'd all manage quite well. I've spent most of these past five years in a fog. Each daughter having her come-out, each one botched spectacularly. But it all worked out in spite of the mistakes I made."

"I don't think loving your children can ever be a mistake."

"No, but sometimes we parents must learn to hold our tongues and trust our children to do what's best for themselves, not to push them into doing what we think is best."

"Ah, yes. Trust." She nodded. "I think I must work on that as well. It's very hard to trust someone you've only known for a day or two."

"You are referring to Romulus Brayden, I assume. Yes, it is difficult. Those bonds take time to develop."

Violet took her aunt's arm as they walked into the breakfast room. The men had already left for the day, and none of the other relatives had come down yet, so they had a rare moment alone. "Unless Lady Withnall relents and agrees to keep quiet about what she saw, I only have one week to learn all I can about him. Last night did not go well for us."

"Ah, I saw him with the Marquis of Herringdon's widow, Lady Felicia. The woman was relentless, never leaving him alone."

"Hard to miss, weren't they? She knew just how to bring out the worst in me. I turned into a green-eyed monster. And I don't even have green eyes."

Her aunt shook her head and laughed again. "Violet, I can only say that the Braydens are men of honor. I don't think Romulus will lie to you about his feelings for Lady Felicia. If he likes her, he will tell you straight out. The truth may hurt, but it is best to know exactly where you stand with him."

When the clock struck ten, Violet walked into the garden to await

Romulus. She was surprised to find him already seated on the bench, his legs stretched before him and his hands propped behind his head as he watched the passing clouds, obviously lost in thought.

"Is it too early to talk about love?" she asked, casting him a hesitant smile. She took a seat beside him and opened her book where they'd left off yesterday.

He appeared relieved to see her, for he responded with a warm smile of his own. "Never too early for that. Shall we talk about last night first?"

"Which travesty would you like to discuss? Shall we start with Lady Withnall? Lady Felicia? Or Lord Forester?"

He winced. "I'd like to shoot all three of them out of my ship's cannons and watch them drop straight into the ocean."

"I couldn't agree more."

He sat up straighter. "Violet, I won't deny there was more between Lady Felicia and myself in the past. It was never anything serious, for she fully intended to marry the Marquis of Herringdon."

"But she's a widow now, and from what I hear, wealthy. She is free to marry whomever she chooses. This time, she can marry for love."

He arched an eyebrow. "Felicia loves herself more than she can ever love any man. More important, I would never offer for her."

"You wouldn't? Why not?" Violet did not doubt him, but she was curious as to his reluctance.

"A thousand reasons. She would demand separate sleeping quarters, for one."

"Isn't this customary? Am I not the one out of step with such arrangements?" She tipped her head up and looked at him with some confusion.

"Yes, you are delightfully out of step. But so am I. This is what I would want in a marriage, a wife who wishes to sleep in my arms. A wife who would never consider taking on other lovers to stem her boredom."

"Romulus," she said with a roll of her eyes, "I don't think any woman would ever find you boring."

"Now, see..." He leaned forward so that they were almost nose to nose. "This is why I would choose you over her always. You may decide that I am boring once you get to know me better, but you would not respond by turning your back on the marriage and discreetly, or not so discreetly, taking on other lovers."

"What do you think I would do?" She knew she was young and inexperienced, but the possibility of giving her body to other men? It wasn't done in the Farthingale family. She couldn't imagine herself breaking this tradition.

He cupped her face gently in his big hand. "You would find a way to make me less boring. Or you would accept me for the dolt I am. The point is, you are capable of caring for others and placing their needs before yours. Of course, being a pig-headed, prideful male, I would want to be the one sacrificing to make *you* happy, not the other way around."

"Would you really?"

"Yes." He dropped his hand and eased slightly back. "But I suppose you'll just have to trust me on that. Violet, let's get back to the book."

"Very well." She opened it to where they'd left off. "We stopped yesterday at the five senses. The strength of this book is teaching us to really see each other, and hear each other, and so on. So, let's start with the sense of sight. What do you see when you look at me?"

"Someone very pleasing to the eye." He grinned. "But I think we've already established that low brain response."

She nodded. "So on to looking at me with your higher brain function."

He chuckled. "Assuming I have one. Well, here goes...you have the loveliest eyes I've ever seen. Violet..."

"Yes?"

He shook his head. "I just mean that they're violet in color. They're intelligent eyes. That's why they sparkle. Otherwise, they'd be dull. You have nice lips. I look forward to tasting them, but I'm jumping ahead a few chapters, aren't I? That's my low brain taking over again."

He cleared his throat and continued. "You are beautiful in a sweet, warm way. I like that, because it means you can also be silly and fun. You don't care if your hair isn't always perfect."

She gasped and put her hands to her hair. "Is it falling out of its pins already?"

"No." He laughed.

She cast him a sheepish grin. "It appears I am vain."

"It will take much more than worrying about your hair to make you vain. We all wish to look presentable in company. But if the wind were to gust and make those pins fall out of your hair, you'd probably laugh and simply accept it."

She nodded. "There is nothing one can do against the wind other than don a hat and hope it stays on."

"A vain person would be angry with the brazen wind for making them less than perfect."

"Ah, well that is not a problem for me. I already know I am less than perfect." She cast him an impish grin.

He regarded her unsmiling, but after a moment, his severe expression lightened. "I think you are closer to perfect than you imagine."

Her eyes widened in surprise. "Well, that's a big step forward. Truth is, I am very far from it. But if you believe I am, then we have made great strides. This is what The Book of Love says is most important. My goal is to become *your* ideal woman. Others may find me lacking, but it is your opinion of me that matters. But do you mean it, Romulus? I heard you tell Lady Felicia I'm not your usual type."

"You aren't. The comment you overheard was about my poor judgement, not about your lack in any way. But that's all in the past and ought to remain buried there, never to be dug up again."

She laughed. "Goodness, now I'm curious to know what you did back then. My past was exceedingly dull." She laughed again. "Nothing in the least scandalous or exciting until those bees came along."

"Ah, yes. I was warned about the Chipping Way curse and chose to ignore it. This is how we had to meet. Nothing tame or polite would do."

"Far better than being introduced at a ball, I think. I doubt you would have remembered me among the crush of guests. Not when so many debutantes were being shoved at you all at once." Of course, she would have remained in raptures over him. But so would every other young lady who met him.

"Had we been introduced in a crowded ballroom, would you have signed my dance card? Or spent time talking to me?" she asked, somehow thinking he would not have done either. More likely, he would have run to the card room and hidden there all evening with his bachelor friends, imbibing brandy or champagne, and commiserating over their misfortune to be hunted like wild boar.

He seemed to read her mind. "I would have noticed you. I would have remembered you. It is even possible I would have dreamed of you for nights afterward. But I would not have pursued you. At least, not yet."

She nodded in agreement. "I didn't think so. You've hardly had a moment to enjoy your bachelorhood."

"Ah, yes. Setting up my own household. Being on my own to do as I wish, not answering to anyone but myself. I was looking forward to that."

"Until me."

"The bees weren't your fault. I could have listened to the warning about the Chipping Way curse and purchased a house elsewhere. I didn't want to. I liked General Allworthy's house. Something about it called to me." He shrugged. "Perhaps it was the beautiful Farthingale I was told lived next door."

She laughed. "You had no idea I existed when you offered to purchase the house."

He shrugged again. "I knew of the possibility of you."

"Warned of the possibility of meeting your doom is more like it."

"No. I was intrigued by the possibility of love."

She clasped the book a little tighter, needing to hold onto something sturdy as her heart began to beat faster. His words sounded quite romantic, but how could they be?

"I did not expect it to slam into me so soon, but I was not afraid of it. Had Lady Withnall not been there as I slathered vinegar all over your body, I might have remained unattached a little while longer. Pretended you did not affect me."

"But you just said you would have avoided me at the upcoming social affairs. Not signed my dance card. Not courted me."

He nodded. "Remaining unattached for now was my plan. But plans are often dashed. I've never been in love. I've never even had a youthful infatuation. But that doesn't mean I disdain it. I always held out the hope of finding the one person who would brighten my heart."

Was he suggesting she was the one?

She didn't believe it.

If anything, he was convincing himself that she had to be the one because fate and the Chipping Way curse had willed it.

"Being alone is not as glamorous as it appears. I realized it almost immediately. My house is a mess. It has yet to be cleaned. I have very little furniture. And the only young woman I've brought there has been you." He grunted, shook his head, and then chuckled. "The movers adored you. They were enraptured by your singing and your family's thoughtfulness. They congratulated me on my good taste in a wife. I didn't bother to correct them. There was no point since we will be married soon anyway."

Her eyes widened in surprise. "Are you admitting defeat already?"

"Not at all. Lady Withnall's edict may have moved up my plans, but the result would have been the same. Once I'd noticed you...I would never have forgotten you. Violet, my dreams of you would not have lasted a mere few days. You would have haunted them all the nights of my life."

Her heart took a small leap. "Really?"

He nodded. "Really."

She sat back, noting that his arm was stretched across the back of the bench. It would take nothing for him to put his arm around her.

She would like to be in his arms.

But he would not reach for her while they were in view of everyone inside the Farthingale house. "May I ask you something?"

He tipped his head in a curt nod. "Certainly."

"What is it about me that would make me memorable to you?"

"First, and this is speaking only from my low brain, you are stunning." He slid her a sideways glance and smiled. "Now, speaking from my high brain, you are stunning on the inside as well. In truth, I don't think you appreciate just how lovely you are in every way."

She blushed. "That is nonsense. There are dozens far prettier and more accomplished than me."

"Not in my eyes, and we know from that book," he said, nodding toward the tome she still gripped in her hands, "this is what counts most. It isn't merely that you are pleasing to the eye. Lord knows you are." He rolled his own eyes and glanced upward before returning his gaze to her. "I also like that you want to be something more as a person. You said earlier that looks fade over time. But a good heart, intelligence, generosity, those attributes don't fade."

Violet listened intently, surprised Romulus was taking their predicament so seriously and reaching deep into his heart for answers. He wasn't merely asking *how do I get out of this mess with my bachelorhood intact?* He'd gone beyond it. *What do I want out of life? What sort of partner do I wish for?*

"This book speaks of the five senses as a means to connect us," he said, the resonant depth of his voice quite soothing and at the same time exciting. "But we can also connect through common goals and aspirations. Or common likes and dislikes. I think our senses form the bond of our attraction to each other, but it would be our common goals that truly bind us."

"Are you suggesting we already have strong connections to each other?"

He nodded. "Yes, isn't it obvious?"

"How?"

She leaned forward, eager to hear his thoughts, because she did not know how a brave and worldly sea captain could have anything in common with a sheltered debutante who felt more comfortable climbing a tree in a country meadow than dancing a waltz in a London ballroom. Why would such a man want anything to do with her? What was their common bond?

"Violet, if your eyes grow any wider, they are going to roll out of their sockets."

"I can't help it. You amaze me. Please, do go on. I am very interested to hear what you have to say."

He smiled and shook his head. "Braydens and Farthingales marry for love. That is one of our strongest connections. We've been raised to respect the sanctity of marriage. Another connection is that we both come from large, meddlesome families."

She laughed. "Oh, dear. Is yours as bad as mine?"

"Possibly worse. You haven't met my Aunt Miranda yet. There is no one quite like her, and I'm not sure I mean it as compliment. I love her, of course. But she can be quite scary, at times. Even Lady Withnall would cringe in fear."

Violet clapped her hands. "I adore her already!"

Romulus gave a hearty laugh, but after a moment, he turned serious. "Braydens are faithful to their spouses. I don't know what you thought was happening between me and Lady Felicia last night, but it is important for you to know that for my part, nothing was happening. Nor will it ever happen with Felicia or any other woman. It isn't the Brayden way. It isn't *my* way."

She nodded. "I hope you know it is the same with Farthingales. We are faithful to our spouses. I'm not sure how we prove it to each other except over time."

"Some things must be taken on faith, Violet. We've had good examples to follow. Big, loving families. That is our common connection, and it is a very good start."

She closed the book and set it aside, then folded her hands on her lap. "How else are we connected? You are a sea captain, used to commanding sailors and doing battle. I am no one of consequence. I'm not saying it to belittle myself. It is a simple fact. I've done nothing of importance in my life. And honestly, you do not look like the sort of man who really needs a woman to support him or to help him make something of himself. I think this is what troubles me most. I am inconsequential to your life. But you would be very important to mine."

"You are looking at it all wrong, Violet. I don't need you handing me cannonballs in the heat of battle or hoisting mainsails. What a man looks for in a wife...I'm not quite sure how to explain it." He ran a hand through his hair in obvious consternation as he struggled to find the right words.

She waited quietly, watching in fascination as he collected his thoughts. Indeed, she marveled at the care and determination he was putting into their situation.

"What a man needs...is a reason to be. Why am I on the high seas tackling pirates? Why do I bother with civility or etiquette when I'm home or out in Society? If only men existed, we'd all be sitting about a campfire drinking ale until we passed out. We'd live in caves and fight over everything and nothing, because men always fight unless they're held back for reasons more important to them."

He reached out and tucked a finger under her chin. "A man adopts civility in order to make a better world for his family. His children, his wife. Even those meddlesome relatives he wishes would go away and leave him in peace."

"I had no idea you were a soldier and a philosopher."

"I hadn't thought of myself that way. But yes, I suppose. When asked who I am, I don't think of myself merely as a captain in the Royal Navy. Nor do I think of myself as the brother of an earl. When asked the question *who am I*, I may respond by stating my military rank. That's the easy answer I would give in casual conversation. But it is only a small part of me. *Who am I* is more about my character and my goals in life."

He released her and leaned back once more. "When James returned from war so badly injured, I grew mad at the world. I was also angry with him. Why did he go off to fight? He could have paid someone to take his commission. Other noblemen did and thought nothing of it."

"He is a Brayden, so he wouldn't. That is his noble character."

Romulus nodded. "The war almost destroyed him. If not for Sophie, I don't think he would be alive today. She is why he wakes up each morning ready to experience the new day. What she offers him is something not easily definable. Truly, I can't explain it. But when I look at you, I see that same quality."

She put a hand to her heart, for this was no longer a lighthearted discussion or even a moderately serious one. It had taken a leap to something quite profound. "Romulus, surely you jest."

"Not at all. I don't know what it is about you, Violet. I just know that if you were in my life, it would be a good life. A happy one." He groaned lightly. "Oh, hell. Why aren't you breathing?"

He was watching her, so he noticed her eyes begin to water. He groaned again. "Are you going to cry?"

"No, of course not. Even if I do, it is only because your words overwhelm me." She wiped a stray tear as it trickled onto her cheek. "I've had gentlemen tell me I'm pretty. I've heard it for years now. Perhaps I should have taken it as a compliment, but inside I always wondered, so what? What else am I? A vase is pretty. A flower is pretty. But what you said just now about Sophie's influence on your brother's life, this is what I hope to be. This is what I'd like to mean to someone. To be needed, to be looked upon as someone's reason to be. Now that is the best compliment anyone can receive."

She wiped away another tear. "Romulus, I know we're only on our second full day. But must we wait?"

"To marry?"

Her heart was in a rampant, roaring beat as she nodded. "Yes. Will you marry me?" As the import of her own words struck her, she gasped. "Oh, dear! Never mind. Forget I said any such thing. I was swept away in the moment." In all her life, she'd never dreamed she would be the one proposing to a man. But how could she not after what he'd just told her?

He laughed. "I'm flattered, but if you will recall, I asked you first. You refused, and my response was *Miss Farthingale, your answer cannot be a rejection of my offer.*"

He took her hands in his and nudged her to rise along with him. "There is something important we must do before this goes any further."

"What is that?"

"The kiss. You insisted upon it, if you will recall."

She nodded.

"I've wanted to kiss you from the moment I unlaced your gown and began rubbing vinegar all over your body," he said, his voice soft and sensual. "Your family, our neighbors, even the villainous Lady Withnall knew exactly what I intended to do to you. Now you know, as well."

He lowered his lips to hers so that they were achingly close but not quite touching. "What do you say, Violet? Are you willing to explore the sense of taste?"

CHAPTER NINE

MOTHER IN HEAVEN.

Was she willing to kiss Romulus?

What a question to ask! He was easily the handsomest man she'd ever met and certainly one of the smartest. She wanted to devour him, breathe him in, inhale great gulps of him, for she loved his rugged, manly scent that hinted of salty air and spices. She loved the strength and power of him, wanted to cling like a limpet fish to his massive shoulders and burrow close against his body.

She knew she would love the muscled strength of his arms as he wrapped them around her.

His kiss.

Most of all, she wanted to taste his lips, allow their warmth to seep through her own and carry her away to a place she'd never been before. "Yes, I'm willing."

Goodness, yes.

She glanced toward the large parlor window, trying to detect whether any of her family was looking out of it. Hortensia was there, her stern and frowning countenance staring back at her, knowing exactly what they wanted to do, and by her frown, she was determined to stop them.

Violet stifled her disappointment.

"What a bother," she muttered.

Hortensia would come charging out of the house like a raging bull the moment Romulus put his arms around her.

He must have noticed the direction of her gaze, for he emitted a soft, laughing groan. "This will take some tactical planning. Do you still want the kiss?"

She nodded.

"Then come with me."

"Where?" She merely asked out of curiosity and did not resist when he casually placed her arm in his as any gentleman would do when walking with a lady down the street. She wasn't certain what he intended, but she went along since he obviously had something in mind.

"The large oak tree will hide us from her view."

He was referring to the infamous tree where the bees once had their hive. "It will? Oh, I see. Yes, it might."

He nodded. "We'll have only a few seconds to conduct this operation."

She laughed. "You make it sound like a tactical naval maneuver."

"Oh, it is. Hortensia is on to me and my evil desires. She will come running out of the house as soon as she loses sight of us behind the tree. We'll have to the count of three to reappear, and when we don't, she'll know exactly what I'm doing to you."

"With my wholehearted approval." Violet could not help but laugh again, for he had a devilish arch to his eyebrows, and he was smiling at her with a most appealingly wicked warmth. "I'll be complicit in this delicate military operation. Tell me what I ought to be doing."

He walked her casually around the garden as they spoke. "All you need to do is respond honestly. There is no right or wrong in a kiss. You'll either like it or you won't. Your body will respond instinctively to it. So will your heart. Just follow wherever it takes you."

She nodded. "I'm ready."

In truth, she had been ready from the moment she'd escaped the bees only to end up in his kitchen, his big hands skimming all over her body as he unlaced her gown, rolled down her stockings, and hurriedly applied the vinegar to her skin. The bee stings burned in a bad way, but his touch burned as well, in an incredibly delightful way.

They strolled near the tree.

"Here we go," he muttered, his arms suddenly wrapping around her as she leaned against the tree trunk and felt its rough bark press through the back of her muslin gown. He turned her so they now switched positions, he leaning against the rough bark as he drew her up against his chest and lowered his head to crush his lips to hers.

She felt the warm conquest of his mouth on hers, the demanding press of his lips, and the tension in his body as he sought to hold back, no doubt afraid he'd scare her with the searing intensity of his desire. She knew he wanted her and felt this same hunger for him.

She clutched the lapels of his jacket, needing to anchor the waves of sensation that began to course through her body. These were elemental waves, it was the only way she knew how to describe them. Air, fire, water, earth. The rush of air that left her breathless, while at the same time, a fire raged in her veins. Her legs had turned to water, no longer able to hold her up. She would have fallen if he were not supporting her, and now she was drowning in the power of his kiss. But he steadied her, his embrace comforting and planting her to the ground so she would not float away.

She was unprepared for the enormity of these sensations, but he'd told her to trust her heart and follow wherever it led her. The answer was obvious. Her heart led her straight to him.

Yet, how could she want him so desperately when she hardly knew him? How could her heart be so certain?

She felt the lick of his tongue along the seam of her lips and opened slightly to take more of him in. He probed, invaded, and yet there was a protective gentleness to the kiss despite its heat and urgency.

She'd lost track of the seconds, for this moment in his arms felt timeless, and she did not want their kiss ever to end.

"Violet! Do not kiss that man!"

Oh, far too late for that.

"Twenty seconds," Romulus whispered, easing his lips off hers with a wrenching groan. He released her and stepped back.

She felt bereft.

She liked being in his arms.

How had he kept his wits together enough to count to twenty? She'd gotten as far as one, two…then completely lost her place. But this was her first time, and she had no idea what to expect.

He'd done this before, quite often if the perfection of his kiss was any indication.

"Caught with my hand in the tin of biscuits. We're in for it now," he muttered, obviously feeling not a whit of remorse for what they'd just done.

In truth, neither did she.

She liked the affectionate warmth of his smile and the emerald fire in his eyes as he gazed at her.

She'd thoroughly enjoyed clutching his muscles and running her hands over the hard planes of his shoulders and chest. Her only disappointment was the impossibility of touching his skin, for there were too many layers of fabric between them.

She had no idea her thoughts could be so wanton.

Was Romulus thinking wanton thoughts of her?

ROMULUS WAS NOT in the habit of strangling old ladies, but Violet's aunt was making his fingers itch to wrap around her throat. He could do nothing but watch the harridan storm toward them.

Violet's chin was tipped up in unexpected defiance.

He smothered a grin, realizing she'd liked his kiss and was not at all pleased with Hortensia for interrupting her exciting experiment.

Her first kiss.

He hoped he'd done it justice.

One glimpse of Violet's starlit eyes revealed he had. He was glad of it, not merely because he was a prideful arse who liked to think he had prowess with women. He cared for Violet more deeply than he thought possible on such a short acquaintance. But it felt as though he'd always known her, that his heart had merely been waiting to embrace her. She was important to him, and it had nothing to do with any possible scandal.

"What do you have to say for yourself?" Hortensia scowled at Violet, the question delivered with the force of an inquisitor at an inquisition.

"I say...hurrah! I'm glad I kissed him and would not take it back for all the world." But she tempered her defiance as she continued. "Aunt Hortensia, don't be angry. You know I had to kiss him. This is what I was explaining to you about The Book of Love and the importance of testing its theories. Yes, this experiment was a few days rushed, but he was the perfect test frog."

Hortensia stared at him as though he was a debauched hound.

He supposed he was when it came to Violet.

"Indeed," Violet said, overlooking the silent exchange between him and her aunt, "I could not bring myself to kiss anyone else. Besides, we are betrothed and ought to be permitted some modicum of privacy."

Hortensia cast Romulus another discerning glance. "So, you were her willing test frog?"

"I hope I am much more than that to your niece. The kiss was harmless enough."

Hortensia snorted.

Violet smiled up at him. "Your kiss was divine. Well done, Mr. Brayden. Thank you for being so...cooperative."

"My pleasure, Miss Farthingale." He supposed these sensations of love and sexual awakening were all new to her and felt like tests at every step. As for him, he was very much looking forward to tasting her rosebud lips again soon. He'd already sown his wild oats. This was no test or new exploration for him.

He'd been sexually awakened years ago.

But with this kiss, Violet had awakened his heart as well.

He was experienced enough to know what he wanted, and it was this girl with the soft, violet eyes and the beautiful smile.

"Impertinent girl," Hortensia said with a sigh of defeat. "Wipe that cow-eyed look off your face and make yourself presentable. You have company."

Violet appeared surprised. "I do? Who would call on me at this hour?"

Whoever it was, Romulus already hated them for interrupting his time alone with her. But he would get more kisses from her later today. He was happy to be the object of her testing if the results were as delightful as their first kiss had been.

Indeed, these love experiments could be quite jolly fun.

He strode to the bench and picked up the book, curious to read it cover to cover. These experiments might be enhanced if he understood better what he ought to be doing to increase Violet's pleasure.

Despite his low brain function presently being in control of his body—Lord, he was in flames over this girl—he was thinking of how to make their lives together as husband and wife happy and fulfilled. This was the pleasure he sought to learn more about.

There, that was a high-brain purpose.

Even if his thoughts were still dug low in that sexual ditch.

"Lord Forester and his sister, Lady Rawley, have stopped by. They apologized profusely, but said it was urgent that they see you."

Violet frowned. "Very well."

She turned to Romulus. "Do you mind if we postpone our..." A pink stain shot into her cheeks. "…discussion until later?"

By discussion, he supposed she meant hot, steamy kisses.

Yes, he minded.

But he could be a gentleman about it. "Not at all."

The sun had broken through the clouds and was now shining down on Violet's hair. Those dark, silken curls looked ready to burst from their pins. He'd probably knocked a few of them loose as his fingers had been buried in her hair.

She was nibbling her lip, driving him wild with the play of her teeth against her plump, lower lip. "You are welcome to join us."

He was going to refuse, but she continued. "After all, we are betrothed. Even though it is a secret betrothal for the moment."

After that kiss? He'd marry her today if it were possible to obtain the special license within the hour.

"But I know what Lord Forester's visit is about, and I don't wish to keep his purpose from you."

"What purpose?" Was there something more between her and Lord Forester? It couldn't be anything romantic. Violet was no accomplished flirt and would never be able to pretend affection for two men at once.

But he'd seen Forester with her in Lady Dayne's moonlit garden last night. Although Violet held no romantic feelings for him, there was no mistaking Forester's amorous intentions toward her.

"It is about my singing."

"Your singing?" Oh, hell. Was he about to be dragged into a music recital? At this hour? He'd need three or four drinks to numb his ears. Not that he would mind hearing Violet sing, but the others?

"I think it is important that you join me," Violet said, casting him a pleading look.

"Of course." Bloody damnation.

Hortensia was still looking at him as though she wanted to bludgeon him, but this appeared to be her natural look.

He walked inside with Violet and was instantly glad he'd agreed. Forester was not happy to see him, and his sister appeared more than slightly alarmed.

This wasn't about warbling a few tunes among friends. "Why are you here, Forester?"

"I might ask the same of you." He turned to Violet. "Lady Rawley and I wished to speak to you in private, but I see we've come at a bad time. When may we call upon you again?"

"Tomorrow afternoon. You've already been invited. Did you receive Aunt Sophie's invitation to come to tea tomorrow?"

"No, we must have gone out before it arrived. We'd love to attend." Lady Rawley smiled at Violet, but there was an undercurrent of tension in her manner that put Romulus off. What did this pair want with Violet?

"We'll see you tomorrow then," Forester said, bowing over her hand and giving Romulus the curtest of acknowledging nods.

Romulus crossed his arms over his chest and frowned at Forester's retreating back. There was something he disliked about the man. It wasn't jealousy, he would have been more polite if it were simply a matter of that.

Of course, he would never encourage another man's pursuit of Violet, but he could understand why another man might want to court her. She was lovely. Sweet. Intelligent. Perfect. But his gut was roiling, and the little hairs on the back of his neck were standing on end. This man was not competing for Violet's affections.

This man was not to be trusted.

Romulus did not yet understand the reason for his unease, only that alarm bells were ringing in his head, and he did not want Violet anywhere near Forester. "You mustn't see him again, Violet."

She laughed off his request. "Don't be silly. We've already invited Lord Forester and his sister to tea. They're old friends. I cannot take back the invitation. Nor would I wish to take it back."

She frowned at him. "What is it you don't like about him?"

"I don't know."

Violet now looked as though she wished to bludgeon him. "You don't know? Yet you expect me to cut an old friend out of my life, just like that?"

He may have been a bit heavy-handed, but he was only thinking of her safety. "Yes."

He caught the disappointment in her eyes and knew he had confused her with a request that seemed illogical. "Please, Violet. I'm not an ogre. Nor am I a jealous, possessive hound. There is more going on here than you realize."

"Such as?"

"As I just said, I don't know yet. But I need you to trust me." He ran a hand through his hair in exasperation. Why ever would she agree? She'd known Forester for years and him for two days.

"Trust," she said after a thoughtful pause. "This is the key to everything, isn't it?"

He nodded. "It is."

She gazed up at him with hurt reflected in her eyes. "Then why do you not trust me to make the right decision?"

CHAPTER TEN

WHY DO YOU not trust me to make the right decision?
Violet's question troubled Romulus, and continued to trouble him as he strode into his brother's townhouse later that afternoon. He'd tried to explain his reasons to Violet, but they'd sounded weak even to his own ears. "I'm an experienced naval officer," he'd told her. "My instincts are finely honed to sense danger."

His instincts weren't merely warning him that Forester was no friend to her, they were shouting it at him.

Her anger had abated somewhat, but she was not happy with him. "I shall offer you a compromise," she'd said with a calm and logic he had to admire. "Let me hear what he has to say, and then I'll talk to you about it. But I must be the one to decide what I must do."

He had opened his mouth to protest, but she would allow no more and frowned at him. "Trust goes both ways, Romulus. How can I marry someone who doesn't trust me?"

That remark still stung.

He trusted Violet.

Blessed saints, there was no guile or malice in her heart.

But Forester and his sister?

He'd check the silver after a supper party to make certain they hadn't walked off with any pieces.

"Rom, you're looking awfully morose for a man in love," his brother teased as Romulus entered the study and sank into one of the soft leather chairs beside the fireplace. James had been seated at his desk, but rose to join him.

His cousins, Tynan and Marcus, were standing with their shoulders propped against the fireplace mantel, each with a glass of brandy in hand.

They grinned at him as he sat down.

"The tadpole is in love?" Marcus teased, referring to him by the name given to the youngest Brayden boys. James, Marcus, and Tynan were the eldest and all of them earls. James was Earl of Exmoor. Tynan was Earl of Westcliff, and Marcus was Earl of Kinross.

Not only were they older, but sometimes insufferable because of their titles. Not that they ever treated him as lesser, but they could never resist playfully taunting him and the younger Brayden boys because that's just what older brothers did.

Marcus's brother Caleb was known as squid because he fell in the middle, between the eldest three and the youngest four. They all still referred to Caleb as squid even though he was General Brayden, and in command of England's finest royal dragoon units.

"Shut up, Marcus," Romulus grumbled, "or I'll tell your wife you were teasing me. Lara will have you sleeping in the outhouse for a week."

Marcus laughingly groaned. "She would do it, too. I don't know why she's so fond of you tadpoles."

Romulus, Finn, Joshua, and Ronan, said tadpoles, were all close in age and the youngest of the Brayden boys...now men, but not in the eyes of their older brothers.

"What's going on, Rom?" Tynan asked, frowning. "How can we help?"

"I need advice." This was also the Brayden way, the eight of them always ready to help each other out.

Romulus flinched as James moved from behind his desk and limped toward him. None of them said anything as he carefully lowered himself into the chair beside Romulus, keeping his bad leg outstretched since he couldn't quite bend it.

James's suffering tore at their hearts, but James would only get angry if he caught any of them pitying him. "You need advice on how to handle a woman?"

He nodded, annoyed the three of them were now grinning at him. But he was ready to take their teasing because he needed answers. "Violet thinks I don't trust her."

James chuckled, but it was one of commiseration, for he'd likely experienced the same when first meeting his wife, Sophie. "Is she right? Do you trust her?"

"Yes, of course I do. It's her so-called friends I'm worried about." He then went on to explain about his gut feeling. "If Forester's unannounced visit was so *urgent*, then why did he and his sister run off like scared rabbits the moment they saw me?"

"Perhaps it was a harmless attempt to court Violet," Marcus said. "You're his competition, and you must admit, we Braydens can be quite intimidating."

"The man is a snake. There's nothing noble in his intentions."

"But you also just told us Forester approached Violet in Lady Dayne's garden last night and backed off when she told him to unhand her. Perhaps he's just inept at courtship, and you're putting him on edge. The ill feeling you sense may be aimed only at you, Rom."

"I hope so. I'll rip him apart if he sets a hand on Violet."

His brother and cousins exchanged amused glances and then responded by chuckling again.

"What's so funny?" Romulus rose to pour himself a brandy and offered one to James.

But James declined. "It warms my heart to see my little tadpole of a brother in love."

He offered to refill the glasses of his cousins, but they also declined, their grins still fixed on their faces.

Romulus sighed. "Hell, James. Stop calling me a tadpole. Do you know what I am to Violet? Her test *frog*. So, I suppose this tadpole is now grown up. Violet has this book her sister gave her, supposedly a scientific explanation of the sensations of love and how to arouse a man's desires to–"

"Blessed saints! What did you just say?" James was smiling so broadly, his face looked about to crack in half. "And her family is allowing her to read this book?"

He nodded. "She claims it's scientific and she is testing the theories out on me. Nothing lewd or suggestive. It's quite interesting, actually. Harmless so far." He shrugged. "But it is about love, and we all know matters can get out of hand rather quickly. If it does, I know she'll be safe with me rather than with some other hound."

"Or frog," Marcus teasingly muttered.

"A hound like Forester?" Tynan remarked.

He nodded again. "Her entire family knows the depraved workings of my mind when it comes to Violet, especially after the bee incident."

James chuckled. "Frog. Hound. Bee. You're collecting quite a menagerie."

Romulus frowned at him. "But how can any man be trusted around her? She's so beautiful. Warm, generous, smart. She's also so damn innocent, I can't help worrying about her."

She still had no idea the power she held over him. One look and she set his blood on fire.

"I hardly spoke to the girl," James said, "but she did not strike me as silly. Sophie likes her, too. I trust Sophie's judgment on such matters. Did you ever consider that women may be smarter than us when it comes to matters of the heart?"

Romulus rubbed a hand across the back of his neck in consternation. "Violet is young and inexperienced. She'd be the first to agree she knows nothing about men. But perhaps she is cleverer about this

Forester matter than I am."

Marcus nodded. "She did agree to talk to you about her meeting with Forester after it happened. Lara would toss a plate at my head if I dared tell her who she could or could not talk to."

"Seems Violet knows how to handle both you and Forester just fine." James cast him a discerning glance. "I think you ought to do as she asks. Trust her."

Marcus and Tynan agreed.

"Very well, I shall." But it still left him with a sick feeling in his stomach.

VIOLET HOPED THIS afternoon's tea would pass without incident. Jameson Forester and his sister, Valerie, had accepted the invitation to attend. However, Violet had also invited Romulus and was worried the two men would butt heads again.

Romulus was the first to arrive.

She greeted him with a smile, her heart leaping within her chest at the first sight of him, for he looked incredibly handsome. "You will behave for my sake, won't you?" she asked, her gaze pleading.

He took her hand in his and bowed over it. "Yes, Violet. My brother boxed my ears and told me not to be an interfering arse. So, I'll be polite and quietly grind my teeth while Forester and his sister take you aside."

She breathed a sigh of relief. "I will tell you what happens. I don't mean to keep anything from you, not even if they swear me to secrecy."

"Thank you, that puts my mind at ease."

When he released her hand, she placed it gently on his arm. "It is important that we trust each other, and just as important to also be willing to share our thoughts and feelings."

"Feelings?" He groaned.

"Yes." She rolled her eyes and grinned. "This is how we build our intimate bonds. Trust is vital, of course. But so is friendship."

"You're spouting that book again."

"And you are showing signs of behaving like a dominant male baboon. I've been doing a lot of reading lately. My cousin Lily is presenting a monograph to the Royal Society on the social structure of baboon colonies. The Fellows have not heard it yet, but they're in high dudgeon and have already got their robes in a twist about it."

He gazed at her in amusement. "Isn't this the Farthingale way?"

She laughed. "Yes, we never seem to do things quietly. Lily is brilliant. She claims men exhibit the same traits of aggression and possessive territoriality as male baboons. She also claims the baboon colonies are set up quite similarly to our societal order. Of course, the Fellows in the Royal Society are up in arms over her assertion and want her banned from stepping foot in their hallowed halls ever again. But she is right, whether or not they admit it. Do you see how you are tense and gritting your teeth at the mere mention of Lord Forester? This is because you view him as an interloper who is attempting to steal the female you covet. Namely, me. You are angry and intend to chase him out of your territory."

Romulus groaned. "Is this what thousands of years of civilization has come to? A book about love and a treatise on the baboon traits of men?"

Violet overlooked his sarcasm. "I won't judge the members of your sex too harshly. After all, it seems to be the male low brain function that also brings about our advancements. The homes we live in, the buildings that form a city, the carriages we ride in. The farms that create our food. The fabrics of our clothes."

"Women contribute as well," he remarked.

She nodded. "Yes, it is a shared effort. But The Book of Love claims it is a woman's instinct to nest, to maintain a home for her children. We are not the builders, the scientists, or warriors, at least not yet."

He placed a finger under her chin and tipped her face up so that their gazes met. "Violet, what are you hoping to find in these books? Don't get me wrong, I'm glad you enjoy reading," he said when she opened her mouth to protest. "But you obviously want to be something more than my wife or the mother to our children. Are you worried that I will hold you back?"

Although she tried to hide it, he saw the uncertainty in her eyes. "I don't wish to diminish the importance of those roles. Good heavens, we Farthingales are all about family and home. But once we marry, you would be a husband, a father, and a naval commander. So why can I not be a wife, a mother, and something else? My cousin Rose is a talented artist and runs her own business. You probably dine on the plates she designs or take tea in her teacups."

"I'm sure my cousin Marcus has had a few thrown at his head," he said, unable to resist the jest.

Marcus was a decorated army general, his fame and popularity perhaps on a par with Wellington. But his wife knew just how to keep him in his place. Lara had only tossed a plate at his head the one time, but no one was ever going to let Marcus live it down.

After all, that's what loving cousins were for, to tease and torment each other. But they would close ranks and defend each other to the death if an outsider ever threatened any of them.

"Lily is a brilliant scientist," Violet continued. "Laurel is one of the finest horse breeders in London. My Oxfordshire cousins, Belle and Honey, help run one of the largest perfumeries in England."

She sighed and shook her head. "Honey and Belle aren't married yet, but the others are. They are good wives and mothers, and dote on their families."

"Which brings us back to that something more you wish to be."

"Yes, only I don't know yet what it is. I expect it will involve my voice since it is a good singing voice." She glanced at him and laughed. "Honestly, Romulus! You are cringing again."

"No, I'm not. Never about you."

He cast her such a warm, affectionate look, she could not take offense. Although it was obvious he did not like singing. He seemed to be a reasonable man. They would work it out.

They spoke no more about the matter as other guests began to arrive.

The house was filled with the scent of currant scones and the lemon, ginger, and apple spice of the assorted cakes elegantly set out on the parlor tables. Mrs. Mayhew and her kitchen staff had been hard at work all morning to prepare the treacle cakes, maids of honor stuffed with apple jam, and other delights on display.

While Violet helped her Aunt Sophie greet the new arrivals and ensure all was in order for the afternoon tea, Romulus occupied his time speaking with Lady Dayne and later with Lady Withnall. Of course, the room went silent at the first sound of the *thuck, thuck, thuck* of her cane, for the little harridan instilled fear in everyone present, even those who held no dark secrets.

Violet was proud of Romulus when he stepped forward to engage her in conversation, showing no fear. Well, there was little to fear now that they had resolved to marry. If Lady Withnall decided to spread word of the bee incident, any scandal would die out as soon as she became Mrs. Brayden.

Violet Brayden.

The name sounded nice.

She thought no more about it when Lord Forester and his sister arrived. "May we speak to you in private?" Jameson asked even before managing a greeting.

"Please, Violet," his sister said, glancing around as though worried they might be overheard.

"Yes, let's take a turn in the garden." They walked out of the parlor, and she led them outdoors, smothering a smile when she glanced at the oak tree where the bees had lived, but also where she'd received her very first, blazing kiss. Hopefully, the first of many from Romulus. "What is so urgent that has you both on edge?"

Jameson regarded her intently. "We need you desperately, Violet."

"For the charity event you mentioned?"

He nodded. "Finances are quite dire at St. Aubrey's, and the buildings are in greater danger of collapse than we imagined."

"We've received another missive from the abbess imploring us to raise funds as soon as possible," his sister said. "You are the only one who can do this for us. Violet, you must do it for the orphans."

They continued to walk slowly around the garden, undisturbed by the other guests who had remained inside. Violet suspected Romulus was watching her from the large, parlor window, just as Hortensia had been watching them when they'd plotted their strategy for their kiss.

"Give me the details," she said, determined not to commit to anything before speaking to Romulus, her Uncle John, and Aunt Sophie. While she knew she had common sense, she was also inexperienced in such matters and could think of no better three people to look to for guidance.

"We thought to let a theater for the evening and–"

"I won't sing in a theater." First, she knew her family would never permit it. Nor would Romulus approve, and she couldn't blame him. "Is there not another more respectable venue available?"

Lady Rawley's eyes widened, and she gasped. "Then you'll do it?"

"No, Valerie!" She frowned at the pair. "I'm merely stating that I won't even bring it to my family for their approval unless I am comfortable with your plans. And I am not comfortable with standing on a Covent Garden stage."

"Ah, I see." Jameson cast his sister a glance. "What our Violet is saying is that we ought to be looking for something more elegant. A royal society hall, a museum. Perhaps an elegant London house or garden, although we'd need a tent for the garden in the event of rain. The Duke of Lotheil has a magnificent home in London. Isn't your cousin married to his grandson?"

He was referring to Lily.

"And your own sister is married to the Earl of Welles. I hear his house is also extraordinary." Valerie smiled at her. "They spend most of their time at his estate in Wellesford now. So what harm is there in allowing you to host the charity affair in their London home? The house is unoccupied presently, is it not? We can bring in our own staff to move their furniture out of the way and set up the main rooms for a night's recital. Perhaps two nights if the response is brisk."

"We'll have an orchestra and plenty of champagne. After you sing, we shall collect the donations." Jameson paused suddenly and shook his head. "No, what am I saying? We must have them pay to hear you. A donation fee just to come in the door. This way we keep out the hangers-on and have only the wealthiest attend. We'll take more pledges from them after you sing. I shall personally take charge of the funds and hold them in safekeeping until we can present the donation to St. Aubrey's abbess."

Valerie took her hand. "What do you say, Violet? Will you ask Lord Welles to give you his townhouse for the evening?"

"Let me see the letter from the abbess. You said she wrote to you."

"Yes, here it is." Jameson dug into his coat pocket and retrieved a rather crumpled paper. "You may hold onto it, if you wish. Show it to your uncle. I know he and your aunt are familiar with the orphanage."

"Thank you, I will." She tucked it securely in the sleeve of her gown.

"Let us know tomorrow," he added. "I hate to rush you, but you'll understand the need for haste once your read the letter. You have the voice of an angel, Violet. Put it to good use. Perhaps a quick song at today's tea to whet the appetites of your guests?"

"Perhaps." It was not unusual for the family to include a song or two during these tea parties. Often, her cousin Dillie would be coaxed to play the pianoforte and Lily, her twin, would play the harp. Violet would sing, although usually in a duet with Dillie. "I ought to go inside now. Aunt Sophie will be wondering where I've disappeared to."

They all walked back into the house and went their own way.

Violet was still uncertain of this venture, but it was for charity, and she did feel better knowing it would take place in a family home, assuming her brother-in-law Nathaniel approved of the use of his townhouse. She could send word and have it reach them within a matter of hours.

Now eager for the tea party to end so she could quietly read the abbess's letter and discuss it with her family and Romulus, she settled on the sofa beside Dillie and distractedly nibbled on her ginger cake.

Dillie nudged her. "If you're not going to eat that slice, I'll take it. You know me, I can never pass up ginger cake."

"And you're eating for two now." Violet glanced meaningfully at Dillie's rounded belly. "Have at it, Dillie. I don't have the appetite."

Her cousin frowned lightly. "What's wrong?"

"Friends have asked me to sing a few songs at a charity benefit they wish to organize. I just don't see how it will work. They need to do this quickly and expect me to be the lure to draw the necessary benefactors and their purses. But no one knows of me. I know I can sing, but so what? If Romulus is any indication, the donors will not rush to hear yet another sweet young thing warble a few songs."

"Well, why don't we give it a try here?"

Violet tipped her head in confusion. "What do you mean?"

"Let's slip into the music room. I'll play while you sing. Let's see how the guests respond to our impromptu recital. What have you got to lose?"

"Nothing, I suppose." She smiled at her cousin. "It will be like old times."

Dillie laughed. "Although I doubt anyone will miss Lily's harp playing. Or should I say, her inability to play. No other person alive is able to evoke the awful sounds she made from those harp strings."

"I'm sure she worked it out scientifically, configuring just the right chords to evoke the strongest cringe response." Violet laughed. "Oh, I do miss her. Jasper and Ewan, too, of course."

"They'll be down from the Highlands by the end of the week. She's giving her baboon lecture at the Royal Society. Can you believe it? The Fellows are in revolt, but the Duke of Lotheil is chairman, and she is married to his grandson, so he's set down the law. She will speak, and he expects every Fellow to attend. He'll take note of those who think to defy him."

"I'll attend," Violet said with a nod. "She'll need our support."

"I'll pick you up. Ian will have a fit, no doubt worried that a brawl will break out, and I'll be in the middle of it." She sighed. "He knows me too well. No one had better insult my sister, or I will come after them with my bare fists."

Violet curled her hands into fists and laughed. "I'll be right there beside you."

"Which is why Ian will insist on attending with us," Dillie said with a roll of her eyes. "He knows he can't keep me away from the lecture. Perhaps Daisy and Gabriel will join us. Ian and Gabriel have both perfected that cold, lethal stare. No one will dare cause trouble while they are present."

Violet nodded, suddenly wondering whether Romulus might like to attend. He'd certainly learn firsthand what it meant to ally oneself to the Farthingale clan. But it would also give him the chance to discreetly back out of the betrothal if he decided a quiet domestic life was what he wanted. Farthingales did not know the meaning of the word *quiet*.

"Come on, Violet. Let's escape to the music room."

The room was empty when they walked in. Dillie sat beside the piano and lightly tinkered with the keys. Violet stood next to her, facing Dillie and her back to the door. She began to hum along to the playful notes.

Dillie began with a country lilt they often sang at family getaways in Coniston. Violet closed her eyes as the tune began to envelop her. Immediately, she felt the air fill within her lungs, and she was soon surrounded by a lightness of spirit. She warbled the first few notes. The music inspired and transported her, the words and melody now floating from her lips as gently as a feather on a summer breeze. She reached the high notes without difficulty, accomplished the playful trills with similar ease.

Her father affectionately called her his songbird, adopting this name for her almost from the time she'd learned her first words.

Songbird.

This is what she was whenever she sang, a majestic bird in flight, its wings outstretched and gliding on the wind.

Free.

Soaring.

Happy.

When the song ended, the room began to fill with a different noise, that of enthusiastic cheers and clapping.

Violet opened her eyes and turned in surprise to the ovation.

The room was packed, all the guests now crowding around her and Dillie to offer their compliments. Romulus stood by the doorway, his arms folded across his chest and his expression stoic.

She stood on tiptoes to catch a glimpse of him, hoping to gain his attention.

He arched an eyebrow and a slow smile spread across his face.

She returned his smile, then lost sight of him as the guests surrounded her to offer their congratulations. Jameson was among the first to approach her. "You must do this, Violet. Look how everyone responds to you."

"They adore you," Valerie said, giving her a hug as she nodded in agreement.

Yes, she wanted to benefit St. Aubrey's for more reasons than anyone suspected. It wasn't only for her singing. That was mere vanity on her part. The real reason was much closer to her heart, and none of her friends knew of it.

Her family never spoke of it.

There was one child who had been raised at the orphanage, one child who was the dearest thing in the world to her.

That child was her mother.

Indeed, it was not something the family ever spoke about. There was no shame involved, only sympathy for her mother's feelings. She had never overcome the pain of being abandoned, of not knowing her blood kin. When her parents had married and Violet's father had brought her into the Farthingale clan, she'd acquired a host of loving relations. Yet, as happy as her mother was, the anguish still festered for the blood connections she was denied.

Perhaps this was a little of what Violet was feeling now. Oh, she knew who her family was. What she did not know was who *she* was. She had yet to answer these questions. Who am I? What is my role in life?

She smiled at Jameson and Valerie, merely nodding as they continued to gush about her singing.

She was relieved when they finally moved away.

"Aunt Sophie," she said when her aunt reached her side and gave her a hug. "There's something I'd like to discuss with you and Uncle John. May we speak after the tea party?"

"Of course, my dear."

Violet glanced over at Romulus who was still standing by the doorway. Detached. Removed. Tensing as Jameson and Valerie strolled past him into the hall. *Oh, dear.* There was going to be trouble between these two men.

How much trouble? And how was she to prevent it?

CHAPTER ELEVEN

"ROMULUS, PLEASE STAY," Violet said as the afternoon tea came to an end and he was about to return to his home.

Many guests had lingered, still talking about Violet's recital and the beauty of her voice. Romulus was the first to admit it was spectacular, but he knew what this discussion would entail, and he was not looking forward to it.

Lord Forester and his sister still made his gut roil with unease. Whenever they got near Violet, he had the urge to draw her behind him and stand protectively between her and that pair. It had nothing to do with his behaving like a possessive arse, although there might be a little of that, for he was not indifferent to Violet.

He didn't care if she thought he was behaving like a jealous baboon. She meant something to him, and he was not going to let anyone hurt her. "Of course, I'll stay."

Night was falling, and as the doors were open onto the Farthingale garden, Romulus could see the brightest stars just coming onto the horizon. The day had been warm, and the scent of grass and roses lingered in the air.

"Thank you," she said, nibbling her luscious lower lip in an obvious sign of worry.

"What is it, Violet?" He was in no hurry to leave her side, for he hadn't been alone with her all day. There was nothing waiting for him at his home since it was still sparsely furnished and most of his newly hired staff would not move in for another day or two.

"I wish to talk to you and my aunt and uncle about the St. Aubrey's charity." There was a look of trepidation in her eyes, as though she was worried about his response to the news she intended to relate.

He knew what she was going to say, for the joy of singing had been evident on her face.

And now she thought he would disapprove.

But he'd heard the magic in her voice and seen how happy she was when singing. The talk they'd had earlier about her wanting to be something more...this was it. This was her calling, to use her voice to better this often-dangerous world.

He took her hand when she started to turn away. "Violet, I want you to know, I'll support you in whatever it is you wish to do."

"Much as you dislike it?" She seemed surprised, but pleased.

He ran his thumb along the delicate curve of her jaw. "Yes. What matters is that it means something to you. But I'd like to hear the details, and if you'll allow me, I will offer my suggestions."

Her smile was as beautiful as starlight. "Yes, of course."

She stood a moment longer, smiling up at him.

He chuckled. "What?"

"You are quite wonderful. I hope I don't disappoint you."

His grin faded. "You never could. I mean it, Violet. You are perfect for *me* in every way." Lord help him, it was all he could do to keep from taking her in his arms and kissing her into forever.

She cast him an impertinent smile and nodded. "I shall make certain to remind you of your words when we discuss the matter of the St. Aubrey's recital."

It took another half an hour before Romulus finally sat with Violet, her aunt, and uncle in her uncle's study. "Tell us what Lord Forester proposes, Violet," John Farthingale said, taking a seat behind his desk and looking a little weary.

"He would like to organize a music recital to seek donations for St.

Aubrey's." She cleared her throat and blushed delicately. But this was Violet, shy about attention being foisted on her. "He thinks your well-heeled friends will pay to hear me sing. The proceeds would all go to the orphanage, of course."

"Where and when does he intend this event to take place?" Sophie asked.

"As soon as possible." She reached into her sleeve and withdrew a folded parchment. "It is all quite rushed, but Sister Ursula, the abbess at St. Aubrey's, wrote to Jameson. I haven't read it yet, however their need is dire and she is urging him to obtain the funds immediately."

She handed her uncle the letter.

He took a moment to read it and then grunted, but made no comment.

Romulus was now curious to look at it as well. "May I see it, Mr. Farthingale?"

"Yes, of course." But her uncle's brow was still furrowed. "Violet, tell me more about this benefit he wishes to hold."

"It's rather simple, Uncle John. Champagne, cakes, and music. I don't know if he plans on having other singers, or perhaps a pianist or harpist. But he thinks my singing will be the lure to draw donors to this event. You know why this orphanage is important to me. I want to help in any way I can."

Romulus eyed her curiously. "Why is it important to you?"

Another blush crept up her cheeks. "I...I..." She turned to her aunt and uncle for help.

Blessed saints! Was she adopted? The possibility never occurred to him, for her resemblance to the other women in the family was too strong. But this may have been the very reason the Farthingales had taken her in.

His heart tugged, watching her still struggling for words. He reached out and wrapped her hand in both of his. "Violet, you can tell me anything."

She nodded, but her lips were tightly pursed, and he could see this was not an easy thing for her. He stroked his thumb gently over the top of her hand. "Do you think I care where you come from? There is no shame in being raised in an orphanage."

Her eyes rounded in surprise. "No, it isn't me." She cast her aunt and uncle another desperate glance, but eased at her uncle's nod, as though he was giving her permission to reveal a dark, family secret. "This is where my mother was raised. She was the orphan."

She took a deep breath. "But she still feels the pain of not knowing who her family is, so we try very hard not to talk about it. I'm glad she and my father are traveling now. This would be very difficult for her. Yet, she'd want me to help the orphanage in any way I can. I am able to do it using my voice. Perhaps this is why I was given this gift, to be able to help in a cause so dear to my mother's heart."

Romulus entwined his fingers in hers. "Then there's no question you must do it. But all the more reason your uncle or I must be involved as well."

Her eyes widened in dismay. "What do you mean?"

"I don't trust Forester or his sister." He felt her stiffen in his grasp, but he would not allow her to slip her hand out of his. "Violet, this is important to *me*. I will support you in every way, but Forester and his sister do not touch the donations. In this I am adamant."

She frowned at him. "He will never agree to your holding the funds. Nor can I blame him. You've disliked him from the first. How can he take this as anything other than a vile insult?"

"I don't care. What I cannot shake off is the oily feeling I get when I'm around the two of them. Why should he care if someone trustworthy is given responsibility for the donations he hopes will pour in? I am not requiring it to be me. I can ask my cousin Finn. While Tynan and James run the Brayden business affairs, it is Finn who manages the family wealth. He does the same for many prominent members of Parliament, be they in the House of Commons or House of Lords." He turned to Violet's uncle. "Of course, I would have no objection to you or any of your brothers taking charge of the purse strings. My only concern is to keep Forester out of the financial end of it."

Violet's uncle gave a curt nod. "I shall discuss this and other terms with my brothers. In the meantime, will you ask your cousin Finn? I know of him, and I think he's a good choice."

"I'll be seeing him for a late supper this evening. I'll discuss it with him."

"Good. I'll meet with Lord Forester tomorrow afternoon to finalize the details. I don't like the idea of holding this function in the Earl of Welles's London townhouse, especially since he won't be there. But I will ask the Duke of Lotheil if he'll allow us to hold the recital in the new Royal Society hall."

"I would like that," Violet said, her eyes now brighter. "The hall is beautiful. To sing among those ancient relics would be quite remarkable."

Romulus said nothing.

The short hairs on the back of his neck were standing on end again. Perhaps he was indeed being a possessive arse, not liking the idea of other men ogling this beauty as she sang her angelic verses in a packed hall.

He would not feel so ill at ease if they were married. Perhaps it was foolish of him, but it would seem quite a different matter if the angel singing among the rare antiques was known to be his wife.

Unfortunately, he did not think Violet would now agree to marry him before this event took place. He glanced at her, willing himself to be patient.

After another few minutes of discussion, Romulus rose to leave. "I'll see you tomorrow, Violet."

She nodded and rose along with him. "Same bench, same time."

He bid her aunt and uncle farewell, intending to walk out and leave the three of them to talk over whatever else was needed, but

Violet followed him out of the study. He was surprised and pleased as she walked him to the front door. "Do we need to discuss my participation in the recital any further?" she asked.

"No." He caressed her cheek. "So, it appears you are to sing."

"Assuming we'll have the Royal Society hall. And assuming Jameson will accept to have your cousin manage the donations."

"He can have no objection. Finn is known and respected among the Upper Crust. If he refuses, it will only confirm my suspicions as to his motives."

She sighed. "I am going to give you Lily's monograph to read. I think you will recognize yourself among the pages."

He grinned wryly. "Are you suggesting I'm behaving like a baboon's arse?"

He ought to have merely bowed over her hand, but they were alone in the hall, and he could not resist giving her a kiss on her soft cheek. "I'll dream of you tonight, Violet."

Her smile was sweet and teasing. "In a high brain way?"

"No, love. Low brain all the way."

Violet's heart simply melted when Romulus strode toward her the next morning with an appealingly boyish smile on his face. However, there was nothing boyish about him. He was all hard-muscled man. "Good morning," she said, hoping not to sound breathless.

He was dressed in his naval uniform, obviously donned for a ceremonial occasion. His buttons and medals gleamed in the sunlight, and his black, thigh-high boots were polished to such a bright shine, one could almost see one's face reflected upon the black leather.

She set aside The Book of Love and rose from the garden bench, returning his smile with a warm one of her own. "Romulus, you look so handsome."

He laughed. "Are your legs turning to butter? It's the uniform. It has that effect on women."

Heat rushed into her cheeks, and she knew her face must now be in flames. Of course, who could resist such a man? Now that she knew him better, she admired his intelligence and his sense of honor, but there was no overlooking the magnificence of his body.

The uniform made him look incredibly daunting. He was muscled, but the cut of his jacket made his shoulders appear massive and chiseled out of solid rock. He was all sinew and strength.

He tipped her chin up so that their gazes met.

She felt like a fool, swooning over him just as any other woman would.

He knew it and was grinning at her. "I had lots of naughty dreams about you last night," he teased. "I'm glad I'm not the only one of us who can't think straight when we see each other."

She laughed.

He always knew just how to put her at ease.

"I want to kiss you, Violet. Ache for it. But little Farthingale spies are all about." He turned toward the oak tree where her two cousins, Charles and Harry, were hiding amid the branches. Their giggles filtered down through the thick cover of leaves. "Of course, your Aunt Hortensia is staring out the parlor window with her usual prune-faced scowl. I don't think she likes me. She knows exactly what I wish to do to you."

Violet shook her head. "She's scowling at me because she knows I won't refuse your wicked advances. However, you'll be pleased to know Pruitt approves of you."

"Ah, your wise, Scottish butler. I am honored." His smile softened. "I can't stay this morning. As you may have surmised from the uniform I'm wearing, I've been summoned to the Admiralty."

She frowned. "On a serious matter?"

"No, just a formality."

He must have noticed the worry in her eyes, for he continued to assure her in a purposely light manner. "I'm not going anywhere before I make you my wife. I mean it, Violet. Make the wedding plans once you're through with the St. Aubrey's benefit. I don't need more lessons out of that book." He glanced at the tome. "It doesn't matter to me whether love begins with the brain or the heart. I don't need to review the five senses to know that the sight of you, or the sound and scent of you, gives me pleasure."

He groaned and kissed her lightly on the forehead. "I want to marry you. I don't need the threat of Lady Withnall's anvil falling on my head to convince me."

"I feel the same way, but I also feel it is important for us to get through this first week. Not only to see what comes of Lady Withnall's threat. Getting through this charity recital will require all my concentration. My heart is wrapped up in it. I know how much the orphanage means to my mother, and I want everything to be perfect, something we can all look back on with pride."

"It will be, Violet."

She swallowed hard, suddenly caught up in ache for her mother.

Romulus regained her attention by caressing her cheek. "My aunt wishes me to bring you to her house for tea this afternoon. Lady Dayne has also been invited. I'll come by at four o'clock to pick you both up. You'll like Aunt Miranda. She is the notorious Lady Grayfell, possibly the only person in London able to strike fear in the heart of Lady Withnall. I think she was Julius Caesar in an earlier life. Perhaps Atilla the Hun."

Violet emitted a mirthful laugh. "Honestly, Romulus, the way you describe her. I'm sure she isn't nearly as daunting as you make her sound."

He rolled his eyes. "Oh, she's worse. But she will adore you. My cousin Finn will also be there. I spoke to him last night. He has agreed to hold the donations for St. Aubrey's."

"Then I may thank him in person this afternoon. I'll let Uncle John know your cousin is willing. He'll include it in his note to Jameson."

She nibbled her lip, a little troubled to be taking the responsibility away from her old friend, but it was a small thing. Jameson could still claim all the glory. No one would think twice about his delegating the financial aspect since it was considered beneath a gentleman to deal with something as crass as the money handling.

"Since you'll be occupied at the Admiralty, I'll ask Uncle John if I may join him at the Royal Society. He's arranged to meet the Duke of Lotheil there at noon. It will give me the chance to view the hall. If the duke gives his permission, then we'll have to work fast to get the place set up properly."

"I hope it all works out, Violet."

She cast him an impish grin. "I've already sorted through my songbook and chosen about twenty songs I think will be appropriate for the recital. I'll have to narrow them down to four or five. But I'll sing them all to you first, and you can tell me which you like best. You won't mind, will you?"

"Gad, Violet. That's just cruel." He laughingly groaned. "But you know I'd do it for you."

His expression had her laughing all the harder, and yet there was something deliciously sweet in the way he regarded her. She was truly touched, knowing how much he detested musicales. However, for her, he'd endure.

"Stop cringing, Romulus. I'm teasing you. It is Jameson and his sister I intend to torture with my singing. I'll let them choose which songs I am to perform."

She glanced up at the oak tree as the leaves began to rustle above them, reminding her that Charles and Harry were listening to their every word, and likely preparing to pepper them with acorns. "You had better be off for the Admiralty. I'll see you this afternoon."

"I'll be thinking of you," he said with a chuckle, looking as though he wanted to wrap her in his arms and kiss her with delightful thoroughness. He wouldn't with the children giggling above them and spying on their every move. "I hope all goes well with the Duke of Lotheil and the Royal Society."

"I'll be thinking of you as well. Are you certain the Admiralty has no surprises in store for you?"

She noticed the fleck of hesitation in his eyes, quickly covered up by a devastatingly appealing smile. "No surprises, Violet. My ship is not yet seaworthy. I doubt they'll assign me another."

But Violet felt a tug to her heart.

Why did she feel as though her time with Romulus was running out?

CHAPTER TWELVE

VIOLET HAD BEEN standing in the entry hall for the last twenty minutes, peering out the front window. It was now four o'clock and still no sign of Romulus. She had so much to tell him, and was worried something had gone wrong at the Admiralty.

Had he been given command of another ship?

"Miss Violet," Pruitt said, clearing his throat, "you'll be more comfortable waiting with Lady Dayne and your aunt in the parlor. Captain Brayden won't turn up any sooner by your staring out the window."

She smiled at the Farthingale butler. "I know. I can't help it." She wanted to say it wasn't like him to be late, but how would she know whether Romulus was the punctual sort or not? Moments like these were reminders of how little she really knew him. Yet, at the same time, she felt as though she'd known him forever. "Oh, thank goodness! There he is. I see him coming up the walk now."

She breathed a sigh of relief and hurried to throw open the door.

Pruitt groaned lightly behind her.

"Training a new butler, Pruitt? A very pretty one," Romulus teased, obviously surprised to find her throwing open the door. "Sorry I'm late," he said, still dressed in his uniform and looking incredibly handsome. "The summons to the Admiralty turned out to be more involved than I expected. I'll tell you about it later. Is Lady Dayne with you?"

She nodded. "She's in the parlor with Aunt Sophie."

Pruitt had left them to notify Lady Dayne. They now stood alone in the entry hall, but would only have a moment to speak before they were interrupted. "Violet," Romulus said with a whispered ache to his voice as he bent his head toward her.

Before she knew it, she was caught up in his arms and his warm lips were pressing against hers with unexpected urgency. There was something wonderful about his kisses, or perhaps she was simply so swept away by him that she was coming to crave him as much as one might crave air.

She circled her arms around his neck, feeling the prick of his medals against her arm and the heat of his body now molded to hers.

She liked that he was hungry for her, the crush of his lips intense and unexpectedly ravenous. But what had happened at the Admiralty?

Before she knew it, he drew away, leaving her lips tingling and her heart yearning for more. "Have you been assigned a new vessel? What is it, Romulus?"

His groan was one of helpless frustration. "They want me back in Cornwall by the end of–" He cut off abruptly as Lady Dayne and Pruitt joined them.

By the end of what?

Violet stifled her own frustration, knowing they would have no chance to speak in his carriage unless he chose to confide in Lady Dayne as well. Although there was no question of the kindly dowager's discretion, Violet was disappointed when Romulus chose not to say a word on the subject. Instead, he directed the conversation to a dozen trivial topics, purposely avoiding mention of his return to Cornwall. When was it to be? By the end of tomorrow? End of the week? End of the month?

She could not suppress her concern. What was so sensitive he could not discuss it in front of Lady Dayne?

She hoped they'd have the chance to talk while at his aunt's tea party, but she quickly realized this was not going to happen. The moment they entered Lady Grayfell's townhouse, Violet was descended upon by giants who turned out to be Brayden cousins.

She thought Romulus was the size and brawn of a Roman gladiator, but even at his strapping height and incredibly muscled strength, he was considered the runt of the litter. Finn, Joshua, Ronan, and Tynan were barely taller than Romulus, but the way they teased him, one would think they were head and shoulders above him.

They were all handsome men, to be sure. But none compared to Romulus. She could not have designed a more perfect male. Everything from the waves of his golden hair, to his exquisite green eyes, and masculine face, to his big, rugged warrior body was perfection.

But it was more than that. He was kind, protective, and took his family's jests in good humor.

How could she not melt when in his presence?

"Is this Violet?" Lady Miranda asked, embracing her without thought of waiting for a proper introduction.

Violet was hauled against the imposing woman's bosom, clutched so tightly she could hardly breathe. Her embrace was obviously meant as a sign of affection, even if embarrassingly uncomfortable. "Let go of her, Aunt Miranda. You'll suffocate my betrothed," Romulus said with a laughing shake of his head.

"Don't be ridiculous, Rom." But Miranda eased her grip and allowed Violet to draw away. She was almost as tall and most definitely as strong as any of the Brayden men.

"It is a pleasure to meet you," Violet said, feeling like a child among them. The size of this family! Fortunately, Sophie and Abigail, the wives of James and Tynan, were also present and came forward to greet her.

The three of them were of similar height, and Violet could only imagine how they must have felt when first meeting these Brayden men.

"I cannot believe one of my tadpoles is betrothed." Lady Miranda gave Violet another hug, this time thankfully brief. However, Violet was not free of her grasp yet. Romulus's aunt took her by the shoulders and gently turned her around to inspect her. "Rom, you've made a fine choice. I like your Violet. What a pretty girl you are, my dear."

Romulus cast his aunt a wry grin. "She's a wonder, Aunt Miranda. Smart, beautiful, and she sings, too. You've never heard anything like it. She has the voice of an angel."

Violet wasn't used to so many people, other than Farthingale family members, staring at her all at once. Of course, the family would all gather around the piano at Christmastide and listen as she sang, but most of these Braydens were still strangers to her.

She blushed as all of them continued to regard her as though she was a pet in a zoo. "Your nephew is exaggerating, of course."

Romulus arched an eyebrow. "I am not. If anything, I am understating your talent."

One of the giants stepped forward and introduced himself as Finn. His hair was darker than Romulus's, and his eyes were a magnificent mix of gray and green. "I'm looking forward to your recital, Miss Farthingale. Do you know yet where it shall be held?"

"Oh, please call me Violet," she said with a nod. "The Duke of Lotheil has consented to our use of the new Royal Society hall. It is a magnificent addition to the building's structure. I think we'll draw a good crowd there."

Finn grinned. "With you singing? You'd draw a crowd anywhere. The hall will be packed."

She laughed in surprise, appreciating his confidence, but knowing he was only being polite. "How can you be so certain? You haven't heard me sing yet."

"But Romulus has. He hates all manner of musical entertainments, thinks most of the debutantes who perform at these functions are insipid. He cringes at the mere thought. But he isn't cringing when he speaks of you. If he claims you have the voice of an angel, then I am sure you do."

"Will you sing for us?" Joshua asked.

Ronan poked him in the ribs. "Shut up, you dolt. She's our guest. It isn't right to put her to work." He bowed politely over Violet's hand. "Ignore my ape of a brother. You needn't sing for your supper."

She thanked him, feeling somewhat relieved. However, she knew she would have to get over her shyness when it came to singing to strangers, for the Royal Society hall would be a crush if Finn's assessment was correct.

She took a moment to thank Finn for agreeing to hold the funds.

"My pleasure, Violet. I'm delighted to help out for a good cause. It's very easy to get caught up in the whirl of wealth and power concentrated in London. But what use is amassing that wealth if it is merely to be kept locked away? I like that we are working toward helping the orphanage."

Lady Miranda cut in when the dinner bell rang. "Enough, boys. Give Violet some room to breathe."

Before Romulus could offer his arm to escort her in, Sophie and Abigail came to her side. "Ignore the men. Walk in with us," Abigail said. "I'd love to hear more about your charity recital. How can we help?"

She turned to Romulus, who merely smiled at her and shrugged.

James arched an eyebrow when Sophie ignored his outstretched arm. "Seems my wife has no desire to be with me this evening. Lady Dayne, may I escort you to the table?"

Tynan escorted Lady Miranda in, although Violet suspected his mother needed no one's assistance. She was a beautiful woman, but definitely capable of defeating a regiment of enemy soldiers all on her own.

Violet liked this about her immensely.

She also enjoyed the dinner table banter between Romulus and his cousins. Although they were obviously on their best behavior, and did feel comfortable with her and Lady Dayne present, they did lapse once or twice into rougher language that brought a stern frown to Lady Miranda's brow. "The eight of them were impossible as boys. Wildebeests, you know."

James leaned over and smiled at her. "But among ourselves, we also referred to the younger cousins, Romulus included, as tadpoles. Caleb was the squid."

Violet laughed. "And what were you, my lord?"

"Good heavens, call me James. I," he said with a wink at his wife, "was the embodiment of perfection. I needed no pet name. Nor did Marcus and Tynan. It was only the younger brothers who required them. You should have seen them when they were boys. Caleb was all arms and legs."

She nodded in comprehension. "Ah, hence the name Squid."

"Rom, Finn, Joshua, and Ronan were skinny, ill-behaved nuisances with spindly legs that could barely hold them up. They were always hopping about, always underfoot."

She nodded again. "Tadpoles. Obviously."

James smiled at her. "Exactly."

Romulus sat back and listened to her jesting exchange with his brother. She could see the relief and joy glistening in his eyes as he watched them chatting. Perhaps she'd also imbibed a little too much wine, for every time Romulus looked at her, she felt a rush of heat through her body.

She knew she'd imbibed too much when the family gathered in Lady Miranda's parlor after supper and Romulus's cousins goaded her into singing a song. "Choose one we know, and we'll sing along with you," Joshua said.

She chose a country ballad about a frog who went courting, knowing only Romulus would get the full meaning in her choice. He was not only one of the Brayden tadpoles, he was her test frog as well. Without musical accompaniment of piano or harp, she and his cousins sang about the bullfrog wooing his female frog love. His cousins held their sides, laughing hysterically when Violet sang the female frog verses to Romulus in a lovingly seductive croak.

Even Romulus laughed heartily.

Sophie and Abigail cheered.

Miranda gave her another suffocating hug when the evening was over, and it was time for Romulus to escort her and Lady Dayne back to Chipping Way. Romulus assisted Lady Dayne into his carriage and then put his hands around Violet's waist to help her up. "Lord, you're beautiful," he whispered. "But you've also had a little too much to drink."

She meant to deny it, but the carriage seemed to spin in front of her, and his touch immediately turned her blood fiery. "I–"

She hiccupped.

Romulus settled her securely, making certain her back was firmly resting against the squabs before he released her. But she wasn't so drunk that she did not notice the twitch of his shapely mouth in amusement or the heated look in his eyes as his gaze raked over her body. He was no less affected in touching her than she was in experiencing his touch.

The way his hands had curled around her waist and lingered, she knew he desired her with fiery passion. Since they were both burning with desire, she wondered if he could be convinced to explore that passion further.

Had they been alone in the carriage, Violet would have leaped onto his lap and smothered him with kisses the moment the carriage drew away from Miranda's gate. She supposed this was why young ladies were never permitted out of their homes without a chaperone.

She sat beside Lady Dayne, so that her kindly neighbor could not see the unrestrainedly heated glances she was casting at Romulus. But he could see them. The look he cast back turned her body into an incandescent flame.

Good heavens! This man!

Fortunately, Romulus was not nearly as giddy as she was, so he chatted amiably with Lady Dayne for the rest of their short journey. When the carriage reached Chipping Way, he dropped Lady Dayne home first, and then walked Violet next door to return her to her uncle's house. They'd just closed the front gate behind them when Romulus took her in his arms and kissed her with enough steam to make her toes curl.

It was a deep, intensely hungry kiss that would have had the family shotguns out and pointed at his head if ever they were caught. His hands roamed over her body, but despite her befogged state, she realized he was not merely pawing her but memorizing every curve, every nuance of her body, as though he wanted to etch her into his brain.

No...into his heart.

The kiss was one of desperation and longing. It wasn't merely an I-want-you kiss. No, this kiss was a farewell kiss.

It could only mean he was leaving her soon. There was no other possible explanation. He had been called back to duty and ordered to leave before the week was out. Tipsy as she was, she understood the import of his kiss.

"Romulus," she said breathlessly when he took his lips off hers and began to trail kisses along the curve of her neck, pausing to suckle on a sensitive spot just below her ear. "Oh, my."

She sighed in delight, only to return to her senses a moment later. "You must tell me."

"Tell you what?" He drew her body closer so they were molded to each other. She felt the heat and yearning building between them.

"About the meeting at the Admiralty. I am not so foggy-brained I've forgotten." But she was certainly in danger of losing her reason as he continued to suckle the sensitive spot on her neck. If any girl needed a chaperone right now, it was her. She would have allowed him to take her right here on the grass, the ache she felt for him was that strong. "What happened? You must tell me, Romulus. No secrets between us."

He sighed and reluctantly stopped nibbling her neck. "They've assigned me to another ship. Marry me tomorrow, Violet."

She blinked, the comment sobering her quickly. "Tomorrow? Why?"

"Because it may be only a matter of a few hours before I'm ordered to leave London."

"For Cornwall?"

She felt every bit of his frustration, for his tension seeped into her bones as he continued to hold her. It was as though he feared to let her go, needing to keep himself anchored so neither of them could float away. "I'm told I will be given command of The Song of the Ocean."

"What does this mean?" She understood the jest in a ship having the word 'Song' in it, but there was more significance to the name.

"It is the escort vessel to the fleet admiral's flagship."

"Oh, Romulus, what an honor!" She studied his features. He had looked glum all afternoon and even more so now. "Isn't it an honor?"

He nodded. "Yes, it's what I'd hoped for during my years of service. But not anymore. Chasing pirates off the coast of Cornwall is one thing. I'm never more than a few days' ride from home. But the Lord Admiral and his flagship are often sent on diplomatic missions around the world. At any moment, I could be given duties that may keep me away from you for years."

She gasped. "Years?"

"I know it isn't fair of me to ask, but I must. I want you for my wife, Violet. I can't lose you. I couldn't bear it."

"Nor could I." She slid her hands around his neck. "Romulus, you won't ever lose me. My heart is yours forever. I don't need a book to tell me this. If we marry, would I be allowed to sail with you?"

"Into danger? Blessed saints! Do you think I would ever agree to put your life in peril?"

A shudder ran through her. "Then this posting is dangerous, not merely diplomacy."

He groaned. "I don't know. One never knows who or what one might encounter when sailing around the world."

"You'll be on the ocean then? Yes, of course. The ship is called Song of the Ocean, so that's where you shall sail. No short forays off the Cornwall coast." She meant to say more, but the wine she'd imbibed and her sharp intake of air caused her to hiccup again.

"The Plover, that was my ship, will soon have a new captain to sail her along the Cornwall coast."

"Why not keep you there in your new vessel?"

"Song of the Ocean is too mighty a frigate to be used merely to chase down local pirates. Besides, she's too big for most Cornish harbors. Her hull would break apart upon the rocks."

She blinked, struggling to make sense of it all. But her mind was in a fog, her brain dulled when she needed to be sober to fully understand the implications of his assignment. She couldn't have had more than two or three glasses of wine, but she'd never had more than half a glass before. It was surprising how quickly the smooth liquid could flow into one's head and make it spin.

Of course, it explained why her inhibitions were loosened enough to play along with Romulus's cousins and half sing, half croak that silly frog song. But there was no silliness now. She was not going to play the coy miss and lose Romulus, perhaps for years.

Dear heaven, perhaps forever if he was killed in battle. "Would you consider resigning your commission?"

He drew her tighter in his embrace. "Do you want me to?"

"I cannot give you an answer. I don't understand what the assignment means for you, so the decision must be yours. I will support your choice, no matter the consequences. But I want you to do what pleases you, not what you think will please me."

"Even if it means we'd be apart for years while I'm escorting the Lord Admiral on his diplomatic missions to India or China?"

She nodded. "Even if it means that...but only if it makes you happy to be doing this."

"Our years apart would not be wasted. When I return, I'll likely be made an admiral of the fleet."

"Your reason to be," she said in a whisper, wanting him and not his accolades. But this was part of who Romulus was, a man wrapped up in honor and duty and love of the sea.

He kissed her lightly on the cheek. "Never mind, Violet. I realize I am asking too much of you. It isn't fair that we should marry tomorrow and then not see each other for years. Nor is it fair to deprive you of having your parents and sister present to witness the most important day of your life."

"Romulus, there is no choice."

He nodded. "I know. Sorry I raised it."

"You misunderstand. My Aunt Sophie is a marvel. If anyone can organize a wedding party by tomorrow afternoon, it is she. A simple one, of course. Only immediate family presently in London. I don't want to wait either. My sister is ripe as a melon, expecting her and Nathaniel's second child any moment now. I doubt she will travel in her delicate condition, nor will Nathaniel dare to leave her side. My parents won't be back from their trip for at least another month. Perhaps longer. I will marry you now. This instant, if it is possible. I'd rather have a day with you as your wife than a lifetime with anyone else."

She cast him a smile filled with all the love she held in her heart. "I don't need to read a book to know this. Whatever happens, I'm yours and will always be."

He kissed her on the lips, a gentle kiss this time, one filled with sweetness and a lingering relief. "Let's talk to your aunt and uncle. Are they home? Or have they gone out for the evening?"

"Home."

He held her back a moment when Pruitt opened the front door to allow them in. "Thank you, Violet," he said softly. "I'm so sorry, but if this new posting is made official, it is also possible I'll be missing your recital."

Goodness, she hadn't thought of that.

She could get over his missing it. What she would not get over was never seeing him again. She knew it was eating at his insides as much as it was eating at hers. She was ready to burst into tears, but force herself to put on a brave facade. She did not want him to remember her as a watering pot. "You won't be there for my recital?"

He nodded. "Probably not. I'm so sorry."

She looked up at him, her eyebrows arched and a skeptical look on her face, knowing how much he detested these evening musicales. But he would have endured for her sake. She would do the same for him. She forced a slow smile to her lips, shaking her head with a merriment she did not feel. She shook her head and chuckled lightly. "No, you're not."

CHAPTER THIRTEEN

ROMULUS DID NOT expect John or Sophie Farthingale to be happy about his desire to make Violet his wife within a day. However, he knew they had no choice but to accept. The betrothal contract had been signed. Consents all around had been given. Lady Withnall was still a loose, gossiping cannon.

Protecting Violet was all that mattered.

If his duties called him away for the next year or two, Violet would remain at risk of ruin if word got out about the bee incident and she was still unmarried.

The matter was simple and obvious. He had to marry Violet now. It was the only way to protect her, no matter what might befall him. "Very well," John said with a sigh, turning to Sophie. "Can you manage on such short notice, my love?"

Violet's aunt smiled at all of them. "I adore weddings. I'll be ready by four o'clock tomorrow afternoon. You had all better show up on time or Mrs. Mayhew and I will be quite put out."

She immediately jumped into action, rattling off a list of what needed to be done. Romulus was not allowed to move from his seat before giving her a list of his family to be invited.

"I'll leave the official license paperwork to you men. Who will officiate the ceremony? Oh, I suppose it doesn't matter. I'll leave that task to you men as well."

Romulus nodded. "I'll take care of it, Mrs. Farthingale."

She gave a curt nod and turned to Violet. "We will have to pack your belongings and move them next door. Good thing you're only moving one house down. When your trunks are packed, Amos will carry them over." She shook her head and smiled. "Good thing he's the size of an ox. He'll manage it in one trip. Oh, Captain Brayden, will you have Violet's quarters ready? Shall I send over–"

Romulus had been holding Violet's hand all the while and now gave it a gentle squeeze. "I've hired Mrs. Mayhew's nieces, Cora and Mary. They'll take care of unpacking Violet's belongings. Everything will be in good order for her."

Violet cast him the softest smile. "I'll hop back and forth between the houses. We'll get everything done in time. Whatever isn't moved tomorrow can always be moved the following day. I'm not going far."

In truth, this eased Romulus greatly. Although he was eager to have Violet in his arms and in his bed, their bliss would only last for a night or two. Perhaps three. After that, he'd be gone, and she would be alone in the house.

The staff would be there, of course.

But Violet would not have him beside her. He did not like to leave her alone and unprotected.

She'd spoken earlier of two more Farthingale cousins arriving shortly for their come-outs. He'd make certain to have his guest rooms cleaned and furnished so that Belle and Honey could stay with Violet while he was away.

He'd ask Finn to stop by every day to make certain all was well. He was involved in the charity recital anyway, so it was a plausible excuse for him to come around, at least until the business of the recital was over. James and Sophie would look in on Violet often, although James did not always have good days. Many times, he was bedridden and in pain.

Romulus felt the familiar ache to his heart at the thought of his brother's constant pain. He would impose on them as little as possible.

As for his sister, Gabrielle, she was married and had her own brood to worry about. Besides, she and her husband lived outside of London. Well, he'd put all the Brayden cousins to work looking after Violet whenever James and Sophie couldn't. The Farthingale clan would also be close at hand, as would Lady Dayne. At some point, Violet's parents would return from their extended trip and lend her a hand.

Lord, would his in-laws move into his home permanently?

He stifled a grimace, determined to endure if it made Violet happy.

Yes, both families would look after her in his absence. He'd get their oaths on it. He'd be mad with worry otherwise.

"I'll send my portfolio of songs to Lord Forester with my apologies that I cannot meet him and his sister tomorrow," Violet said, breaking into his thoughts. "They can choose the songs without me. They don't need my input. I'll sing whichever ones they select. Finn can meet with them to discuss the financial arrangements and set up the charity bank account. Dillie and Daisy have already volunteered to help with the donors since they know everyone in town."

She sighed. "I suppose this recital is a good thing in more ways than one. It will keep me busy while you prepare to leave."

Romulus merely grunted. It bothered him that she would be around Forester and his sister, but he said nothing. After all, this recital was important to her, and he had no intention of undermining it. Also, Violet's aunt had the wedding arrangements well in hand. There was little Violet could do to contribute when Sophie Farthingale was a master at last minute arrangements for a horde of unexpected guests.

Singing was Violet's solace. If it helped her get through losing a husband within a day or two of marrying him, who was he to complain? What would she do once the recital was over? He hoped they would have the chance to discuss it before he was called away.

John Farthingale smacked his hands on his desk and rose. "I suppose that takes care of everything. I'll see you first thing in the morning, Brayden."

Romulus nodded and rose as well.

As they began to disband, Violet suddenly threw herself into his arms and hugged him fiercely. He was caught unawares and laughed softly. "What's this?"

She burrowed against his chest. "I'm so happy and yet so sad at the same time."

He wrapped his arms around her. "I know, sweetheart. Me, too."

"I won't let you down, Romulus."

"You couldn't, Violet. Not ever."

It still troubled him that she felt she had to prove herself worthy of him.

Of him, dear heaven!

He was ready to erect a beehive shrine to the bees who had brought them together. He was determined to place The Book of Love under museum quality glass to preserve it forever. He was grateful for whatever magic had brought them together.

By this time tomorrow, Violet would be his wife. He was going to explore every sensation written in that book in intimate depth. He couldn't wait to touch her silken skin, taste her rosebud lips, breathe in her delicate scent. He'd already had fantasies about rousing her passion and evoking her breathy moans as she reached her release.

He would claim her in every way possible.

Low brain.

High brain.

Low brain again.

Yes, his low brain would be fully in charge as he embedded himself in her body as deeply as she was embedded in his soul.

And she was worried to disappoint him?

Blessed saints! He was on-his-knees grateful for her... and worried as hell over what Forester's real intentions were for Violet. The man would do nothing while Romulus was around.

But what would happen once he sailed from England?

THE DAY WAS warm and filled with sunshine, a perfect day for a wedding. Violet squinted up at the sky and smiled. She had a bit of work to do before the ceremony, but none of it felt daunting, for each moment that passed drew her closer to her heart's desire.

She'd carefully wrapped her music parchments in a large portfolio last night and had also written a note to Jameson before retiring to bed. She brought both to Pruitt. "I need a footman to deliver these to Lord Forester this morning. Can you spare a man?"

"Consider it done, Miss Violet." He took her bundle and note, and immediately went off to summon one of the Farthingale footmen.

She returned upstairs to help her maid pack her belongings. But Martha was most efficient, and the chore did not take long. Within the hour, they were ready for Amos to cart the trunks next door. "I'll walk over with him and start hanging them in your new quarters, Miss Violet."

"Thank you, Martha. I'll be along in a moment." She'd brought to London little more than gowns, shoes, and the accessories required for making one's come-out in fashionable style. She hadn't had cause to wear any of these gowns in the quiet Cotswolds town where she'd grown up. The assemblies and routs held in the countryside were far more casual. These delicately embroidered silks and satins would never suit.

She realized they would not suit now either.

These demure, white silk and lace confections were not worn by married ladies. Perhaps she'd have them altered with an overlay of sarcenet in blues or greens to better suit her marital status.

Better yet, she would give the gowns to Belle and Honey, for they were all of a similar height and weight. Knowing their parents and their utter devotion to their perfume shops, it was quite likely her two cousins would arrive in town with no suitable gowns to wear.

She watched Martha and Amos take her wardrobe to Romulus's home, and then hurried downstairs to see if her aunt and Mrs. Mayhew required help. All was in hand, and she was merely underfoot, so she walked next door to see if she could be useful in what was to be her new home.

She was a little disappointed to learn Romulus was not home yet. He'd gone off with her uncle early this morning to secure the minister and the special license. She hoped he would return soon. However, she was excited and her brain was so scattered at the moment, she doubted she could hold so much as a simple conversation with him.

She'd be a squealing, giggling simpleton.

But this was not how she wished the staff to think of her, so she gathered her wits about her and informally introduced herself to those she encountered as she wandered from room to room.

The Mayhew sisters knew of her, of course. Since the elder was the new housekeeper, it went a long way to making the rest of the staff feel at ease around her, but not so at ease they'd forget she would be the mistress of the house within a few, short hours.

She tried to remain cool and efficient as she entered the bedchamber she and Romulus would share. After all, it made sense that she should direct where her clothes were to be placed. But Farthingales simply did not know how to hide their thoughts or feelings. She blushed to her roots the moment she stepped inside and saw the massive bed.

Well, it wasn't really massive, just the usual size of a marriage bed...if one knew about such things. Which she didn't. But she understood what would take place there tonight. Suddenly feeling all eyes upon her, she turned to leave, and bumped into a solid, muscled wall.

Romulus!

"You're back," she said, breathlessly stating the obvious.

He grinned and patted his hand against his breast pocket. "All is arranged. I have the license right here." He grazed his knuckles affectionately against her hot cheek. "If your face were any hotter, it would burst into flames."

She sighed. "I should not have come up here."

"Why not? This is to be your bedchamber as much as mine." He nodded toward the bed, and his grin widened when he noticed her blush deepen. "Ah, this embarrasses you."

"Everyone is aware what will take place here tonight," she said in a whisper. "I have no one to blame but myself. I insisted upon this."

He took her hand. "Are you having second thoughts?"

"No. Dear me, no." She was still whispering, which he obviously thought was extremely amusing. "But everyone knows, and they're all smirking."

"Let them." He chuckled, and then continued in a low voice that surely was easily heard by the staff in the room who were doing their best not to appear to be listening in. "This may not be a common arrangement among the nobility, but we're not part of that elevated society. I haven't any titles to my name."

"Nor do I."

"You don't?" he said with a teasing arch of his eyebrow and wrapped her in his arms as he feigned indignation. "I've been had. Trapped by a scheming, young miss and her loyal, bee minions." Since the maids were now giggling at his remark, Romulus led her downstairs. "Come with me."

"Where are we going?"

"To the kitchen. I'm starved for food as well as for your delectable body. Since I can't have you…yet, I'll have to settle for a meal. A big one. As I said, I'm starved."

She rolled her eyes. "Haven't you noticed? Your house is in upheaval. Mrs. Mayhew's niece takes her job as housekeeper quite seriously. She's making certain every room is thoroughly cleaned from top to bottom. This includes your kitchen."

"Am I not permitted to enter my own kitchen?"

She laughed. "Not if you value your life. Besides, your newly hired cook is out shopping for supplies while her scullery maids are busy scrubbing out the hearths and stove. We'll only be in the way."

"I'm master of this house. I can never be in the way. I need food."

"I had no idea you were such a petulant child when hungry. She'll be back shortly. Can you not wait...no, I see that you will eat the furniture if you're deprived another moment."

Smiling, she eased out of the arm he'd tucked around her waist. "I'll see what I can grab from Aunt Sophie's kitchen. I'll put together a basket for us and bring it back here. They're busy preparing for this afternoon, and I don't want to put them out any more than necessary. Since your house is being cleaned from top to bottom, we can picnic in the garden. It will be perfect. We'll be out of everyone's way and able to enjoy the lovely outdoors."

"With the added benefit of privacy."

She nodded. "So no one can overhear us as you speak sweet nothings in my ear. Although, I'd much rather hear more about what you did today."

When his smile faltered, she wondered whether something other than obtaining the special license and the minister had occurred. Perhaps the slip of his smile had to do with yesterday's summons from the Admiralty. She could not tell by his expression.

"I'll be back in a trice." She hurried to the Farthingale kitchen which was bustling with activity and quietly gathered some apples, bread, and slices of ham left over from last night's supper.

Mrs. Mayhew caught her digging through her pantry. "Miss Violet, what do ye think yer doing in here?"

"I do apologize, but Captain Brayden was hungry, and his kitchen still is not set up. Oh, it will be in a matter of an hour." She grimaced. "But he can't wait that long. He is already grumbling and must be fed now."

Mrs. Mayhew tossed back her head and laughed. "Needs to keep up his strength, does he?"

"Yes, I suppose." Although from the leering grins on the faces of Mrs. Mayhew and her scullery maids, she sensed the comment had nothing to do with his eating a hearty meal.

The basket was heavier than expected, but Violet was determined to manage it on her own. She carried it into Romulus's garden and set it down with a grunt on one of the wooden benches beside a bed of bluebells and daffodils. Old General Allworthy did not spend much time outdoors, but he enjoyed looking out upon his rows of flowers.

Violet thought it was quite a beautiful garden.

As she hurried to the front of the house and was about to enter it to call for Romulus, a carriage drew up at the gate. To her surprise, the wicked widow, Lady Felicia, stepped down. "Why, Miss Farthingale, I did not expect to find you here."

Lady Felicia looked stunning, her gown a tastefully elegant ecru silk with an intricate band of seed pearls sewn at the high waist. Her hair was styled in a fashionable chignon and her hat was an exquisite ecru silk with pearl beading and two dove feathers.

Violet was overheated from lugging the basket, and had no idea what her hair looked like just now. But she smiled politely, hoping not to show a hint of her irritation or dismay. "Nor did I expect to find you here, Lady Felicia. To what do we owe the honor of your visit?"

"We, is it?" She arched a cool eyebrow. "Seems I underestimated you, Miss Farthingale. You've got your talons into Romulus rather quickly. But I'm on to that sweet, innocent act of yours. You may have him fooled, but you cannot fool me."

"Oh, dear. I've been found out. I am bereft." The woman was insufferable. Violet knew she ought to have held her tongue and not engaged her, but she could not hold back her sarcasm. The woman's superior manner rankled her.

"And I am not so easily deterred." She cast Violet an imperiously snide glance, staring down her nose at Violet. "You may believe you have won him, but I always get what I want. No one, certainly not the rustic likes of you, will get in my way."

Romulus stepped out of the house in time to hear Lady Felicia's remark. "Bloody hell, Felicia. Must you be so destructive in your boredom? Go amuse yourself elsewhere."

He placed a protective arm around Violet's waist.

Lady Felicia tossed back a laugh. "How adorable. Do you think to shelter your new mistress from me?"

Romulus did not appear to be at all amused. Indeed, Violet would have felt a shudder run through her if he ever tossed her the dark, threatening look he was now tossing Lady Felicia. It was as though his every feral, protective instinct had been aroused. "Watch what you say, Felicia. Violet is *lady* of this house. It is as much her home as it is mine."

He drew Violet closer which she understood was his signal to stay quiet and not contradict him. They weren't husband and wife yet, but would be in a few hours.

"You married her?" The remark had obviously caught the vulgar woman by surprise, but predators like Felicia always seemed able to recover quickly. Her malicious smile returned. "Ah, here I thought I was interfering in your courtship. I shall have ever so much more fun destroying your marriage."

She turned abruptly and returned to her carriage, ordering her coachman to drive off the moment she'd climbed in.

Violet stared at Romulus, her mouth agape. "Well, that was fun."

He groaned. "There aren't words...I can't even...I'm so sorry, sweetheart."

A sickening sense of unease churned in Violet's stomach, but she would not allow the unpleasant confrontation to ruin her wedding day. She knew to the depths of her soul Romulus would be faithful in their marriage. This is who he was, noble in heart, loyal, and protective through and through.

Still, the woman's words troubled her. "Romulus, do you think she means it?"

He snorted. "I don't know. But it doesn't matter. There is nothing she can do to break us apart."

Violet's stomach was now twisted in Gordian knots. "We've known each other less than a week. How can you be so certain our marriage will survive?"

He gave no response, merely regarded her grimly.

Those knots in her stomach twisted even tighter. "How silly of me. How can you be? You're not even certain you will ever love me, are you?"

CHAPTER FOURTEEN

ROMULUS COULD NOT take his eyes off Violet as they stood in front of the minister to exchange their vows. Violet's aunt had decided the ceremony should be held outdoors, under the cloudless blue sky. After all the work she'd done to make this a perfect affair, neither of them wished to contradict her. She could have insisted the ceremony be held in the root cellar, and they would have agreed.

He and Violet now stood in the shade of the oak tree where the bees had resided and first brought them together. "Do you think they'll return?" Violet asked, glancing at the branches and then up at him.

Romulus grinned. "The bees? I certainly hope not today. I'd rather get through this ceremony without incident."

Violet looked exquisite, like a woodland sprite in a gown of white silk that draped perfectly over the gentle curves of her body. She had wildflowers threaded through her lush, dark mane. Her hair was partly done up and some curling strands had been left loose, styled to fall in a soft cascade over one shoulder.

Her violet eyes sparkled.

It filled him with pride to know her eyes shone with love for him. "Violet," he said softly, knowing there was so much he wished to say to her still. But they'd only met a few days ago, been forced to wed in haste, and were still unsure of their feelings for each other.

No, that wasn't quite right.

He loved Violet and was certain she loved him.

Their only hesitation was in declaring their feelings too soon.

But did love ever work on a proper timetable? There was such a thing as love at first sight, although Violet's book was filled with reasons to be cautious. Only time could build the high brain connections needed to form a strong marriage, the author declared.

Romulus wasn't sure about that.

He'd felt that deeper attraction almost from the first. The first moment he'd unlaced her gown and touched her velvet-soft skin. The first time he'd put his arms around her. The moment he'd run his hands up and down her shapely legs.

It wasn't merely lust that had shot through every throbbing pulse and pore of his body. It was her softness, her smile, the lovely lilt of her voice that got under his skin and shot a path straight to his heart.

This girl is mine.

He'd known it, felt it to the depths of his soul.

He ought to tell her now. After all, he hadn't been placed in charge of one of the finest ships in the royal fleet because he was hesitant or cautious. "Violet," he repeated, hoping to tell her what was in his heart before the ceremony started.

Her smile shone in her beautiful eyes. "I know, Romulus. I feel it, too."

He nodded.

He hadn't said the words aloud, but he was pleased she understood how he felt.

The minister cleared his throat. "Shall we begin?"

From behind them, his cousin Ronan jokingly called out, "Gad, yes. Start the ceremony already. The apple pies are cooling on the window sill."

"The birds will have at them before we do," Joshua chimed in. "Is that cinnamon in the pies?"

Violet's laughter was as gentle as the breeze. "Uh, oh. The wildebeests are restless. We'd better get on with the wedding. But who invited Lady Withnall? I thought this was to be family only."

"I did. She brought us together." He cast her a deliciously wicked grin. "I wanted her to know how much I appreciated her holding my bollocks to the fire."

Violet's laugh came out as a snort through her nose.

The minister frowned at both of them, casting Romulus a particularly reproving scowl. "Captain Brayden, this is a solemn occasion. Behave yourself."

Like hell.

But he knew better than to embarrass Violet in front of all their family, so he did reluctantly behave himself.

The kiss he gave Violet when the ceremony ended was light and restrained.

The kiss he gave Violet later that evening and when he'd carried her over the threshold to the bedchamber they would now share, was deep and devouring. His hands roamed over her body with shocking lack of restraint. He did not think it was possible for a man to hunger so greatly or feel such happiness.

At the same time, he also felt an agonizing misery.

Violet was now his wife, and he would claim her in every way, but how could it ever be enough?

He would have no more than a few days with her before he was called away.

His heart was already aching.

He shook out of the thought and concentrated on the beautiful angel before him who was surrounded in that moment by the last rays of sunlight slanting through the window and bathing her in golden twilight.

They were now in his townhouse, in their bedchamber, and he noticed the staff had left a tray of fruit, cheese, and scones atop his bureau, along with a bottle of wine and two glasses. Candles were lit to cast a fiery illumination around the room.

They were well provisioned and would not need to come out for at least another day or two.

He glanced at the food, knowing they would sup later. At the moment, the only thing he intended to nibble on was Violet.

He removed his jacket, cravat, and vest, knowing she would be shy when he began to unlace her gown, and hoping it would help if he removed some of his own garments first. He made no protest when she assisted him with his shirt, liking the softness of her hands upon his skin as she helped slip it over his shoulders and head.

Her eyes were as round as teacups and her cheeks were stained a bright pink as she looked her fill, taking no pains to hide her admiration of his body.

He was no coxcomb, but he knew Violet was eager to couple with him. She wanted to touch him, taste his kisses, as much as he wanted to devour her. "Your turn, sweetheart. Allow me."

It took no more than a few tugs at the lacings of her gown to slip it off her shoulders. Unlike the bee incident, he did not stop there. His hands slid along her slender shoulders to nudge the gown off her body. He watched it pool at her feet in a silken puddle.

He'd meant to lift her in order to move the delicate garment out of the way, but the frugal part of Violet was already thinking ahead. She hopped out from amid the silk and picked up the gown to carefully hang it over a chair.

He grinned, knowing she was still thinking practically and not fully aroused yet. But he soon meant to have her hot and purring as she clawed his body and moaned his name.

She was now clad only in her chemise and stockings, having kicked off her slippers when she'd laid out her gown. He could see her body outlined beneath the gossamer fabric, a lightly veiled temptation amid the glow of candlelight. His own body responded immediately, thrumming with excitement at the sight of the dusky tips of her breasts and the dark patch between her thighs.

He could no longer hold back the urge to taste her, to feel the heat of her arousal against his lips and inhale the scent of her essence. Light. Lavender. Liquid and fiery.

He unpinned her hair, catching his breath as her curls tumbled in a wild cascade down her back and over her shoulders. Her hair was longer than he realized, falling below her waist and curling at her hips.

He buried his hands in her hair and crushed his lips to hers, his control about to snap. He wanted Violet so badly, even his skin was prickling and his loins were aching as they'd never ached for anyone before. "Lord, you're beautiful."

Wanting nothing more between them, he removed the last of her clothes and carried her to their bed. He set her down in the center of it, pausing only to remove his boots. He now wore only his trousers, but decided to keep them on for the moment.

There would be time to take them off after he pleasured her.

He sank onto the bed and gently rolled Violet beneath him.

Her eyes were wide in anticipation, and her lips were softly parted. He meant to go slow, maintain control, but as he pressed lightly down atop her body and felt the lushness of her breasts against his chest, felt the silky heat of her skin, he knew he was lost. "Violet," he said in a husky groan that tore achingly from the depths of his soul. He crushed his mouth to hers once more, slanting his lips over her soft, pliant lips, and at the same time cupping one of those lush breasts in the palm of his hand.

He ran his thumb lightly over its budding peak.

She gasped when he replaced his thumb with his tongue and began to lick and suckle, unable to restrain himself, unable to go slow, for a tidal wave of heat and insatiable desire was crashing all around him.

"Romulus!" Violet wrapped her arms around his neck and arched toward him, as though needing him to take more of her in. Mother in heaven! He was going to swallow up this girl, he was so hungry for her.

His swollen member strained against his breeches.

But he kept up the onslaught on her body, swirling his tongue around the rosy peak of one creamy breast until it hardened, and then moving to the other. He suckled and licked one and then the other, evoking soft, moaning gasps from her lips. "Romulus, these sensations…"

"I know, love. Close your eyes and take them in."

As for him, he was drowning in desire for this girl, desperate to soak all of her in. The lavender scent of her body, the warmth of her skin, the excitement in her sultry, breathy moans.

Her voice was kitten-soft as she purred and arched her body in surrender to his touch, now responsively wild beneath him, squirming, rubbing herself against him, gasping, clutching his shoulders, grabbing onto the back of his head, and tugging at his hair to keep his lips upon her breasts and upon any other part of her body he saw fit.

He nibbled the sensitive spot by her ear.

He kissed his way back down to the tip of her breast.

He kissed lower.

His lips brushed lightly against the patch of hair between her thighs.

She froze, uttering not a gasp, emitting not a breath.

"Trust me, sweetheart."

"I do," she replied, closing her eyes and releasing a sigh as he eased between her parted legs.

She clutched the sheets as he touched her core, light and gentle at first. He wanted to give her a moment to get used to his lips and tongue probing the most intimate part of her. He slowly grew bolder, keeping up the onslaught until she was close to the edge of soaring, and then intensifying the pleasurable sensations.

He felt her tightening, and then felt the nub of her essence quiver. She was nearing her release, about to soar to a never before experienced height. She moaned and tugged at the bed-sheets, her grip on them fierce as she wound and twirled them between her fingers. He extended her pleasure, unrelenting as he touched her and tormented her with each swirl of his tongue.

He kept his hands around her waist to hold her firm as he pressed his mouth to the most intimate part of her responsive body. He could feel the heat emanating from her. He heard her soft, purring breaths that ended on one sobbing moan as she finally gave in to her pleasure. "Romulus!"

"I know, sweetheart." He wrapped her in his arms and held her close until her beautiful body experienced its soaring climax, and she drifted back to earth.

He caressed her, kissed her on the forehead, on her cheek, on her lips. He rolled her atop him, loving the feel of her hot, damp body against his. He felt the pounding of her heart as she wrapped her arms around his neck and kissed him similarly, on his neck, his jaw, his lips with ardent sweetness.

"I had no idea." She laughed breathlessly and burrowed against his body.

"Neither did I," he admitted, for nothing had prepared him for joy that shot straight to his heart and had him reeling as she experienced her release. Nor had any of the wild, rakish moments of his past prepared him for this deep stirring of his heart, this *recognition* in his soul.

He'd found his mate.

More than that, it was as though his soul had been asleep until now, waiting for her, and now aroused by her familiar scent. Lavender. Aroused by the taste of her liquid sweetness. The silky warmth of her skin.

Mine.

She is mine.

It was a primal recognition stretching beyond the bounds of time.

Did she feel it as well?

"VIOLET..."

She knew he'd held back to give her this pleasure. Dear heaven, his voice was raspy and straining from the effort. She felt his rigid fullness against her thigh, and now she was determined to give him a similar pleasure. The only problem, she did not know quite what she needed to do, for although her cousins had spoken to her about what would take place on her wedding night, and her aunt had talked in circles about it, none of them had given her explicit details.

"Romulus, tell me what I should do."

He gave a groaning laugh and caressed her.

She loved the look of him, his muscled strength and the taut planes of his body as he lay on his back and reached one arm around her to draw her closer to his side. His muscles rippled upon his golden skin as he nudged her atop him.

But as he did so, she noticed that a few, thin lines of white marred his chest and arms. Scars from naval battles, she imagined. Some of them appeared new, still thin, red and puckered. "What you should do?" She rested her head against his chest, her breasts pillowed against him, and her legs entwined with his, although his were much longer.

He gently ran his fingers through her hair, studying her as the long strands spilled across his arms and over his chest. "Yes, tell me what to do. Neither The Book of Love nor the women in my family went into detail about this moment. I should have spent last night reading an altogether different sort of book."

He chuckled. "You don't need reading material for this. You're doing just fine."

He took a moment to remove his breeches.

Her eyes widened, not expecting...but she'd felt his stiffness against her thigh, and should not have been surprised by the aching need that suddenly swept over her. She wanted him inside her, wanted their bodies intimately connected.

What they could not yet say in words, they would say with their bodies.

"It may hurt a little at first, Violet."

She eased onto her back and opened her arms to him. "You won't hurt me."

It was all the encouragement he needed.

His big, solid body settled over her, the weight of him exciting even though he was careful to carry most of it on his elbows that were propped on either side of her. She ran her hands across the spray of gold hair on his chest and along the rock-hard bulge of muscles on his arms.

As she closed her eyes and breathed him in, she caught the familiar bay spice scent on his warm skin. She kept her eyes closed as he settled himself between her legs, but her heart pounded with the uncertainty of what was to come. Of course, she trusted him and was calmed by the sweet words he whispered in her ear.

To her embarrassment, it took nothing before she was ready for him, for he worked every part of her at once with his fingers and lips, building her desire with deep, probing kisses and a light, magical touch. He cupped his hand around her breast and rolled his thumb over it to tauten its tip. At the same time, she felt the press of him along the most intimate part of her.

His thrusts were uncomfortable at first, but the discomfort quickly melted away, leaving in its wake sensations of pleasure she never dreamed could exist. She held on to his massive shoulders, felt herself carried along on a beautiful wave that ebbed and flowed, dipped and rose with his every thrust as he eased himself inside her.

She marveled at the hot glisten of his skin, ran her hands, palms flat, along his body, and felt every strain and stretch of his powerful muscles.

Somehow, she felt the intense build of his own need along with hers, and was amazed she could evoke such feelings in him. The Book of Love had explained a man's urge to mate with any desirable female, but this was something more, something that could only exist between Romulus and her.

As his own wave began to swell, hers did, too. They were both carried on magnificent crests that pulsed and pulled them along on an endless, quivering tide. He spilled himself inside her. "Violet," he whispered, his breaths short and her name spoken in a groan. In this moment, she knew they were united forever.

He held her close.

He'd given her everything.

The most precious gift he gave her was his heart. He trusted her to love him and hold him dear forever.

She hugged him fiercely.

He grinned at her. "How do you feel, sweetheart?"

"Spectacular."

He growled low in his throat, obviously pleased by her answer.

"What did you think of *it*, Romulus?"

"I don't know if I can quite put my feelings into words." He shifted off her, but continued to gaze at her, now frowning.

"Oh, you didn't like it." She tried to mask her disappointment. The moment had felt so special for her. She thought it meant something special to him as well. Was she mistaken? "This was my first time. I wasn't–"

He kissed her on the mouth. "I liked *it* very much. You stirred something deep inside of me, something I did not think could ever exist."

"What sort of thing?"

He caressed her cheek with his knuckles. "You awoke a sleeping dragon. I don't know how else to describe what I experienced while holding you in my arms and claiming you as my wife. Mythology has it that a male dragon takes only one mate for life. There is no courtship involved, for he knows her instantly. By her scent, I imagine." He cast her a wicked grin. "By his first glimpse of her luscious, scaly skin. By her wing span that carries her lithe body through the air."

"Romulus–"

"I know." He cast her another grin, this one appealingly boyish. "Your skin is silky smooth, not scaly. Nor do you have wings. My point is, I knew you instantly in that way. In that deep recognition of the soul. It is said dragons roar together when they couple."

She inhaled lightly. "Was I noisy?"

"Delightfully so. But so was I. Could you not hear me roar in victorious conquest? My throat is strained. The noises I made are still rattling between my ears." He kissed her again and drew her into the circle of his arms. "When one dragon dies, the heart of the surviving dragon dies along with it. This is what I felt when coupling with you, that we are one now. One heart. One heartbeat. That if I ever lost you…I would lose the greatest part of me."

She nestled against him, overwhelmed that he should feel this way. He was noble and handsome and heroic. That she would feel this oneness with him was not surprising. What made her so special that he should feel it with her?

It still made no sense.

Did love ever make sense? Or was it just a wondrous, magical sensation meant to be accepted and not dissected and debated until all the magic washed away?

"You are quite the romantic poet, for a sailor. But this explains how I felt the first time you touched me. When you pulled me into your kitchen and unlaced my gown to rub vinegar on me, it was as though I recognized you from somewhere deep in my soul, out of the eternal mists of time." She glanced up at him and smiled. "Do you think there is such a thing as a dragon song?"

"Oh, Lord. Violet, are you going to sing to me now?"

She laughed. "No, you wonderful but still horrid man. You're cringing again. I was merely curious how one dragon mate calls to the other."

"It is a silent call that carries through the air from heart to heart. The operative word being *silent.*"

"That is nonsense. You were roaring. I was making all sorts of ghastly purring sounds."

"I liked your sounds. I'd like to hear them again, if you're not too sore to have me inside you again so soon."

"I'm not too sore."

He shifted their positions so she was under him again. His gaze intensified, his eyes a beautiful, opalescent green. "Violet," he said, stroking his hand lightly along her body, "there's something you must know."

"About this second coupling?"

"Yes. No. About us. To hell with books and their advice. To hell with how we ought to feel and when we should say something."

"Or when we should keep silent?"

His smile was devastating. "We needn't stay silent any longer. We were both thinking it at our wedding ceremony. We should have said it to each other then. It is obvious we've felt this pull to our hearts from the first. We don't need dragon metaphors to state the obvious. Or fear it is a mistake to say it to each other now. I love you, Violet."

Her heart felt ready to burst with joy. "Say it again, Romulus. It sounded so nice."

He growled and nuzzled her neck. "I love you, Violet."

"I love you, too."

They coupled again, laughing with awareness as they exploded in bursts of starlight together, he roaring and she purring, their limbs hopelessly entangled. Their hearts rampantly beating as one. Their lips upon each other's lips to keep their laughter and their noises muted. But mostly, it was because they liked to kiss each other.

As they calmed, their bodies side by side and their fingers entwined, for Romulus had taken her hand and not let go of it, he turned to her with a wicked smile. "Are you hungry?"

She arched an eyebrow. "For you? Yes, but are you recovered so soon?"

He shook his head. "I'm wrung dry. You do that to me. But I meant actual food. We ought to keep up our strength."

"For more coupling?"

He gave her a light, affectionate kiss on the lips. "No more tonight. You'll be too sore to walk in the morning. I wasn't as gentle with you as I meant to be."

She placed a hand to his jaw, the short, bristly hairs of his new stubble of beard rough against her palm. "You were wonderful. Did I complain?"

"You'll feel it in the morning. It's like any exercise or exertion. Feels great in the doing, but you ache to your bones the following day."

"I'll take your word on it. Right now, I feel warm and giddy. Still tingling." She reached for her chemise and drew it over her body. It was one thing to be naked under the covers, but quite another to strut about without...well, Romulus did not appear to feel that way.

He rolled out of bed and crossed to the bureau to collect the tray and place it on the small table by the window. He drew two chairs to the table. Moonlight spilled through the window, illuminating his lean, warrior body.

She thought him incredibly handsome when clothed.

Romulus unclad...

"Like what you see, Violet?" He chuckled. "I think your tongue just rolled off the bed."

CHAPTER FIFTEEN

ROMULUS HAD SILENTLY sworn to himself he'd give Violet the day to recover. But he broke that oath the moment he awoke the next morning and saw her asleep beside him, her dark hair splayed across her pillow and the sheet not quite covering her breasts. Their dusky, rose tips beckoned him.

He groaned, knowing he should not wake his beautiful wife. She was sleeping peacefully, her breaths even and relaxed. He could tell by the light rise and fall of her magnificent chest.

His wife.

He loved the sight of her, especially in his bed.

As he contemplated what to do next, she stirred and stretched, and then opened her eyes and turned to him.

Her smile lit up his heart, for it was as brilliant as a ray of sunshine. "Good morning, Romulus."

"Good morning, my love." He meant to ask her how she felt after last night, but he didn't want to know the answer. He wanted to be inside her again, holding her warm, creamy body against his.

He kissed her.

She kissed him back with ardor.

He cupped her breast.

The fleshy mound felt warm and soft.

She arched her back and moaned.

It was all the encouragement he needed. Blessed saints! He'd take any crumb she offered, but she was not holding back her love. She offered him everything.

He did not hesitate to take it. The two of them were suddenly wild things, groping and laughing as they writhed and twisted in the sheets, desperate to wrap themselves around each other. He would have refrained, although it would have killed him. She only needed to refuse him, and he would have understood.

But she wanted him, surprising him as she took the lead and encouraged his less than proper behavior.

Her face hid nothing of her desire.

Her eyes were closed and her lips sensually parted. Her skin was pink and flushed. And her breasts...he dipped his head and closed his mouth over one sweet bud, suckling it, guiding her to her shattering climax before he claimed his own.

"Violet, that was...Lord help me, I'll be dead by thirty."

She laughed and rolled atop him, her hair in a wild, silken tumble around her shoulders. "We shall both meet the same fate, I fear. I doubt we'll go quietly. What you do to me, Romulus...the things you make me feel."

"I know, my love."

She sighed. "I was peacefully waking, and the next thing I knew, I was on fire and consumed in the burning heat of you. We shall go together in a burst of flames. You roaring, me purring. Or perhaps I shall be singing to you as we turn to ashes. I know how much you love to hear singing. Especially first thing in the morning."

He liked her teasing manner.

He liked that she awoke happy and smiling.

Was there anything he did not adore about her?

The light rap at their door surprised them both.

Romulus slipped the sheet over her shoulders to cover her, and then hastily donned his trousers before crossing to the door and opening it just enough to speak to whoever stood on the other side of it.

His newly hired valet was before him, his expression strained. "Captain Brayden, I'm so sorry to disturb you." He shrank back, as though fearing Romulus would sack him on the spot.

"What is it, Winwood?"

The man stared down at his feet, terrified to so much as glance up lest he accidentally glimpse the woman occupying Romulus's bed. His wife, of course. But the poor valet obviously was not used to husband and wife sharing a chamber. They would have to work a practical schedule before his valet and her lady's maid each ruptured a kidney over this situation.

Winwood cleared his throat. "This letter was just delivered. The messenger said it was important and he would await Mrs. Brayden's answer."

Romulus arched an eyebrow. "Mrs. Brayden?" He grabbed the note, expecting it was a mistake and he would recognize the Admiralty seal affixed to it.

No mistake.

The note was from Lord Forester.

He already disliked the man. What right did he have to disturb Violet on the morning after her wedding?

He wanted to rip it up before Violet read it, but that would rank among the stupidest things he'd ever done. She'd never trust him again. Besides, Violet might not be looking over his shoulder, but her ears were surely perked and she'd heard the note was for her. "Have the messenger wait in the kitchen. Ask Cook to offer him a cup of tea."

Just because he detested Forester did not mean he had to punish the messenger.

When Winwood strode away, Romulus shut the door and turned to Violet. "It's for you."

"Me?" She had already hopped to her feet and was tossing on her chemise, rushing to pull it over her slender body. *Lord, her body.* "I was sure it was for you, from the Admiralty."

She took the note from his outstretched hand and opened it, reading it where she stood. "Jameson wants me to meet him at the Royal Society this afternoon. His sister will be there, of course. They want to set up the hall for maximum effect and want me there to test my voice and see where it carries best."

"Can't they do it with another singer?"

She frowned at him. "It wouldn't be the same."

He wanted to argue the matter, but couldn't. He understood only Violet's presence would do. He would never allow just anyone else to perform his duties as captain on his ship. As much as he did not like or trust Forester, this was about Violet and her *reason to be*. She'd been given the voice of an angel. Her father called her his songbird. The orphanage was where her mother had been raised.

He had to give his all in supporting her or risk breaking her heart. "I suppose we had to get out of bed sometime today. Of course, we'll go."

"We?"

"Violet, we've been married less than a day. I'm not letting my new wife out of my sight."

She arched an eyebrow, looking very much like an imp. "There will be singing."

"*Your* singing. Something I can easily tolerate. I'll remain with you the entire time. I'm sure I'll be transported by your every lilting note."

"What a load of hogswallop." But she threw herself into his arms and wrapped her arms around his neck. "Thank you, Romulus. This means a lot to me. I'm so very grateful."

He twirled her around, laughing. "Just how grateful?"

"Oh, I'm sure I'll find a way to reward your low brain tonight. You forget, I've been reading more than The Book of Love."

"What do you mean?"

"My cousin Lily's baboon study. Baboons mate, too. In the wild. In the raw. Perhaps I'll teach you a baboon mating trick or two."

He groaned. "My heart has stopped beating. You'll have me dead before I reach twenty-nine."

She put her ear to his chest. "Nonsense, Romulus. You are in perfect health. Even your heart is strong."

"It's beating so hard, it's about to pound a hole through my chest."

She gazed up at him innocently. "Oh, then perhaps we ought to forget all about those baboon sex tricks."

"What?"

"Shall I give you a sample now?"

"Hell, yes."

ROMULUS PROPPED HIS shoulder against one of the columns in the rear of the impressive Royal Society hall, a magnificent, white marble homage to the great civilizations of ancient Greece and Rome. Violet stood in front on a stage that must have been erected for another function but appeared to serve perfectly for the charity recital.

He listened to the soft trill of her voice, amazed by how effortlessly she reached the high notes. He felt a deep stir of pride in his heart when she sang one of the songs chosen for the recital.

It was as though the melody floated across the room on angel's wings.

He heard the magic in her voice. Felt its gentle beauty flow through his body.

Others responded the same way. Within moments, workers and visitors began to wander in to quietly listen, their eyes wide with enchantment, knowing they were hearing something quite special.

Violet's eyes were closed as she sang.

She had no idea of the effect her voice had on others.

Despite his instinctive dislike of Forester, Romulus had to give the man credit for recognizing Violet's gift of song. He'd shown more faith in Violet than he had. Indeed, he was disappointed with himself, for he had quickly dismissed it as just singing, albeit excellent singing.

He was wrong.

Her gift was so much more.

Violet opened her eyes when her song ended and was taken aback by the crowd that had gathered and the cheers now filling the great hall.

She blushed and gave an embarrassed bow.

Her gaze sought his. It wasn't hard for her to spot him leaning against one of the columns. Braydens were tall. He was no exception.

Relief shone in her eyes when she saw him, and her smile was as sweet as melted sugar.

"I love you," he mouthed, hoping she could read his lips.

People began to come up to her to offer their compliments.

Romulus was uncertain about the steadiness of the stage, so he plowed his way forward to be close to Violet should matters get out of hand. Forester came up to him, a wry smile on his face. "You married the little songbird, I hear."

Romulus nodded.

"I ought to be insulted. I wasn't invited to the wedding even though Violet's family and mine have been friends for decades."

Romulus decided to be civil to the man. "It was immediate family only, and many of them could not be present on such short notice either. We wanted to keep it a small affair."

"Ah, I understand. She's delectable. Turned out quite beautiful, although she showed none of that promise when she was younger. Obviously, you were caught in a compromising position. What was it? A mere kiss? Or did you manage more?"

Romulus curled his hands into fists. Why had he bothered to be civil? "Nothing at all like that," he said, speaking calmly although he wanted to knock out a few of this scoundrel's teeth. "It was a matter of love at first sight. Why delay when you know it's right? She felt the same. We married."

The crowd had now started to disperse, so Romulus climbed onto the stage to stand beside Violet, knowing he was responding like a possessive arse, but he did not like Forester anywhere near her. Nor Forester's sister, for that matter. Where was she? He'd noticed her earlier, so there was no question she was around.

As he surveyed the hall, he saw her slip back in from a small door off to the side. To his surprise, Finn strode out after her. Perhaps they'd been discussing the donations and where within the Royal Society offices they were to be held for safekeeping until deposited in the bank.

After all, the recital was to be an evening affair, a time when all banks were closed.

Finn had an odd look on his face. Had he been doing something more than merely discussing bank deposits with Lady Rawley?

Romulus was no hound, but he had far more experience with women than Finn had, and certainly more experience with women like Lady Rawley. She was not to be trusted. Blessed saints! He hoped Finn had more sense than to be swayed by her kisses.

Forester had also climbed onto the stage and now followed his gaze to where Finn and Lady Rawley stood. "Ah, I see my sister has been amusing herself with your cousin."

"Are we through here? Violet and I have things to do today." *Such as undress and have wild, baboon sex in bed. Or on the floor. Or on the table.*

Lord, he thought Forester was depraved. How was he any better? The thoughts he had of Violet would make a pirate blush.

However, he was going to speak to Finn first. His cousin was a wizard with investments, but a dolt when it came to women. In truth, it was quite possible Finn was still a virgin. If so, it was even more important they speak, for Lady Rawley was not the right woman for his first experience.

He knew her sort, bitter about her lot in life. Never satisfied. Ready to blame everyone for the poor choices she'd made. Felicia was much the same. These women had married for the title and were now bored out of their minds. Not even widowhood and the freedom it afforded, satisfied them. Felicia was proof of that.

But Lady Rawley was still married, albeit unhappily.

He did not care if the dalliance was consensual. The last thing he wanted was Finn involved in a scandal, called out by a humiliated husband.

How were he and Finn to have this discussion in front of Violet? Obviously, they couldn't. But neither did he wish to let Violet out of his sight. He glanced around. There were still a few of the Royal Society Fellows milling around the hall. He could steal outside with his cousin for a few minutes. "Finn," he said, hopping off the stage and striding toward him. He gave a nod to Lady Rawley and then impolitely hauled Finn away, "I wanted to ask about your mother. Lady Miranda did not look well yesterday."

"She didn't?"

Gad, Finn was even more naive than Violet. How had the wildebeests failed in looking after their own? "No, not at all. She looked quite yellow."

He marched his cousin outside so that they now stood on the steps leading into the hall. The air was cool and crisp, and the sun shone down on them. Finn was immediately defensive. "What's this about? My mother has never been sick a day in her life."

"What were you and Lady Rawley doing just now?"

"Nothing." But a blush shot into his cheeks.

"I knew it. Did she try to kiss you?" Romulus ran a hand through his hair in irritation. "And you let her?"

"Christ, Rom. I'm not a three-year-old. So what if she kissed me? It isn't as if I made the first advance. It didn't mean anything. There was no more to it than that. She's married." He shrugged. "What was I supposed to do? Push her away? Blubber and wail like an infant? Declare she offended my delicate sensibilities?"

Romulus frowned.

"Fine," his cousin said, sighing heavily. "I'm not proud of kissing a married woman. I never would have considered it. She surprised me by throwing herself at me. I was caught unprepared. And don't you dare repeat any of this to anyone."

"I won't. I give you my oath on it. But you must watch out for her, Finn. She and her brother are up to something shady. I think they're after the donations."

"What?" Finn shook his head and gave a dismissive laugh. "Why? Is this because you're convinced no woman would want to kiss me unless she had an ulterior motive?"

Damn it. Now he'd insulted his cousin. "No. Don't be daft. I don't give a fig about your experience with women. This is about avoiding a disaster for Violet. I don't trust Forester or his sister. Keep alert. Don't let her seduce you into doing something stupid."

"When have you ever known me to do something stupid?"

"Never," Romulus muttered. "But men go mindless when sex is involved. Just be careful if she offers you more than kisses. You aren't the prize. Those donations are what she's really after."

Finn folded his arms across his chest. "Are you through insulting me in every way possible?"

Romulus winced. "Yes. I'm sorry. Truly. But this is important. Violet will be devastated if those funds don't get to the orphanage. I hope they do. I hope I'm wrong about all of it, but I feel this pair is up to something. I dare not even discuss it with Violet. She thinks they are her friends. Now it is your turn to give me your word. Please say nothing about my suspicions to Violet or anyone else, for that matter."

"What about our cousins?"

He sighed. "Fine, you can tell the wildebeests. But only if it proves absolutely necessary."

Finn nodded. "We're good then. You have my word. I'll keep it between us for now. I'll let the others in on it if I sense danger."

"Thank you. I'd want the family looking out for Violet, especially if I'm called to duty and can't be here for the recital."

His cousin gazed toward the door. "You had better go inside. I'm sure Violet will be missing you, although I can't imagine why. You're just a big pain in the arse."

He cuffed Finn. "Just keep your breeches buttoned."

He strode back inside.

The hall was empty.

His heart shot into his throat. Where was Violet? She had been out of his sight for less than five minutes. Damn it, she wasn't a toddler. But it wasn't merely that she was missing. It was that she and the Foresters were missing together.

Since she hadn't gone out through the main doors, she must have—
"Violet! There you are. What happened? Where did you go?"

She hurried to his side and rolled her eyes. "Ugh! Can you believe those old fossils who run the Royal Society? Jameson and Valerie were late for another appointment so they hurried off shortly after you left. Their carriage was waiting for them in the alleyway outside the hall so they ducked out the back way. I went in search of a ladies retiring room. I finally found it behind the relics room." She pointed to the small door through which Finn and Lady Rawley had earlier emerged. "It's a tiny chamber near where they store their musty artifacts. Obviously, comforts for the ladies were added merely as an after-thought. Men!" She grunted in disgust, then smiled at him. "I like you, though."

He laughed in relief and kissed the tip of her nose. "I like you, too. Shall we go home?"

His heart was still in a rampant roar. He hadn't been able to calm himself down yet, even though Violet was perfectly fine and nothing untoward had happened.

"I'm a little hungry. Blakney's Confectionery is not far from here. It's a wonderful little sweets shop. They make the most heavenly pies. Do you mind if we stop there first?"

He nodded. "Sounds perfect."

Blakney's was just as Violet had described it to him. Cozy. Cheerful. Wrought-iron chairs painted white and colorful linens in vivid red. He ordered an apple pie with cinnamon topping. Violet ordered a lemon tart. He had just finished his first slice and was about to dig into the second when Violet cleared her throat. "Would you mind terribly if we dined at Uncle John's and Aunt Sophie's tonight?"

He froze with his mouth open and his fork raised.

"You see, my cousins, Honey and Belle, are expected, and I thought it would be nice to see them."

He lowered his fork, sparing only a glance at the tempting chunk of baked apples sitting on the gleaming tines of silver. Those warm, savory apples should have been rolling in his mouth and preparing to slide down his gullet. "Can't it wait until tomorrow? I thought we'd…"

She blushed. "Yes, of course. If you insist. It isn't as if I *must* see them today."

"But you'd like to." He laughed silently, realizing his wife was not quite so guileless as he suspected. She'd lulled him into this state of glutted satisfaction—Lord, those pies were good—before asking him to agree to more hours *out* of their bed, her exquisite body achingly *out* of his arms. "I don't mind. We'll go if it means that much to you."

She placed her hand over his. "Thank you, Romulus."

He'd warned Finn to keep his wits about him, but Romulus knew he ought to have taken his own advice.

Violet left him witless.

He would jump through fire if she asked him.

He had no idea how severely marriage could turn a man's brain to pudding. He'd thought that particular idiocy occurred before marriage, stupid boys doing stupid things with the wrong sort of woman.

The institution of marriage was supposed to sober a man. Make him responsible. Respectable. Wise. Once sowed one's wild oats before entering into said permanent arrangement, got the *stupid* out of one's system.

Completely wrong when dealing with love marriages. Making love to the woman one loved was a bountiful harvest of delights, but it left one's brain soft-boiled.

He kept hold of Violet's hand, not caring that they were gathering stares. She tried to slip her hand away discreetly. He wouldn't let go of it. "We're married. We can do this."

She smiled at him. "I know. And I do love holding on to you. But I would love another bite of my lemon tart, and I can't while you have my hand."

He chuckled and released her. "Gad, you have me wrapped around your little finger, and we've only been married a day."

"You have the same effect on me. Isn't it exciting, Romulus? I feel so lightheaded. I'm still tingling all over from this morning, and giddy with delight at the prospect of what comes next." Her eyes sparkled with happiness as she spoke. "I know where you'd rather be right now. Your gaze is hot enough to burn through the wrought iron of our table. I would rather be home with you, too. But I also like being out and about in town with you, being seen with my new husband."

"Is that so?"

She nodded. "I'm not perfect. Indeed, I know I'm being quite prideful right now, wanting to show you off. Wanting to shout out loud, this man is the handsomest man in the world! This is my husband."

"Well, all right then. I'm feeling quite proud myself. This beautiful songbird is mine. How the hell did that happen? I feel I was rewarded for my bad behavior."

"It wasn't so bad. You did the honorable thing and asked me to marry you. Which reminds me of another thing we ought to do."

"And that is?"

"Stop by Lady Withnall's townhouse and personally thank her."

He sank back in his chair and groaned. "Gad, Violet. Now you are going too far."

CHAPTER SIXTEEN

A NOTHER MESSENGER AWAITED them when they returned home, this one for Romulus. "It's from the Admiralty." He looked at Violet in dismay. "I've been summoned."

Her hand tightened on his arm. "No," she said in a broken whisper. "It's too soon. We've only had a day."

"I know, love. It's probably just a preliminary meeting."

She gazed at him with hopeful eyes. "Do you think so?"

"Yes." Although he wasn't as certain as he made it appear. Still, he did not think it likely he would be sent off without a few days' warning. "I had better go with the messenger. I'll meet you at your aunt and uncle's for supper."

Violet nodded. "I'll go over there early and see if my Oxfordshire cousins have arrived. My other cousins may also be there, Dillie and Daisy. We were going to discuss the charity recital."

He gave her a lingering kiss. "It will be a wonderful success. You affect people, Violet. You are amazing."

She blushed. "Hurry home, Romulus. You have a wanton for a wife, and she is hungry for you."

"I will, love." Romulus kissed her and then hurried to the Admiralty. The sooner he learned what this message was about, the sooner he could return to Violet.

The late afternoon sun was bright and glistening upon the murky Thames water as he rode to meet the First Lord Admiral. In the distance rose the mighty Tower of London. It was not long before he strode into the massive stone Admiralty building that housed the naval administration offices and climbed the stairs to what looked like a war room of a sort.

The wood-paneled chamber was filled with maps set upon a long conference table. The First Lord Admiral was seated at the head of the table. He knew the man, Viscount Melville, and gave him his due respect. Several high-ranking naval officers and a few politicians were also seated, apparently in wait for him.

He recognized most of the men, a powerful lot who could make or break a man's career.

"My lords," Romulus said, taking the nondescript seat offered to him. He was a mere captain, fairly low in the order of precedence among those at the table. Indeed, possibly the lowest. Yet, the Lord Admiral spoke to him first. "The Cornwall pirates have struck again, Brayden. Quite serious, this time. They've sunk one of our best ships."

Romulus frowned. "How did it happen? Captain Ashcroft is an experienced—"

"Captain Erskine was put in command," said a man he recognized as Lord Marbury, Marquis of Chester. Not a man to have as one's enemy.

Oh, bollocks. This was going to be a mess. Erskine also happened to be a nephew of the marquis, who presently looked as unhappy as a man could look and not be in tears...or raging. Romulus drew in a breath. "It was Erskine's frigate that sank?"

The marquis nodded.

Which meant Erskine was in danger of losing his commission. It was standard procedure for a captain to stand for court-martial if he lost his ship. Is this what they had planned for the poor man? It wasn't Erskine's fault. The Admiralty was to blame for putting this inexperienced nephew of the Marquis of Chester in charge of an important command. "What happened to Ashcroft? Was he reassigned?"

The Lord Admiral cleared his throat. "He's still there, of course. Erskine ordered him to take their fleet and give chase to a pirate wolf pack."

"He ordered Ashcroft to lead the charge? So where was Erskine when he lost his ship?"

The air became thick with tension. Finally, the Lord Admiral spoke up. "He stayed behind in Port Isaac. His frigate was moored in the harbor. Pirates burned it."

"Christ, he remained alone in Port Isaac? How many casualties on our side?" His heart ached for the men who'd had no chance to escape the burning vessel.

"No casualties. Not a scratch on Erskine or his crew. No one was on board," the Lord Admiral said, staring pointedly at the Marquis of Chester.

Romulus shook his head. "No one on...where were they all?" Was Erskine that much of an idiot to leave his ship completely unprotected? Not even a few men to stand guard? Not that it would have helped. Perhaps his misguided decisions had actually saved his crewmen.

Port Isaac was a pirate stronghold. The place was infested with those scoundrels. The harbor master and his underlings had to be in the pocket of those pirates, handsomely bribed to look the other way. All sorts of activities took place in the harbor under their very noses.

Several of the town magistrates had to be on the take as well. Perhaps every damn official in the seaport town. Erskine knew this. He should have sailed out with his fleet. He should have been leading–

He broke off the thought. "So, the burning of his ship was merely meant to humiliate the Royal Navy. Retaliation for my capture of McFlynn and his pirate wolf pack, I presume."

"We believe so," the marquis said.

Oh, damn.

He saw the look in the marquis's eyes and knew he was going to try to pin the blame on anyone but his nephew. Romulus stifled the shudder of apprehension that slithered up his spine. How could this be blamed on *him*? It was Erskine's bloody ship. He was miles away when the ship burned, right here in London, ruining the luscious Violet Farthingale. He'd be damned if he'd allow them to pin the sinking of Erskine's ship on him.

He paused a moment, knowing he was about to cause an uproar. "Why wasn't Ashcroft put in command? He was the obvious choice." Of course, he knew the marquis must have put pressure on the First Lord Admiral to promote his nephew. This is how it was often done. Letters sent to the Lord Admiral petitioning for a coveted commission for a son or brother or nephew. "We're lucky the morning papers aren't filled with accounts of a bloody slaughter, which is what would have happened to Erskine and his crew if the pirates had really meant to do more than taunt us."

"Enough, Brayden. We didn't call you in here to box our ears," the marquis intoned.

He gritted his teeth and nodded, knowing he needed to get this man on his side, and he knew just how to do it. "What are you going to do to Captain Erskine? He is a decent chap, just inexperienced. The sinking isn't his fault."

The marquis stared at him. "Then you would vote against my nephew's court-martial?"

"Of course, I would. As I said, this isn't his fault. You promoted him too soon. He should not be blamed for what happened."

The marquis released a breath of relief.

"However," Romulus continued, hoping to tread carefully, but not certain he could manage it, "he cannot be left in command. You cannot trust him with the lives of our sailors. You know this. A battle-tested commander has to be put in charge."

Every man around the table understood they had averted a disaster. Pirate captains did not gain their status by being stupid. They were blood-thirsty rogues, but also wily when it came to their own survival.

Pirate common sense had saved Erskine and his crew. Not even the officials they bribed would have protected the rogues if Royal Navy blood was shed in their harbor.

Not that the Admiralty would have done much if a few sailors had their throats slit. But if they'd touched a hair on Erskine's head? The marquis would have demanded the might of the Royal Navy come down on them, crushing the scourge once and for all.

Romulus almost wished they'd broken Erskine's arm or done something harmless enough from which he'd heal. It would finally put pressure on the government to end the rampant piracy. But the corruption extended deep within the echelons of government. Everyone had their hand out, from high government officials down to the men who built the ships or loaded its cargo. It did not matter whether it was a merchant vessel, passenger ship, or naval frigate.

Hands were out, it was merely a matter of how much each man grabbed.

The Lord Admiral frowned. "Erskine will be given a promotion and assigned to the Admiralty here in London."

Romulus rolled his eyes, too angry with these pompous toads seated around the table to hold his tongue. "Have him shuffle papers all you like, but you cannot give him decision-making authority. You cannot put our lives in his hands."

"Watch what you say about my nephew, Brayden. I'll have you put in shackles."

Bollocks. Time to get this marquis back on his side again. "Lord Marbury, if he is your heir, then do him the favor of getting him out of the line of battle command as soon as possible. He is inept at it. He is fortunate not to have been their target, or he would have died a horrible and painful death at the hands of these merciless fiends."

He scanned down the table. One of the lords seated here could be the very one protecting the harbor master and others, for those men running Port Isaac should have been tossed in prison years ago. "I am glad he is safe. In truth, I like him. But it is important that our men patrolling St. George's Channel and the Irish Sea also remain safe. We need men in command who know what they are doing. Who will not be duped into making foolish decisions that cost the lives of thousands of sailors."

He turned to the marquis once again. "I sincerely hope your nephew is safe and unharmed. He is a good man at heart, just not meant for military service."

The Lord Admiral nodded. "There was not a scratch on him or his crew."

Which confirmed he had done nothing to save his vessel or chase the men who'd burned it. Erskine should never have been put in charge. He had no experience. But as the heir of a marquis, he had been quickly elevated in the ranks.

No one around the table had to say it aloud, but they were all thinking the obvious. They were fortunate the pirates hadn't meant to spill blood that night.

Still, an expensive frigate had been lost.

That had to hurt the royal treasury.

The king must have been blazing mad.

"I hate to send you back, Brayden. I had bigger plans for you," the Lord Admiral said. "I wanted you in my own fleet command. But we need you back in Cornwall. You know the territory better than anyone. The pirates respect you, especially now that you've taken down one of the most vicious among their ranks. But they know you're gone, and they've become emboldened. They're easily outsmarting our patrols. The English merchants are howling."

The Duke of Grambling now spoke up. "So is His Majesty," he said, confirming what Romulus had suspected. "He is most displeased. So, let's fix this as soon as possible before all our heads roll."

The Lord Admiral nodded. "You are to return as soon as your ship is repaired."

"My old ship? The Plover?" He'd been told he would be given a new vessel in the Lord Admiral's fleet, but he doubted that majestic frigate would now be put in service in Cornwall.

They would give him back his old command, give him back his crew, his small but sleek and agile frigate. He was pleased. He knew this vessel, her every creak and groan. He knew how fast she sailed and how tightly she turned.

He knew how many hits she could sustain.

"She won't be ready until next week," the Lord Admiral said, regaining his attention. "I'll expect you to remain in London until then."

He eyed the Lord Admiral curiously, surprised it would take so long when he'd expected the vessel to be seaworthy in a matter of days. She'd only cracked a mizzenmast. And why was he required to remain in London until then? Was the man purposely doing him a favor?

How could he know about Violet and how desperate Romulus was for even a few more hours with her? Putting off his departure until next week would give him time to see her recital and make certain the funds were properly deposited in the orphanage account.

"I hear your wife is giving a charity recital." The Lord Admiral grinned at him, responding to the surprise surely evident on his face. "I happen to be a Fellow of the Royal Society. Some of the Fellows heard her sing today, just a practice song or two. I understand she has the voice of an angel."

Romulus tried to keep the smile of pleasure off his face, but he doubted he'd succeeded. "She has, my lord."

"Then it is fortunate you will be here for her recital." He turned to the other men as they all rose, the business concluded. "You all must go hear Captain Brayden's lovely wife sing. It is for an excellent cause. St. Aubrey's orphanage." He came to Romulus's side. "I have reason to know it," he said quietly. "I will be there to support her."

"Thank you, my lord. She will be honored."

"Oh, and Brayden…"

"Yes, my lord." He silently cursed, for here it was, the hammer about to drop on his head.

"I'll be assigning you a new cabin boy."

One of the Lord Admiral's by-blows? No, he didn't seem the sort. More likely the by-blow of someone important. Perhaps someone connected to his family or that of a close friend. Likely, someone quite powerfully connected to whom the First Lord Admiral owed a favor. Why else would the man take personal interest in a cabin boy?

Romulus did not particularly care who the lad was, for anyone put under his charge would receive the same treatment and protection. He'd keep this lad safe and well cared for.

Indeed, if that was all demanded of him, then it was a relief.

He needn't be told to guard the boy with his life. It was ingrained in him. He'd fight to the death to protect a child. "Very good, my lord. I'll watch over him."

"I know, Brayden. It puts my heart at ease."

Bollocks, he'd better not lose the boy.

Who was this important lad?

CHAPTER SEVENTEEN

"ROMULUS, YOU'RE BACK early." Violet took his arm as he strode into their townhouse. She kissed him lightly on the cheek and cast him a cheerful smile to hide her worry, but her stomach was in knots. Would he now confirm he had been ordered to sail to some distant shore and would not return for years?

Somehow, she managed to remain calm. "I didn't expect you until suppertime. I was about to go over to Aunt Sophie's, but there's no rush. I'm sure Honey and Belle are still unpacking. Anyway, I'd much rather hear what happened at the Admiralty."

He led her into his study and poured himself a brandy while he told her briefly what had transpired. They had another week together. It wasn't nearly enough time, but she was grateful for every moment. She hung upon his every word as he related what had happened in Port Isaac.

"So, this was a well thought out plan." She shook her head in amazement. "The pirate fleet lured the ships under Erskine's command out to sea on purpose? And he stayed behind? Making it easy for them to burn his frigate right there in the harbor? Oh, dear."

Her eyes widened. It felt as though she was listening to a tale of adventure written in a book. Unfortunately, these pirates were all too real.

"Do you know who led the pirate attack?" she asked, now seated on the settee beside him and still hanging upon his every word.

"No. But I'll find out soon enough. This pirate captain thought he was being clever, showing off to the other pirates, smugglers, and assorted vermin who haunt the town. But all he's done is rouse the ire of the king. Frigates are damned expensive, and the loss fell squarely on the royal treasury. The king will want his revenge for that."

"May I ask one last question?" In truth, she had a thousand more she wanted to ask, but he was obviously fatigued and the strain of his meeting showed in his eyes.

He laughed. "Yes, love. Go ahead."

"Why haven't the harbor master and Port Isaac council been replaced? They're obviously in–"

"Involved up to their eyeballs in smuggling and piracy? Quite possibly. But they are also protected by someone very high up in our government. Perhaps even within the king's own inner circle. Some of the ill-gotten lucre may even be getting back into the king's own hands. Who knows? It would be quite the jest, him burned—quite literally—for his own misdeeds."

Her eyes widened in horror. "Do you believe the king himself is involved?"

"I don't know. I don't care. I'll leave it to someone in government to handle that rattling snake."

She rang for light refreshments to be brought in. "How many lords do you think are in business with these smugglers and pirates?"

"It could be all of them. I truly don't know. I detest the politics of the situation. I'm a warrior, not a windbag. We are very different animals. I doubt we are in any way related. Warriors are trained to defend their country and place their own interests last. Politicians think of themselves first. They'd throw their own grandmothers to the wolves if it would advance their careers."

"I had no idea you were so cynical."

"It's hard to patrol the Cornish coast and still feel optimistic about the charitable nature of man. Perhaps I am being too harsh. There are good men, lots of them. But the smuggling in and out of Cornwall seems to attract men of greed."

"Do you believe the king is one of them?"

"No, not in any significant way. He is aware of what goes on and chooses not to do much about it. However, there is probably more damage to be done if he does come down too hard. It cannot be easy for him to control all these lords, and the general populace would be howling if they could not get around some of the taxes imposed. The king is no fool. He has to appease so many factions. I'm not there to stop the piracy and smuggling so much as to control it so it does not get too far out of hand."

He sighed and ran a hand through his hair. "Let's speak no more about it, love. The upshot is, I've been given back my old command."

"Patrolling the Cornish coast."

"It will keep me closer to home. Closer to you."

She nestled against him when he wrapped his arm around her to draw her close. "I said I had one last question, but I have another. Do you mind, Romulus?"

"No, love. Ask it."

"What of the cabin boy? Do you know who he is?"

"Not a clue."

"I'll prepare a package for him. A sweater, mittens, scarf, and cap. I understand it can get cold out on the water. I'll pack the same for you. Do you think he reads? I'll add some books, too." She nibbled her lip. "But what if he doesn't read?"

Romulus emitted a deep, rumbling laugh. "I wonder if his mother gives as much thought to him as you do. If he doesn't know his letters, then I'll read to him. Satisfied?"

She nodded. "You're a good man, Romulus Brayden."

He lifted her onto his lap. "No, I'm not. I'm a lecherous fiend who has an insatiable appetite for pretty brunettes with violet eyes."

She kissed him lightly on the lips, then drew back grinning. "I seem to have developed a fascination for big, green-eyed captains in the Royal Navy."

Romulus dipped his head to kiss her properly, but Violet darted off his lap as their butler rolled in the tea cart. "The refreshments," she said breathlessly, trying not to look so guilty. It did not help that Romulus made no effort to hide his amusement or his hot gaze.

It also seemed a little ridiculous that Romulus should eat before walking next door for supper with Violet's family, but the two slices of pie he had devoured earlier in the day was not enough to sustain a man his size.

Shortly afterward, Romulus walked her next door and settled in the library with her uncles while she skittered upstairs to greet her newly arrived cousins. They were unpacking their trunks in the bedchamber once shared by the twins, Lily and Dillie. But now that the twins were married, their room was used for visiting relatives. "Belle! Honey!"

Violet's cousins rushed to hug her. "Violet! You've been busy," Honey said, not taking a breath before continuing in a mix of squeals and giggles that was so unlike her usually staid and composed cousin. "Aunt Sophie told us everything. I cannot believe you're married! I thought we three would be attending the balls, soirees, and musicales together, comparing our dance cards and commenting on the young bucks who seem most promising."

"And those who are to be crossed off our lists immediately," Belle added with a grin.

"Is your husband here?" Honey asked. "Oh, goodness! It sounds so odd. I still cannot wrap my head around the news."

"You'll meet Romulus when we return downstairs. He's wonderful."

Honey gave her another hug. "I can tell by your smile. Does he happen to have a brother of marriageable age for Belle?"

Belle now frowned. "Stop, Honey. I don't need you matchmaking for me. And what about you?"

"Never mind about me," she said with a roll of her eyes. "You're the one who ought to marry."

Belle turned to Violet. "Our parents will be furious when they find out Honey has no intention of finding herself a husband. She's only here to keep me company."

"We'll see about that," Violet said. "Things happen, as I can attest. Romulus has no available brothers, but he does have some very handsome cousins. You'll meet at least one of them soon. His name is Finn Brayden, and he's helping me out with the charity recital. Has Aunt Sophie told you about it?"

"Yes, we got an earful about all that went on this past week." Belle shook her head and chuckled. "We're so sorry we missed all the fun. Poor Aunt Sophie! Between worrying over her daughters and you, I'm amazed her hair has not turned completely gray. She begged us to stay out of trouble. We promised her we'd behave, but she merely sighed and gazed heavenward. I don't think she believes us."

Violet couldn't help but laugh. "It's this street, Chipping Way. Things just happen." She locked her arm in Belle's. "Come, meet my husband."

The men walked out of the library when they heard the women come downstairs. Romulus was impossible to overlook, for he was much bigger than the other men. "Oh, my heavens," Belle whispered. "That's him?"

Violet nodded.

"Blessed saints," Honey muttered. "And there are more just like him? Belle has to meet one of these eligible Braydens."

Belle frowned. "What about you?"

"I told you, I'm taking over the family business. A husband will only be a hindrance."

Violet knew she had to have a serious discussion with Honey, but now was not the time. She'd take her aside after the charity recital.

The right partner opened up opportunities, not shut doors. But Honey could be stubborn and would take a good deal of persuading.

After introductions were made, they all entered the dining room to sit for supper. The conversation was lively, mostly about the progress of the recital. Dillie and Daisy joined them shortly afterward, along with their husbands, happy to report they'd already collected a substantial number of vouchers they would turn over to Finn tomorrow. "Ticket sales are brisk," Dillie said, "but most will simply pay at the door." She glanced at her own husband and smirked. "Ian will see to that."

It helped that Dillie was married to a duke, especially one as powerful and respected as Ian Markham, the Duke of Edgeware. The notion of actually paying up front was foreign to most of the Upper Crust, but they would not dare defy Edgeware.

It seemed he and Daisy's husband, Lord Gabriel Dayne, were quite enjoying setting down the law to these lords and ladies. "Some of them are insufferable," Gabriel muttered. "They think they can run up tabs wherever they please. Most pay up eventually, but there are always a few who never do and never will. I can understand those who suffer from a desperate lack of funds. But there are those who do so merely out of disdain for their inferiors. And they conveniently believe everyone is their inferior. I look forward to tossing those churls out on their ear."

Daisy cast her husband a warning glance. "There will be no unpleasantness at your charity affair, Violet. Never you worry. No fists will be raised."

"I'm so grateful to all of you. This is wonderful," Violet said, her eyes aglow and her heart beating with excitement. "I wish the abbess of St. Aubrey's was here, but this affair is all so rushed, I doubt she'll respond to my letter until after the recital. She'll want to write to each of you to thank you personally."

"None required. It is our pleasure," Dillie's husband said, glancing at Dillie with so much love gleaming in his eyes, that it stole Violet's breath away. Would Romulus grow to love her as much as Ian obviously loved Dillie?

The gossip rags had been brutal in their description of Ian as well as of Daisy's husband, Gabriel. They were called wastrels, devils, disreputable rakehells. Mothers were warned to hide their daughters from these rogues.

Good thing Dillie and Daisy had paid no attention to the whispers.

Looking at these two couples, Violet was convinced love worked miracles.

The evening, as enjoyable as it was, ended early. The recital planning was mostly done, and Belle and Honey were stifling yawns after their long journey.

Violet was eager to return home with Romulus, for every minute alone with him was precious. He'd been reassigned to his old command, so there would be no grand tour or honeymoon for them, just a few days to get to know each other better before they were forced apart.

They walked home and immediately retired to their bedchamber.

Violet expected Romulus to have her undressed and in bed the moment the door closed behind them, but he strode to the window instead and appeared to be gazing at the moonlight.

Violet walked to his side and peered out as well. "A beautiful moon tonight, isn't it?"

"Yes, love." He turned to her with a wistful smile.

"What are you thinking?" she asked when he returned his gaze to the moon.

He shrugged. "I was wishing that time would stop, right here. Right now. I want to capture this night alone with you and hold it forever."

When he turned to face her, she tugged lightly on his cravat to unknot it. "Then let's get to it, Captain Brayden. There isn't a moment to waste." But her smile faded as she studied his features in the moon's glow. "You're still worried. What is it that has you so tense? My recital? Your return to Cornwall?"

A muscle twitched in his jaw as he reached out to turn her in his arms so that her back was now pressed lightly to his chest and his arms were around her as they both gazed out the window. "I rarely see such a clear sky when I'm on patrol off the coast. Fog usually swirls in deeper waters, like a gray cloak draped over my ship. But some nights, there is not so much as a wisp to be seen. On such a night, the moon is bright and full. It sits like a huge, silver ball, silent and glistening over the dark waves. The stars blanket the sky. They can blind a man with their shimmering sparkle."

"Sounds beautiful."

"It is. On those nights, the sea is gentle and quiet. One can hear the waves lapping the hull. I hope to share this sight with you before too long. Once I'm settled, I'll send for you. But not until I'm certain it's safe."

She nestled against him, her cheek resting upon his broad chest. "I look forward to the day. I can't wait to see your ship, to sail away on it with you. To stand in your arms as you show me the moon and stars."

"There's nothing like it, Violet. The beauty of it seeps into your soul." He turned her and kissed her deeply. "As you have seeped into my soul."

He lifted her into his arms and carried her to bed. Violet could see that he was still worried, even as he lowered his body over hers and made sweet, slow love to her.

What troubled him?

Her recital? The new cabin boy? The pirates who were overly emboldened? Jameson Forester, of course?

His worry now nagged at her, remaining in the dark recesses of her mind even as his hands slid magically along her body, caressing her and rousing her so that she was hot and ready when his big, magnificent body joined with hers. He sent her soaring to the silver moon and sparkling stars he had just been talking about. "I love you, Romulus."

"Thank The Graces," he teased. "I was worried you were bored and not enjoying yourself."

"And you? Are you bored?"

He groaned. "Hell, no. My low brain is in spasms and ready to go again."

"Is it physically possible for your body to recover so fast?"

"Men are like salmon during spawning season. They will ignore the laws of gravity, defy the impossible for the chance to mate."

But he did little more than hold her in his arms and stroke his fingers gently along her skin for a good, long while. Only after a length of time had passed, did he shift her under him, pressing his body over hers and stoking the fires within her. Their coupling felt different this time, perhaps a little more desperate, as though Romulus's soul ached. It was as though a sadness had overwhelmed him even as he thrust into her and found his release.

Their separation would be harder on him than it would be on her. She would have her family and his to keep her company and occupy her time. Belle and Honey would be a distraction for certain. But Romulus would be on patrol, chasing down pirates and enduring sudden squalls.

Perhaps it was merely a commander's nature to think of all that could go wrong. Those worries would not leave him, not even while he was in the throes of ecstasy. She was not hurt or angry. She knew he took pleasure in her body. But he was also thinking of his impending return to his old command and resuming his old life, one that did not include her.

She sensed he was already missing her.

Worrying about being apart from her.

His worry was infectious, and this insidious, inkling of doubt crept into her heart as well, leaving her with unsettled dreams.

Would she ever have the chance to stand in the circle of his arms on the deck of his ship?

Or would it all go horribly wrong and she'd never see Romulus alive again once he returned to Cornwall?

CHAPTER EIGHTEEN

T HE RAIN CLEARED off early Saturday morning, the day of Violet's recital. She was relieved, for the dampness was not good for her throat and she was tense enough already. A mere eight hours left until the big event.

She'd hardly touched her breakfast and was now picking at her noontime meal. The thought of a hundred spectators paying to hear her sing, ogling her, and expecting to be dazzled by her performance, had her stomach tied in knots.

"Violet, love. Are you all right?" Romulus asked, frowning as he watched her from across the table.

"Yes, perfect." She flashed him a smile and quietly tried to calm her nerves by reminding herself of all that was in readiness. "Perhaps I ought to try on the gown once more. Just to be certain–"

"What? Just to be certain you haven't suddenly grown too tall for it? Or too big for it? I don't think you have anything to worry about. It fit you to perfection yesterday." His frown of concern eased into a rakish grin. "Gad, you looked so good in it. I wanted to strip you out of it so badly."

"That makes no sense." Her gown was more of a costume piece, an opalescent, pearl-colored silk confection in a medieval style that had a silk overtunic in hues of blue and green, the colors of the ocean, and a silver belt that circled her hips and fell to a V in front. It had been freshened and was neatly laid out on her bed.

"It makes perfect sense. You looked spectacular in it, so where else was my low brain to go but to wish to see you naked out of it? You look spectacular right now, by the way."

She gasped. "We are not going upstairs to bed. I'm not about to let you get me hot and sweaty, then I'll have to bathe all over again." She had been treated like a queen this morning, the tub brought up to their chamber, hot water poured into it along with exotic, fragrant oils that Belle and Honey had brought with them from their Oxford perfume shop.

She'd enjoyed a good, long soak, and then her maid had washed her hair before the water turned too cold. There was nothing more to do but style her curls now that they had dried.

Romulus took a sip of his coffee, then set down his cup. "I'm available to assist you with another bath should you change your mind. Not that I'm insisting, mind you. I just want to be clear about my willingness to help."

She couldn't help but laugh. "Is that right? You'd lather me up? Wash me down?"

"Why not? I did a commendable job rubbing vinegar all over your body when the bees attacked, if you will recall. I can do the same with scented soaps or oils."

"I'm impressed," she teased. "You are quite versatile."

He cast her a seductive smile. "Care to find out just how versatile?"

"Oh, you wicked, wicked man!" She was so tempted, but she dared not. Still, he was incredibly...no! She began to fuss with her hair.

Jameson had suggested she leave it down tonight, as part of the theatrical effect, so that it tumbled long and loose over her shoulders and down her back. He said it would give the impression of youth and innocence, not to mention beauty. He vowed they would haul in another thousand pounds from the well-heeled, London set because of it.

"Why are you suddenly fussing with you hair, Violet?"

189

"I was thinking how I ought to style it."

"I thought you said Forester wants you to keep it unbound."

She nodded. "He does."

"So, where's the problem? I can see why he suggested it. Every man watching you will believe you walked out of his dream. He'll imagine running his fingers through your dark curls."

Of course, she knew Romulus would seriously maim any man who attempted it.

"They'll all be wishing you were theirs and believing you are singing to them alone."

"I can't believe you are agreeing with him."

He cast her a wry smile and arched his eyebrow. "In truth, neither can I. But he's right about this. Your medieval costume will have them thinking they are heroic knights and you are the damsel in distress they must rescue. I can't repeat what else they'll be thinking. I can only say this is what crossed my mind."

She sighed.

"Men spend their blunt freely when their low brains are engaged. You, my innocent and utterly ravishing wife, will have them in a low brain frenzy. They'll be hurling wads of pound notes onto the stage."

"Fine. Enough. I've agreed to wear the medieval gown and keep my hair unbound." She snorted. "Damsel in distress, indeed. Two of the songs in my repertoire are medieval ballads. I suppose this outfit makes sense."

She'd rehearsed those ballads and others each day at the Royal Society hall with one of London's best-known pianists to accompany her. Jameson had mentioned they would have to pay the man out of the proceeds, for he would not play without being compensated. Violet hoped his fee was not exorbitant, but since Jameson had already agreed to the terms, there was little she could do about it.

Belle and Honey had gone with her to each rehearsal. Also with them was a burly, watchful footman. Neither Uncle John nor Romulus trusted the three of them to be left on their own, even though they were never alone in the Royal Society building.

It mattered not that the place was crawling with scholars and stodgy professors, as well as the occasional nobleman who came to admire the ancient swords, artifacts, and bones kept under glass in the Society's small museum near the hall.

Violet toyed with her own cup of coffee, absently twirling it in her hands as she took a deep breath for the twelfth time this morning.

Romulus arched an eyebrow. "You'll be perfect, Violet. Don't work yourself into a state."

"I can't help it. It's hitting me like a wall of stone tumbling off an ancient fortress. I–"

Their butler strode in with a note for her. "Ma'am," he said, bowing as he handed it to her.

She opened it and groaned. "Belle isn't feeling well. It's this weather. The morning rain and now the sudden chill. I knew it would affect her lungs. Honey will likely stay with her, and I'll have neither of them with me tonight."

Romulus set aside the newspaper he'd obviously been hoping to read while he finished his coffee. "Love, your Aunt Sophie will be there with John and your other uncles. So will Daisy, Dillie, and their husbands."

"But they'll be occupied in the front of the hall, making certain everyone pays the entrance fee. I suppose Jameson and Valerie will calm me down."

"And Finn will be guarding the receipts. His brothers will be helping out as well."

She managed a smile. "The Brayden tadpole-wildebeests."

He leaned forward and grinned. "Lady Miranda will be in the audience as well. She'll take a battle axe to anyone who dares disrupt your performance." He reached across the table to take her hand, enveloping her cold fingers in his big, warm palm. "I'll be there, too. There's that little matter I must tend to at the Admiralty, but it shouldn't take up more than an hour of my afternoon. I'll be home in plenty of time to escort you to the recital hall this evening."

She shook her head. "Picking up your cabin boy is no little matter. How odd that you should be asked to bring him to your home and have him ride with you to Cornwall, don't you think?"

Romulus shrugged. "It is a bit unusual. I usually meet my cabin boys when I'm on my ship, but since The Plover is still under repair, I suppose it is just as efficient to bring the boy along with me. I'm riding to Cornwall anyway. He'll be no bother."

"The Lord Admiral will know the boy is being well looked after while in your care. I wonder if he's related to the king."

"If the lad is, then he'll be my commander by the time he's eighteen. I had better stay in his good graces."

Violet knew he was jesting, but the sudden summons to collect this boy struck her as odd. "He's welcome here, of course. I wish they had waited until tomorrow. After all, didn't you say the Lord Admiral himself will be in attendance tonight? Surely he understands how important it is for me to have you by my side."

Romulus nodded. "Which is why he arranged for me to retrieve the boy well before your recital. It is quite likely this matter could not wait."

"Do you know the boy's name yet?"

"No. Wasn't mentioned in the note."

Violet shook her head. "Most odd. I'll lay odds he is related to the king."

"Then I'm honored to be entrusted with his care."

Violet rolled her eyes. "Ugh, and you really mean it, too. Sometimes, I wish you weren't so wonderfully noble. Should we bring him with us to the recital? I hate to leave him on his own mere hours after you bring him home. The Mayhew girls will take excellent care of him, but it isn't the same as having us. He might enjoy an evening of music."

"Said no boy ever," Romulus muttered. "We'll ask him which he'd prefer. How's that?"

"Perfect. And he can stay in the ancient relics room with me if he begins to tire and doesn't wish to remain in the hall with everyone else. They've thoughtfully placed a settee and small table in there for my use tonight. Let's bring along a pillow and coverlet. Perhaps a few apples and toys. He can eat, play, or sleep in there while I'm singing on stage. No one will disturb him, other than Finn when he locks the receipts in the vault where they keep the smaller relics." She cast him a triumphant smile. "There, all figured out."

She noticed Romulus was not smiling along with her.

"Do cheer up Romulus. It's a perfect solution. What can go wrong?"

THE ROUTE TO the Admiralty was becoming quite familiar to Romulus. He'd been riding back and forth each day this week, the Lord Admiral having suddenly become his most ardent supporter and seeking his opinion on naval tactics, battle preparedness, ship design, even which wines to stock in the flagship wine cellar. Romulus hardly considered himself an expert on that matter.

"Ah, Brayden. Just in time. Let me introduce you to your new charge, Lord Innes Buchan, son of the Duke of Buchan."

The boy stepped forward. "It is a pleasure to meet you, Captain Brayden. I look forward to serving under your command."

Blessed saints! A duke's son? And not just any duke, mercy one of the most powerful men on this sceptered isle. How in heaven did his offspring get sent off as a cabin boy? "My lord, the pleasure is all mine," Romulus said, quite impressed by the poise of this nine-year-old who had a thick mass of curly blond hair and green eyes the hue of an English meadow in summer.

"Thank you." He cast Romulus a nod of acknowledgment. "Lord Admiral Melville speaks quite highly of you. I look forward to sailing with you on The Plover."

Was the lad a tiny forty-year-old in disguise? He'd never met a child who appeared so grown up. As the boy was escorted out of the war room to bid farewell to the governess who had brought him down from Castle Easingwold, just north of York, the Lord Admiral gave him a quick account. "He's the fifth and youngest son of Buchan, sired by the duke and his second wife."

"And she sent him away?" He could not comprehend why a mother would wish to be rid of such a boy.

"Wife number *three* has insisted he be sent away. The boy's mother, wife number two, died in childbirth when he was born."

Romulus felt a tug to his heart. "Poor lad." Violet would be beside herself to fuss over him. Indeed, the Farthingales might quite suffocate the boy with love, something he doubted Innes had ever experienced. Certainly not a mother's love, and certainly not from his stepmother.

"The duke loves the boy, but he cannot have him underfoot right now."

"What about preparatory school? The boy is old enough."

"His father would like him to experience life aboard a ship. I suspect he wishes to groom the lad as a future First Lord Admiral," he said with a wry smile.

Romulus nodded. "The country will be fortunate to have him leading the Royal Navy."

"I heartily agree. So, try to keep him alive and uninjured, Brayden. He'll be sent to Eton when he's older, but for now, he is all yours."

The boy walked back in the room.

"Come along, my lord. My wife is eager to meet you. She'll have lemonade and ginger cake waiting for us. Do you like ginger cake?"

The boy nodded, his blond curls bobbing with vehemence. "My

favorite."

Romulus decided it was a good thing he'd been ordered to take charge of the boy today.

Violet melted at the sight of him and had to struggle to hold back her tears when Romulus took her aside a moment to tell her of the boy's circumstances.

"It is unpardonable the duchess would insist on sending him away," she whispered.

"She views him as a threat. Perhaps the duke sees too much of his second wife in the boy. I suspect his second marriage was a love match. Wife three does not wish to compete with that."

"How is this the boy's fault? The duke might grow to love her if she showed love toward his son."

Romulus kissed her on the forehead. "Then she'd be you, and the duke would fall hopelessly in love."

She rolled her eyes and tsked. "My lord," she said, turning to the boy, "would you care for more ginger cake?"

"Yes, I would."

Once Innes had finished, she asked him if he enjoyed playing marbles. When his eyes lit up, she went next door and came back a few moments later with two boys slightly younger than Innes. "These are my cousins, Charles and Harry. They are champion marbles players."

Charles held up a pouch and rattled it. "I have aggies and alleys, and shooters and taws."

"Any mibs and ducks?" Innes asked quite seriously.

Harry, the youngest, nodded. "Bumblebees and jaspers, too. Charles has them all."

"Bumblebees," Romulus remarked, grinning over their heads toward Violet. "Those are my favorite."

The boys played for over an hour, stretched flat on their stomachs on the parlor floor and rising only to grab a milk biscuit or currant scone before dropping to their knees for another round of marbles.

By six o'clock, Charles and Harry were returned next door, escorted by Violet and a footman.

Romulus took the opportunity to ask Innes if he'd like to remain at home under the care of the Mayhew girls, or come with him and Violet to the Royal Society hall. "My wife and I would be delighted if you joined us. But the choice is entirely yours."

"Truly? She won't find me inconvenient?"

"Not at all. In truth, she'll probably miss you and worry about you if you don't join us."

His eyes lit up. "She would? Then may I go with you, Captain Brayden?"

"Yes, my lord. You are most welcome." Bollocks, the boy tore at his heart.

By seven o'clock, Romulus and Innes were standing in the entry hall, waiting for Violet to descend the stairs. When she did, the blood rushed into Romulus's head...and lower, of course, because his low brain had taken control again.

Young Innes gaped at Violet, his jaw dropping and his eyes about to pop out of their sockets. "Is she an angel?"

"She certainly looks like one, doesn't she?"

Innes nodded.

Hell, if a nine-year-old boy could fall in love with her on sight, how would the grown men in the audience respond? He was glad the wildebeests would be joining them. He'd position them in a line in front of the stage to catch any fools who attempted to run onto it.

As for him, he'd do his best to keep an eye on Forester and his sister, although it would be harder to do now that Innes was coming with them. He'd draw Finn aside and issue another warning about that pair.

Finn would be angry with him, for the caution would be taken as an insult. He'd apologize to his cousin afterward.

He took Violet's arm and helped her into the carriage, then gave the lad a boost in. Romulus took the bench opposite them, stifling a smile at the look of wonder on Innes's face. Of course, the boy was staring at Violet, and she was smiling back at him, a lovely, openhearted smile that would shoot straight to any man's heart.

He suddenly became wistful.

He would be leaving for Cornwall shortly, leaving Violet behind. They'd coupled often enough that she might be carrying his child. They would not know it for some time yet. But in watching her gentle manner with Innes, his love for her swelled. She'd be a good, kind mother to their children.

He gave silent thanks for whatever had brought them together. Those bees. The Book of Love everyone was beginning to believe was magical. The tiny termagant, Lady Withnall. Perhaps all three played a part in uniting him with Violet.

He supposed it did not matter.

Whatever the reason, he was grateful for it.

Now all he needed was this night to pass without incident. Why were the short hairs on the back of his neck still spiking in alarm?

CHAPTER NINETEEN

A CROWD WAS already gathering in front of the Royal Society by the time Romulus's carriage drew up to the building. However, the carriage was steered to a spot toward the back of the hall, and they were all escorted inside through a side entrance that led down the small passageway directly to the ancient relics room where Violet and Innes would remain until her performance began.

The relics room, as the Duke of Lotheil had promised, now contained a settee and small table. Atop the table was a pot of tea and several cups. "How thoughtful of the duke," Violet said. "Would anyone like tea?"

"No, love. But I shall pour you a cup if you wish to have some. How about you, Innes?"

"I'm fine, Captain. None for me."

Violet nodded. "Nor for me. I can't put anything in me so close to my recital time or I'll be belching out the songs." She then belched a few notes.

Innes thought her antics hilarious.

He exchanged a glance with Violet, loving her more for this. She wanted the boy to laugh.

Innes now looked at her in adoration.

Romulus understood why. Here was an angel who could belch. What more could a man want in a woman?

"Love, I'm going to see what's going on in the grand hall. Innes, do you want to come with me?"

His eyes grew wide. "May I?"

"Yes, of course. But stay close to me. The hall will be packed by now, and the First Lord Admiral will not be pleased with me if I lose you." As much as Violet liked the boy, Romulus knew she needed a moment alone to concentrate on her performance and do whatever throat exercises one did in preparation...or whatever one did before walking on to the stage, ready to appease a hungry audience.

To his dismay, he realized he did not even know which songs she was going to sing. The list had been planned between Violet and the Foresters, but she had told him which songs and it now escaped him.

Not that the song list mattered much. What mattered was that she had told him, and he had forgotten. He'd been so caught up in Admiralty matters, he'd dismissed this recital as unimportant.

Yet, Violet was the most important thing to him. How could he have shown such lack of interest? He felt worse because she had never once called him to task for it.

He shook out of the thought and concentrated on locating the Foresters amid the crowd. He couldn't see them, but they had to be in here somewhere. He knew they'd arrived ahead of him and Violet.

He expected to find Jameson Forester front and center, taking all the accolades for himself. He led Innes in a turn about the hall before going out front to where Violet's cousins and their husbands were collecting the entrance donations. Finn would likely be with them, and wherever Finn was, Lady Rawley was certain to be close by.

He quickly introduced Innes to Dillie and Daisy and their husbands, then asked them about Finn. "Have you seen him?"

Daisy nodded. "Our box was full, so we gave him the receipts taken in so far. He went to place them in the vault in the relics room."

"He went alone?"

Ian frowned. "He's a big, hulking Brayden. Who is going to mess with him?"

"Besides," Gabriel added, "the hall is a crush. Perhaps there are a few pickpockets about, but no one is going to steal the donations in front of a hundred people."

"Lady Rawley accompanied him," Dillie said.

"Christ! And where's Forester? Have any of you seen him?"

Ian's frown deepened. "Not in a while. He was here earlier, but–"

"Innes, stay here. I'll be right back for you." But Innes clung to his hand and wouldn't release it, no doubt petrified he was about to be abandoned again.

"Come, Lord Innes," Dillie said gently, "take the seat between me and Daisy. You can help us take in the last of the donations. I promise you, Captain Brayden will return shortly."

Romulus shouldered his way through the crowd and back to the relics room the moment Innes let go of his hand. He heard Ian calling behind him. "What's going on?"

Romulus briefly confided his concerns about the Foresters. "I could be wrong."

"I hope you are. Tell you what, I'll check around back."

"Alone? I know your feats of valor are legendary, Your Grace. But your wife will mutilate me if any harm befalls you. Are you armed?"

He nodded. "To the teeth. You can't tell by looking at me, can you? My tailor is quite talented. Hidden sheaths for daggers, pistols, garrote, manacles. I'll give you his name, if you like."

"Lord, I'm glad you're on our side." He saw his cousins, Ronan and Joshua, standing close by. "Take them with you."

"Gad, they're big fellows. Any runts in the Brayden litter?"

Romulus grinned. "I'm the runt."

He quickly explained the matter to his cousins and hurried to the relics room. If the Foresters planned to steal the donations, now would be the best time to do it. The Farthingales were at the front door collecting the entrance fee. The Braydens were in the grand hall, ready to protect Violet when she took the stage.

If he were Forester, he would grab whatever he could while everyone was occupied. The Foresters would not get all, of course. More would come in after Violet's recital. But they would get the thousands of pounds already brought in. Finn would turn over the donations without hesitation if the Foresters had pistols trained on Violet.

Violet. The thought she might be injured sent his heart pounding through his ears. *Stay safe, love. Don't resist. Let them take it all.*

The narrow hallway leading to the relics room was dark. Someone had put out the candles mounted on the wall sconces, for they had been lit when he'd left with Innes moments earlier.

He crept along in darkness, hardly breathing. Hardly daring to make a sound for fear it would cost Finn and Violet their lives. The laughter and general buzz of chatter filtered in from the grand hall. This area had been closed off, so he knew no one else would saunter down here. He was quite alone in this passageway and preferred it. He did not want the Foresters to panic and do something desperate.

He dared not simply burst into the room. Instead, he leaned his ear against it, hoping to hear something and locate the positions of Forester and his sister, Lady Rawley. If he could hear what they were saying, he could determine if they had pistols trained on Finn and Violet.

But all was quiet.

Then he heard a pistol shot and burst in like a raging bull, his only thought to shelter Violet and praying hard that she had not been injured...or worse. His gut twisted. Finn was lying motionless on the floor, and Violet was struggling with Lady Rawley and Forester. Pound notes were flying in the air, and some had already landed on the floor, now strewn all over place.

He realized immediately what had happened.

Violet—and he was going to give her a good talking to when the recital was over—had grabbed an ancient spear and used it to knock the box of donations out of Lady Rawley's hands. She was now swinging that spear wildly as Lady Rawley was trying to grab it away.

As Forester raised his pistol to aim it at Violet, Romulus grabbed the blackguard and flung him across the room, hearing the crack of bone as he slammed into the opposite wall hard enough to leave him dazed. His pistol had fallen from his hands, and Romulus hastily picked it up.

Then he grabbed Lady Rawley. She tried to hit him with her pistol, but that meant she had been the one to spend her shot. On Finn, obviously.

He handed Forester's loaded weapon to Violet. "Keep it aimed at Forester. If he stirs, shoot him. I'll be right back."

Violet set the spear back on its mount and turned breathlessly to Romulus. "Where are you going?"

"I sent Ian and my cousins out back. They must be there by now. If there are more ruffians waiting outside, I don't want you anywhere near them." But he still held on to Lady Rawley. She was struggling against him with all her might, although rather uselessly. All she could do was flail at him with her gloved fists.

He did not like the idea of carrying a woman into a possible fight, assuming one was going on out back. But neither could he leave her with Violet. And she'd been the one to shoot Finn.

He wanted to break the woman's neck. He might have, had he not blamed himself more for getting Finn involved in the first place. But as his rage was mounting, and he truly feared he would snap this woman's neck, Finn chose that moment to groan and attempt to rise.

He's alive. Blessed saints.

Romulus wanted to weep with relief. "Stay where you are, Finn. Help is on the way. Violet is safe."

Finn nodded. "Hurts like blazes. It's only my shoulder. But someone cracked me over the head...or I hit my head when I fell. I don't know."

"Doesn't matter. We'll sort it all out afterward. Lie still. It isn't quite over yet." He carefully opened the back door.

In the moonlight, he could make out a carriage. As his eyes adjusted better to the dim light, he saw that Ronan had the driver subdued. Joshua was holding on to a woman who was trying to kick him as she hurled epithets at him.

He recognized the sound of her voice. "Damn it, Felicia. What lunacy possessed you to get involved with these fools?"

She turned to him with open hatred in her gaze. "You bastard! You humiliated me."

"How? By marrying Violet?" He did not bother to hear her answer, for Finn was wounded, hopefully only a shoulder wound. "Ian," he said quietly, not sure how to break the news of their brother being shot to Ronan or Joshua just yet, "fetch George Farthingale and bring him to the relics room as fast as you can. Finn's hurt. And then summon the Duke of Lotheil to take care of these three and Forester."

He wasn't certain what to do with Lady Rawley who was still in his arms and had now joined Felicia in cursing him. The widow of a marquis and the wife of a viscount tossing out insults like the bawdiest bawds in any seedy dockside tavern. He'd laugh if this haughty pair hadn't caused so much damage.

He turned to his cousins. "Can I trust you to watch all three of them?" He wanted to be rid of Lady Rawley so he could hurry back to Violet. He'd been gone less than a minute, but it would only take a matter of seconds for Forester to do something rash. He didn't think Violet had it in her to shoot him if he lunged at her. But that bastard would not hesitate to shoot her if he got his hands back on his weapon.

"We'll watch them," Joshua assured.

Romulus hurried back.

Violet still had the pistol aimed at Forester.

"I'll take that, love." He eased it from her tense grasp. "Your Uncle George has been sent for. He'll tend to Finn."

"I think you broke Jameson's collarbone when you hurled him

against the wall. He ought to treat him as well."

"He will, after Finn."

Ian came in a moment later. "Lotheil's men are taking care of the driver and the ladies. I'll have them take Forester as well."

"No, he's injured. Uncle George should tend to him before he's removed," Violet said, her voice and hand obviously trembling.

Ian glanced at Romulus. "What's wrong with him?"

"Busted collarbone."

Ian nodded. "I can fix that. Done it often enough during the war." He strode toward Forester and helped him out of his jacket. Then with a brief warning to "hold still," he worked the bone back in place.

Forester howled.

Violet gasped.

Romulus took her in his arms. "Violet, love. Are you hurt at all?"

"No, just had the wits frightened out of me. Let's pick up all these donations and put them in the vault where they belong."

"I'll do it. Have a seat, and I'll pour you a cup of tea. It might help calm you down."

"No," Finn said, his words strained, for he was in obvious pain. "Don't drink it. I think they put something in it intending to knock you out, Violet. At least, I hope that's all they intended." He turned to Romulus. "They were mumbling something about tea, and it all makes sense to me now. They wanted Violet unconscious so they would only have to deal with me."

Romulus ran a hand through his hair. "And Innes was here, too. You both might have had that tainted brew. You both might have…"

His voice trailed off.

You both might have been killed had it been poisoned.

George arrived, took one look at Violet standing among these men, and frowned. "John is going to burst his spleen over this. Are you all right, Violet?"

She nodded. "I'm fine. Finn's been shot."

"I don't have my medical bag with me. I'll have to get him to my infirmary."

"Take my carriage," Ian said, having returned with George. "I'll have it brought around and will instruct my driver to wait so he can deliver you both to your homes once your work is done. In the meantime, I'll deposit Forester with Lotheil's men. Dillie and I can ride home with Gabriel and Daisy."

He hauled Forester to his feet.

Forester turned to Violet. "Sorry, Violet. But you know how it is."

"I don't, Jameson. You and Valerie were given every advantage in life. These orphans had nothing. You thought nothing of stealing from them."

He tossed back his head and laughed. "Want to know the irony of it? Their roof would not have crumbled. My father intended to give the abbess the funds to have it fixed. That's what gave me the idea for this recital. Save the orphans. Fix their roof. But we intended to take the proceeds for ourselves all along. Would have worked, too. We had it all arranged to be held up in front of witnesses as I took the donations to the bank."

Romulus wanted to strangle the fiend.

Violet looked ready to grab the spear she had just replaced on its mount and run Forester through with it. "You used me to steal from others. Perhaps destroy my reputation. Who would do such a thing to a friend?"

"Friend?" His expression turned vicious. "My sister and I hated you and Poppy. You were always the perfect children. Never complaining, always smiling. Sweet as treacle. We both thought it would be great fun to somehow pin the blame for the theft on you. But we really just wanted the donation funds. It wasn't worth plotting to implicate you. You simply weren't worth the bother."

"But the two of you would have known what you did and laughed about it behind my back."

"The plan would have worked if you hadn't suddenly married Brayden and brought him in on the planning."

She put a trembling hand to her throat. "Romulus never trusted you. He sensed you were up to no good. He was right all along."

Romulus wrapped an arm around Violet and drew her close, worried she was about to lose her composure. In truth, he was amazed she'd held herself together this long. She shivered against him and looked ashen, but he knew better than to suggest they cancel the recital. Ian had just hauled Forester out when applause began to filter down the hall into the relics room.

Romulus groaned. "It's time, Violet. Can you manage it?"

She wiped a tear off her cheek and nodded. "I'll be fine once I'm on stage. I'll sing my heart out. I'm so sorry I dragged you and your family into this mess."

He kissed her on the forehead. "No place I'd rather be than beside you, my love."

She took a deep breath and nodded.

The crowd roared as he escorted Violet to the stage. Her accompanist was already seated beside the pianoforte. Romulus scanned the crowd, still tense and worried something else might happen before the recital was over.

But after several glances around the hall, he eased. All was well in hand. Lotheil and his men were taking care of the culprits. George was treating Finn's wound. He wasn't certain whether he should tell Finn's mother, Lady Miranda.

No.

Miranda was a hellion. A riot would break out.

He would tell her after the recital, for this was Violet's night to shine, and he was not going to allow anyone to ruin it. Miranda would be angry with him, but better she take it out on him. It wasn't in her nature to stay angry for very long. Besides, Finn was a grown man. He did not need his mother getting in the way of whatever George had to do to treat his wound.

He turned back to the stage and stared at Violet, unable to look away.

So achingly beautiful.

Truly an angel.

This was her moment, and he was so proud of her.

He forced himself to return his attention to the crowd, for he had to remain vigilant. As his gaze drifted over the lords and ladies filling the hall, he saw Innes seated up front between Dillie and Daisy. These Farthingale sisters were quite beautiful, but the lad had his eyes fixed to the stage and the enchantress who now captured everyone's attention.

Violet started out with a medieval ballad that every Englishman knew. She then sang a Scottish ballad that had every Scot in the crowd wiping the tears from his eyes. Then a religious hymn, no doubt in honor of the abbess who ran the orphanage. She ended with another popular English madrigal about a brave medieval king and his knights who went off to fight for their kingdom.

The crowd would not stop cheering.

They wanted more.

Apparently, Violet had prepared for this. She sang another madrigal and then another ballad. When she finished the last, she stepped forward and raised her hands for quiet. After a moment, the audience hushed. "This last song is dedicated to my husband, Captain Romulus Brayden, and all the valiant sailors who serve in the Royal Navy. It is known as the Song of the Selkie."

Every seaman knew of this song and had heard it before, but never like this. Violet had a spectacular voice, yet this rendition of the popular Celtic legend left Romulus breathless.

Everyone felt the power of it.

The vast hall was as quiet as a tomb, the ethereal notes seeming to cast a spell over all of them.

No one dared breathe.

It was as though her voice rose from the depths of the ocean. Sad. Plaintive. Beautiful. It was a fairy song. The words were wistful. The refrain haunting.

Romulus felt himself transported to a rocky shore on the edge of the ocean. He imagined himself looking out on the windswept waters, blinking in disbelief as the other-worldly selkie of legend appeared before him and changed into the form of a woman...Violet.

For him, it would always be Violet, for only she had the power to steal his soul.

This was the lore of the selkie.

No man could look upon her and not fall hopelessly in love.

Romulus closed his eyes and allowed Violet's song to surround him, to carry him into the sea. His heart now beat to the rhythm of the waves as they swelled and ebbed, as they washed upon the shore with a soft *whoosh* and then drew back with the strong tug of the tide.

Romulus felt this ensorcelling tug, it drew all of him in and he was helpless to resist. It drew his soul into the watery depths. He was no longer in the Royal Society's grand hall but on that rocky beach. With each refrain, he heard the lapping waves, caught the salty scent of the sea filling his lungs, heard the cries of gulls and plovers who flew along the coast.

Her music continued to surround him. He saw his frigate with its sails unfurled, catching the wind and cutting across the water like a sleek, powerful dolphin, and the sun sinking over the horizon, turning the distant sky and sea waters a fiery gold.

Her song.

Her song.

Everything about it was magical.

She was magical.

He opened his eyes, surprised to find even himself tearing up. He feared to blink the tears away, afraid to somehow lose her. In this moment, she was the selkie who would one day slip back into the ocean, never to be seen again.

When the song ended, no one moved for the longest moment.

Men were sniffling, some were openly sobbing.

Then in one wave swell, everyone rose and began cheering.

Violet looked upon the audience in confusion, genuinely unaware of the profound impact of her song. She blushed and gave a quick bow, obviously wanting to hurry off the stage. But the Duke of Lotheil was not about to allow this night of brilliant triumph to pass without speeches. This grand hall had been named in his honor since he'd paid for its construction. He was on the board of the Royal Society.

He viewed this as his moment to shine as much as Violet's.

He meant to bask in all its glory.

Violet politely stood and smiled at his side.

As the duke spoke, Gabriel and Ian collected more donations.

Romulus had not been far off the mark when he'd told Violet the donors would be tossing wads of pound notes at the stage.

Five new orphanages could be built from the proceeds collected. He and Violet would speak with the abbess of St. Aubrey's about what to do with this bounty. The donations were sufficient to keep the place solvent for decades, allowing Sister Ursula to take in more children. Perhaps she would be open to acquiring a place in London to house the older children who now had to make their own way in the world.

Well, all this was for a later time.

Right now, Romulus wanted to take Violet and Innes home and see them comfortably settled before he rode to George's infirmary to make certain Finn was all right. He wouldn't leave Violet if she was too shaken, but he also had to tell Miranda that her son had been shot. He dared not put it off much longer.

He intended to do it before they left the Royal Society. It wasn't fair to keep her in the dark. Since Finn would likely be taken back to her home, Romulus hoped she would go straight there and prepare a bedchamber for Finn instead of running off like a crazed mother hen to George's infirmary.

He would have a lot of explaining to do to his family.

He would deal with it all tomorrow.

Right now, all he wanted to do was take Violet in his arms and never let her go.

His brother limped up to him and clapped him on the shoulder. "John and Sophie warned me these Farthingale girls were dangerous. I did not appreciate just how much." He clapped Romulus on the shoulder again, his grin now fading. "Seriously, are you all right, little brother? I heard there was some trouble."

"Yes, not a scratch on me. Violet, as you may have noticed, is also fine."

James nodded. "She sang like an angel. I've never heard anything so beautiful in all my life."

"Finn was hurt."

James nodded again. "Ronan just told me about it. He also mentioned Violet is quite handy with a spear."

Romulus emitted a long, deep breath. "I'm still shaken by the whole affair. I want to make certain she is truly all right. Having to go on and sing probably helped her. I'm amazed she managed to perform without her voice cracking. But I suppose singing is as natural to her as breathing."

"Still, it might hit her once everything quiets and she has nothing to distract her."

He nodded. "This is what worries me most. I want to take her home."

"Do it. The Braydens, Farthingales, and the Duke of Lotheil can deal with whatever's left to attend to tonight. Stay with Violet." He grinned at his brother. "You look ashen. Perhaps you are the one in need of calming."

He snorted. "I am. I stopped breathing when I saw her wielding that spear and Finn lying motionless on the floor. But I think his wound is superficial, thank goodness."

"I suppose I would have done the same if I'd seen my Sophie in that situation. But these women, as gentle as they may be, seem able to take care of themselves. Not that we'd ever admit it to them or ourselves. Your Violet is quite special. Look after her, Rom. I'll talk to you tomorrow." He turned to leave and then clapped him on the shoulder yet again. "I love you, little brother."

"Love you, too." He gave him a light punch on the arm.

Romulus cleared his throat and turned to smile at Violet who was now descending the steps of the stage. He reached for her hand. "Never letting go of you," he muttered.

"Did you say something? Sorry, I can't hear you over the chatter of the crowd."

He wanted to laugh. So much for amorous declarations. Violet couldn't hear a word

She lightly slapped her palm to her ear. "I think my ears are clogged. The Duke of Lotheil was bellowing his speech, and I couldn't back away."

Romulus laughed, loving how unaffected she was by the adoration of the throng. "I'll figure out something to unclog them."

She rolled her eyes. "Low brain at work again?"

He was still laughing. "Perhaps." He took her arm as they began to make their way through the rows of slowly exiting bodies. "Only if you are agreeable, Violet. Surely, you know I would never take advantage. I'm not that much of an oaf to force you into doing something you have no wish to do. You've been through a lot today."

He expected a response from her, not really minding if it was a jovial *yes, let's go at it like rabbits* or a more serious *no, don't touch me.*

But she said nothing.

Which worried him most.

What was going through her head?

CHAPTER TWENTY

V IOLET WAS GLAD to have Innes with them in the carriage. The
boy's youthful exuberance was a balm for her. His chatter kept
Romulus from asking prying questions she did not think she was able
to answer yet. What could she say? Perhaps beg his apology for
dragging him into this wretched recital. Apologize further for almost
getting his cousin killed.

She nibbled her lip, fretting about Finn. What if he did not heal
properly? What if he was left with complications from the shooting?
Could Romulus or any Brayden ever forgive her?

Now that the recital was over, the impact of what had happened
hit her all at once. People could have died because of her foolishness.
She'd been so caught up in her love of singing, she had dismissed
Romulus's concerns. It was only luck that neither she nor Innes had
taken the tainted tea. It was only luck that Finn had not been shot
straight through the heart.

She clasped her hands together as they began to tremble.

In truth, her entire body was trembling.

When they arrived home, she forced herself to smile at Innes and
wish him sweet dreams. She kissed him on the forehead.

The boy seemed to float up the staircase, he was so taken by the
gesture. Had no one ever kissed this boy goodnight?

"Oh, Romulus. Please see that he's properly tucked in," she whispered, her heart aching for this neglected boy.

"I will, love." He eyed her as though searching for something from her.

She managed another smile.

"I'll join you in our chamber in a few minutes." But he was now frowning at her.

She nodded, but kept silent as they climbed the stairs together.

She dismissed her maid, for the medieval gown was easy to slip off, and her hair was already unbound. There were only a few pins to take out. She removed her garments and laid them out across one of the tall chairs, then donned the nightrail set out for her on the bed. She poured water into her basin and scrubbed her hands and face, somehow feeling the need to scrub the dirt of this evening off her.

But as she sank onto the bed and sat atop the covers, she suddenly broke down and cried. What if Romulus hated her forever? How could she bear it? She loved him so much.

She must have been crying too hard to hear him when he entered, only realizing he'd come in when he sank onto the mattress and took her in his arms. "Violet, love. I was afraid of this."

"I am so abjectly sorry," she said between tearful gasps of breath.

Romulus lifted her onto his lap and tipped her chin up, forcing her to face him. "You have nothing to apologize for. You are not at fault for any of what happened tonight."

"Are you mad? I am responsible for all of it."

He put his arms around her. "You are responsible for loving your mother so much, you wanted to do something to benefit the home where she grew up. Where is the wrong in that?"

"The Foresters used me, knowing how vain I was about my singing."

He kissed the top of her head. "You have one of the most exquisite voices in the world. Your voice is magic and lightens the heart of all who hear it. If I sang even one-tenth as well as you do, my head would be so enormously swelled, it couldn't fit through our bedchamber door. If anything, you are ridiculously modest about your talent."

He put a finger over her mouth when she opened it to protest. "No, love. And don't you dare blame yourself for Finn. You didn't shoot him. I'm the one who brought him into the charity affair and demanded he be put in charge of the donations."

"Still…"

He groaned. "Violet, there is nothing you can do to make me hold you responsible. There is nothing on this earth that will ever stop me from loving you for all the days of my life."

"Romulus…" She took a deep, shattered breath.

"I mean it, Violet. You overwhelm me. I never expected to love another being as deeply as I love you. I did not think such depth of feeling was possible. But it is. I don't care what your Book of Love says about developing connections over time. We are connected. Irrevocably. Profoundly. Perhaps across time."

"But my singing–"

"Was wonderful. You reduced every man to tears with the beauty of your songs. That last one about the selkie was magnificent. I think Innes and I will stand on deck at sundown every evening and blubber like infants as we watch the sun sink into the water. My men will think we are deranged."

She laughed. "I still feel so badly."

"I know. But don't blame yourself for the evil of others. No one else does."

She nodded, more to placate him than to take his words to heart.

"Let me kiss you, will you, love?" He bent his head to hers and tasted her plump, yielding lips. In short order, his clothes were off as was her nightgown. She stood before him, her beautiful body illuminated in moonlight.

He set her on the bed and settled over her, purposely taking his time to worship her luscious body. Mostly, he worried about how she was feeling. He did not want their coupling to be merely her duty, or her way to compensate for Forester's betrayal. Sex with her was one thing. An act of beauty. A *willing* act.

Forgiveness sex was quite another, an act of contrition. Remorse. Sacrifice. Atonement. She had done nothing that required anyone's forgiveness, least of all his. "Violet, are you all right with this?"

"With me in your arms? With you loving me?" She put her arms around his neck. "Yes, Romulus. I love you. It's me I don't care for very much at the moment. I'm still upset with myself."

Romulus propped up on his elbows, not quite knowing what to do to make her feel better. What concerned him most was that he would be off for Cornwall in a few days and did not want her tormenting herself over this during the months of his absence. "Forester wins if you continue to blame yourself for what is squarely his fault. I'll take you to see Finn tomorrow." He hoped his cousin would be in decent enough condition to see them. "Will you believe his assurances?"

"Your Aunt Miranda—"

"Is probably angry she wasn't in on the fight. We're a military family, love. The Brayden men are big and fearsome, but we are nothing to the women. Have I told you how Miranda took a fire iron to some very nasty fellows attempting to destroy my cousin Marcus's wife and her father? Marcus had to haul Miranda off them. She was out for their blood."

Violet's eyes widened in surprise. "Are you saying this to make me feel better?"

"No, I'm saying it because it's true. You'll see for yourself tomorrow." He kissed her softly on the lips. "Don't punish yourself. I can't bear to see you unhappy. Smile for me, Violet. This is how I want to see you in my dreams. Happy. Your eyes aglow. A beautiful smile on your face."

She nodded.

"And one more thing...Miranda will be jealous as hell when we tell her how you beat off the Foresters with a spear."

Violet laughed and reached out to draw him down atop her. He felt the shift in her temperament, knew she was letting go of her anguish, for her body was beginning to relax and she was no longer curled inward and erecting walls. He breathed a silent sigh of relief when she responded to his renewed caresses.

When he cupped her breast and began to suckle it, she gasped and clasped her hands to his head so tightly, his nose became buried in her creamy flesh. He meant to breathe through his mouth, but his lips and tongue were also occupied. This was the beauty of a man's low brain. The low brain would rather starve the man of breath than warn him to peel his mouth off a soft breast.

He kissed a trail to her other breast, licking and suckling it while at the same time stroking his hand downward until his fingers found her slick, intimate core. She moaned softly and whispered his name. "Romulus."

Their coupling was tender, their bodies hot as they rubbed against each other with every thrust. The feel of her soft skin against his rougher flesh was exciting, igniting. He rolled her atop him and guided her movements, his hands gripping her hips and his eyes practically lolling back in his head with the exquisite pleasure of watching her move.

Her firm breasts were thrust out, their rosy peaks an agonizingly sweet temptation.

Her hair cascaded down her back, reminding him of a waterfall of dark silk.

Everything about her aroused him.

His hands remained clasped on either side of her hips as he guided her to heightened pleasure. He slowed his thrusts. She responded, moaning and moving her hips, urging him to sink deeper inside her until she lost herself in the moment, in the feeling. In her ecstasy.

He felt the heat and shuddering release of her climax, her body so beautiful as it soared toward starlight. Only once she began to calm did he take his own release, and followed her soon after toward that same starlight. "Violet, I love you."

She fell asleep in his arms, her warm body curling around the hard muscle of his. She awoke the same way in the morning, curled like a kitten against him, her back to his chest and her arms wrapped around one of his.

Romulus had intended to get up early, but there was something about the way she clung to him, and he felt it was more important to remain in bed. He needed to be beside her when she opened her eyes.

He knew he'd made the right decision when she blinked her eyes open and cast him a glowing smile. "Good morning."

He rolled onto his side and kissed her. "Good morning, love."

"Oh, dear. What time is it? I'm sure we've overslept."

He did not stop her when she scrambled out of bed, but merely rose along with her. "Not too late. It's only eight o'clock."

"Innes must be awake."

"Possibly. The Mayhew girls are taking good care of him, I'm sure." He watched as she tossed on her robe. It hugged her soft curves, the light fabric sensually draping over her breasts. *Magnificent breasts.* "How do you feel, Violet?"

"About myself?" Her smile faltered. "I'm not sure yet."

"Then let's start with an easier question. How do you feel about me?"

She laughed softly and shook her head. "About you? That is an easy one. I'm wildly in love with you, Captain Brayden."

"Feeling is mutual, Mrs. Brayden." As tempted as he was to carry Violet back to bed, Romulus knew there was too much to do today. His first task was to get that giant weight of blame off Violet's slender shoulders.

Next was to prepare for his departure. Lord, this was going to be difficult. He was tempted to take her with him to Cornwall, but dared not suggest it now. There was work to be done first to subdue the emboldened pirates. But once they had chased down the culprit who had burned Erskine's ship, he expected activity to quiet down.

He would send for Violet then.

After washing and dressing, they walked downstairs together and entered the dining room. Innes was already there, sitting quietly and toying with his eggs. He brightened as soon as he caught sight of Violet and jumped up to politely greet her.

She hugged him as though it was the most natural thing in the world, and then crossed to the buffet to serve herself from the salvers set out upon it.

Romulus smothered a grin as he followed Violet's lead and helped himself to eggs and slices of cold ham. Innes could not stop staring at Violet. He realized the boy believed she was a selkie, and he was waiting for her to transform back into a seal…or mermaid…or other magical being.

"It's only a song, Innes. Violet will not shed her skin and disappear into the ocean. She'll be waiting for us right here when we return to London in another three months."

The boy seemed disappointed to learn she was not a mythical creature. But he quickly got over it when they told him Charles was waiting for him at the Farthingale residence next door. "To play marbles?"

Violet nodded.

The boy cheered.

Within the hour, they were all ready to walk next door.

Romulus was eager to find out what had happened after he'd taken Violet and Innes home. Sophie and John had remained at the Royal Society and would know. He wanted to ask about the donations as well as learn more about Finn.

Had John received any news from George? It would help Violet's spirits immensely to hear positive news about Finn's condition.

Innes went off to play marbles with Charles.

Romulus was relieved, for he preferred the boy to be upstairs playing and not beside Violet if she became upset. Although he was optimistic about Finn's condition, it was possible his injuries were worse than anyone thought.

"How is Belle feeling this morning?" Violet asked when Sophie greeted them and ushered them into John's study.

Drat, in all the excitement, Romulus had forgotten about Violet's cousin.

"She's doing better," Sophie said, taking a seat and motioning for them to make themselves comfortable. "But still not fully recovered. This London weather isn't very good for her. George thinks she ought to be fine in another few days, that she only needs another day or two to adjust to it. Eloise has invited us all to tea at her home next Friday."

Romulus glanced at Violet. "I may be gone by then. I'll do my best to put off my departure to Saturday. But Violet will attend. I assume Lady Withnall will be there."

Sophie rolled her eyes. "Yes, they are best friends, although I can not understand why dear Eloise is friendly with that gossipmonger. Lady Withnall seems to have a nose for scandal. She is always present whenever it is afoot."

Violet laughed. "Well, I think we'll be safe enough at Eloise's tea. Romulus and I are already married. What can possibly happen?"

Romulus and Sophie exchanged glances and then laughed.

When John joined them, he and Sophie told them what had happened at the Royal Society after they'd left. "After securing the donations, Ian and Gabriel went off with the Duke of Lotheil to deal with the Foresters and Lady Felicia. All three are well-connected. They won't be put in prison, of course. Lady Rawley's husband will deal with her. Lord Forester's father will deal with him. Unfortunately, Lady Felicia is independent and answers to no one."

Violet frowned. "She's an odious woman. Is there anything we can do about her?"

"The Duke of Lotheil will deal with her," John said. "I would not be surprised if she suddenly left town on an extended voyage."

"Good riddance," Romulus muttered.

Violet clasped her hands together and took a deep breath. "What about Finn?"

Her uncle smiled. "George stopped by after dropping him off at Lady Miranda's house. He's fine. That is, he will fully recover. The shot grazed his shoulder, tearing mostly through flesh."

"But you'll see for yourself when you visit him," Sophie added. "Would you mind if Innes stayed here? He and Charles play so nicely together."

"Thank you, Aunt Sophie. It would be very helpful." She nodded toward Romulus. "We ought to stop by the Royal Society to pick up the donations. Finn was going to take care of it, but I'm sure he is in no condition to do it now."

Romulus took hold of Violet's hand. "We'll take care of it tomorrow once the bank opens. I'll bring Ronan and Joshua along with me. No one is likely to take on three Brayden men. But you and I can look in on Finn today."

John cleared his throat. "I know today is Sunday and the bank is usually closed. However, the Duke of Lotheil happens to be chairman of the bank. He's offered to open it for you this afternoon since there's a tidy sum to deposit, and he knows you won't rest easy until it is delivered to the bank. You may prefer to get it done today. No one will expect it."

"That's quite generous of him. Yes, I'd like to have the funds safely deposited as soon as possible," Romulus said.

By the afternoon, the donations were securely in the bank's orphanage account, and they were now calling upon Finn. To Violet's relief, he was seated in Lady Miranda's library, dressed and seeming quite comfortable while reading a book. Only the sling on his arm gave away his injury.

He rose to greet them, showing little difficulty in his movements. "Ah, the Viking shield maiden has come to visit."

"More of a spear maiden," Romulus said with a chuckle, winking at Violet.

"Finn, I–"

Finn raised a hand to interrupt her. "Before you say anything, let me apologize to you. Romulus warned me about the pair, but I did not fully appreciate the danger. I was careless and put you in peril."

Violet shook her head. "No, it is I who should be begging your forgiveness. I was so swept away by the chance to sing, I believed whatever they told me. I wanted to trust them, even though Romulus instinctively knew the sort of people they were. How do you feel?"

Finn arched an eyebrow. "Truthfully?"

She nodded.

"Pretty damn good. I can now show off my wound and tell all the ladies how I acquired it foiling a robbery. I'll embellish a little, of course. And I hope you don't mind if I say nothing about your saving me. Lady Rawley's aim was dead on. She would have killed me if you hadn't knocked her arm askew with the spear."

Violet rolled her yes. "Oh, yes. Do keep me out of your swashbuckling tales."

Finn took Violet's hand and raised it to his lips. "Thank you, Violet. I'm sorry for the trouble they caused, and I'm most sorry I had to miss your recital. I heard it was the event of the season. You sang like an angel, my mother said."

Romulus nodded. "She did. She was magnificent."

"I look forward to hearing you sing next time. I'll try my best not to get shot."

Violet shook her head vehemently. "No, this was a one-time affair. I have no intention of making a spectacle of myself again."

Romulus frowned. "You were brilliant, Violet. You lightened the hearts of everyone in the audience." An idea had been taking seed in his mind. He'd said nothing earlier, but decided this might be the right time. "Would you consider giving a recital for the wounded sailors returned from war? They've fought around the world for England. Most will never return to sea, never be taken back into the Royal Navy. But the sea is in their blood. Your Song of the Selkie will stir their hearts, give them hope as nothing else will."

Violet gazed at him in confusion. "You want me to sing?"

He nodded. "Your voice is a gift. Share it however you wish. But you mustn't hide it."

She nibbled her lip. "I'll think about it. But I won't do another recital on such a grand scale. I felt like a nightingale trapped in a cage."

"These homes for forgotten seamen are not very big. Even the largest would house no more than fifty."

"Fifty?"

"Violet, love. I want you to do whatever makes you happy." He took her in his arms and peered over her head to where Finn stood grinning. "I'm not telling you what to do, but I think this is a perfect solution. The men in these homes as well as the military hospitals are in desperate need of cheering. They would appreciate your recital more than words can say."

"I like the idea," Finn said. "These old warriors do need something to look forward to in their difficult lives. You would ease their hearts, Violet."

"Your reason to be, my love." Romulus spoke softly.

Her heart lurched. Yes, to use her gift of song to do some good in the world was all she'd ever hoped for. Also, to be able to help out the retired seamen would make her feel closer to Romulus, perhaps ease the pain of their separation. She sighed. "It's perfect. I'd love to do it."

CHAPTER TWENTY-ONE

"VIOLET, LOVE. I'LL be back in three months," Romulus said yet again, needing to reassure himself as much as he needed to reassure his wife that their separation would be relatively brief and tolerable. It was Friday, the day of Lady Dayne's tea party, and they were walking the short distance, two houses down, to the kindly dowager's residence.

Violet placed her arm in his. "Belle and Honey are here for the season to keep me company, and my parents will return shortly. Until then, the Mayhew nieces and our other household retainers will take care of me. Not to mention Uncle John and Aunt Sophie live right next door and will look in on me every day. I'm sure your family will come by often as well." She smiled up at him. "I doubt I'll be alone for a moment. Indeed, I'll be glad when you and Innes return so I may finally have peace in the house."

He and Innes were to leave first thing tomorrow morning, but for the moment, the boy was hopping beside them, happy to be anywhere near Violet. "Innes," she said, "I'll pack three tins of ginger cake for you to take on your journey. They are for you, and you needn't share them with anyone, not even my husband."

His eyes widened, and he cast Romulus a questioning glance. He released the breath he had been holding when Romulus nodded his approval. Innes turned to Violet. "Thank you, Mrs. Brayden!"

She laughed lightly, the sound a sweet, melodic trill that warmed

Romulus's heart. "But you mustn't devour the cakes all at once. They'll last for a while in their tins."

The boy nodded and skipped ahead, for Lady Dayne had also invited Charles and his bag of marbles to the tea. Innes and Charles had become good friends. Romulus knew the pair would duck out of the parlor and ensconce themselves somewhere out of the way to play with their aggies and mibs.

He glanced at Violet, noticed she was nipping her lower lip, and wondered what she was thinking of now. "Are you all right, love?"

She nodded. "I gave The Book of Love to Belle this morning."

"Ah, the magical tome notorious for bringing reluctant bachelors to heel." He shook his head and laughed. "Does something more need to be done? Now that Belle has it, some poor sod is going to fall hard."

"It is gaining a reputation, isn't it?" She shook her head. "I acted on impulse, and now I'm worried that I ought to have given it to Honey instead. She's the elder. Belle is my age, and Honey is two years older. Did I make a mistake in handing it to Belle first?"

"Does it feel like a mistake?"

"In truth, it doesn't. Now that I am so spectacularly happy and have married the man of my dreams..." She paused to cast him an impish grin. "I know the book needs to be given over to someone else. Belle or Honey, of course. Logically, it should have been Honey. But my heart told me to give it to Belle."

"Then don't fret. You made the right choice."

Romulus held her back a moment and gave her a soft kiss on the lips, not particularly caring who saw them. Violet was his wife, and he was a besotted fool when it came to her. He never imagined marriage could feel so good. "Go with your heart, love. After all, it led you to me."

She nodded. "What do your instincts tell you?"

"Oh, no. Don't get me involved in your matchmaking schemes." He laughed and raked his fingers through his hair. "My instincts are telling me to forget the tea and carry you back to our bedchamber where I can explore your delectable body for uninterrupted hours on end. You're frowning at me, so I see that I have spoken out of turn. Well, you asked me. I can't help it if my beautiful wife stirs my low brain lust."

"Belle," she quietly blurted as they were about to walk into Lady Dayne's parlor and mingle with her other guests. "It must be Belle."

"You're suddenly certain?"

"The feeling just came over me." She scanned the crowd in search of her cousin but did not see her. "Oh, Romulus. Something's going to happen. My body's tingling, and the air feels charged."

"Here? Now?" He grinned. "I could make another stupid comment about my low brain and carry you home. Just say the word."

She rolled her eyes. "Oh, I see Lady Withnall."

He gave a mock sigh. "Ah, there she is, eyeing us both with her beady, weasel eyes from across the room."

Violet slapped him lightly on the shoulder and laughed. "Be nice to her, you wicked man! Oh, there's your cousin, Finn. I'm so glad he accepted Lady Dayne's invitation. He looks well, doesn't he? He isn't even wearing a sling on his arm. I'm so relieved."

Romulus escorted her through the crowded parlor. "Let's greet our hostess and then we can chat with Finn. Unless you'd rather find your cousins first." He looked around the room. "I see Honey, but I don't see Belle."

"She must be somewhere around. I know she's here. Probably in a quiet corner. She's shy. I would have heard if she wasn't feeling well and had decided to stay home. She was in the pink of health when I saw her this morning. Looking quite lovely, actually."

They greeted Lady Dayne and Lady Withnall.

Romulus stifled a grin as Violet impulsively reached out and gave the tiny termagant a sincere hug. "Thank you again, Lady Withnall," she whispered. "Thank you again and again with all my heart."

To his surprise, the old woman's features crumbled, and she appeared genuinely touched, almost as though she was about to cry. "I'm glad to see you both so happy, my dear. But it is the bees who must be thanked for bringing you and your scandalously gorgeous husband together."

Whatever Violet meant to say was cut short when Charles and Innes tore into the room. "Captain Brayden," Innes said breathlessly, his eyes once again wide. "Something's happened."

The boy tugged at his hand, but Romulus held him back a moment. "What is it, Innes?"

"It's your cousin, Finn, and Mrs. Brayden's cousin, Belle."

He groaned. "Oh, no. What happened?"

No, no, no. It can't be. It's just a book.

He cast a glance at Violet who clearly looked confused, horrified, and perhaps gleeful. Was that a matchmaking glint in her eyes?

By this time, the boys were gathering a crowd. Mostly Farthingales, but there were other guests present. Lady Withnall's nose was twitching like a rabbit's and her ears were wiggling. This could not be good. "Innes. Charles. You ought to tell me what happened in private."

"There isn't time," young Charles said, hopping on one leg. "They're in the garden. Belle touched him like this..." Charles slid his hand up and down himself, directly over his little crotch.

John Farthingale had just taken a sip of his tea and now sprayed it out of his mouth. His wife pounded him on his back as he began to cough. "Oh, John. Surely, it's all an innocent misunderstanding," Sophie crooned, but her words did nothing to soothe John's mounting ire.

"Then Finn grabbed her in his arms, because she started making strange sounds," Innes added unhelpfully.

"What sounds?" Violet asked before Romulus could stop her. Despite being married to him, a low brain cad who could not get enough of her in a primal, carnal way, she was still remarkably innocent.

"Um, she was breathing heavily," Innes replied.

"This kind of sound." Charles began to moan.

"More like this," Innes corrected and made suggestive sounding gasps.

"Brayden, I'm going to kill your cousin," John muttered.

"Boys, there must be some mistake." Blessed saints! Was Finn…what the hell was he doing to Belle?

Lady Withnall's nose was now madly twitching.

Romulus had to get to his cousin before anyone saw whatever the idiot was doing to Belle. Only Finn wasn't an idiot. He was one of the smartest men in London, but perhaps not when it came to women. "Where are they?"

"In the garden," Innes said. "They toppled on the grass. She was still moaning when we ran inside to tell you."

Romulus tore out of the house, Violet on his heels. "Finn! Are you insane?" His cousin had his hand on Belle's chest and was pressing down on it. At the same time, he had his mouth on Belle's mouth. There was a logical explanation, of course.

The damn Book of Love.

Finn looked up, shocked to see the crowd gathering around them. "She can't catch her breath. Where's her sister? She'll know what to do."

As Honey raced forward, Romulus drew Violet back. "This explains her heavy breathing. But…why was she touching him?"

Violet's eyes were still wide in horror, confusion, and yes, glee. "I don't know." She turned in dismay to Lady Withnall who was now hovering close to Finn as he took guidance from Belle's sister while he lifted Belle into his arms.

"Why are your pants wet?" Lady Withnall asked Finn. "Did you spill tea all over yourself?"

Finn merely scowled at the incorrigible snoop.

Belle appeared to be over the worst of her attack, her breathing less erratic now.

"Put your arms around my neck," Finn told her, now carrying her toward Lady Dayne's parlor.

Romulus remained in the garden with Violet as the small crowd followed Finn back inside. "Did you have to give her that book before the tea?"

Violet's mouth gaped open. "I'm so sorry, Romulus. It was just sitting there on our bureau, and I suddenly felt compelled to bring it over to Belle." She stared at him. "Do you think...?"

"No. It can't be." Even though he had been thinking the same thing himself only a moment ago. "It's just a damn book. An old book. Faded red cover." He ran a hand through his hair in consternation. "Lady Withnall saw it all."

Violet gave a laughing groan. "There's also the Chipping Way curse. Poor Finn. He didn't stand a chance. If the book didn't get him, the bachelor curse of this street did. I'll talk to Lady Withnall. I'll explain about Belle's difficulty breathing. Those attacks can be frightening when they occur, and there's rarely any warning when they do. Should we follow them in? Finn might need your help."

"No, love. Too late. Nothing to do but hope they'll be as happy as we are in wedded bliss." He took Violet in his arms. "Lord, I'm going to miss you. The lavender scent of your body. The silky warmth of your skin. Your spectacular violet eyes."

"My singing," she teased.

"I love your voice. I love you, my beautiful songbird." He scooped her into his arms.

She gasped. "What are you doing? People are watching."

"No, they're not. All eyes are on my addle-pated cousin. Oh, Lady Miranda will be happy as a lark when she learns Finn's going to marry."

"Don't be ridiculous. Belle will not agree to it."

"You weren't inclined either. Look where it got you?" He kissed her on the lips. "Got you into my bed, that's for sure. And I'm not complaining." He started to carry her out of the garden.

"Romulus! We can't leave."

"Of course we can, love. No one gives a rat's arse about us now. But I care. I'm going to enjoy my wife until the moment I have to leave for Cornwall. Your aunt will bring Innes home once the tea is over. You'll have all day tomorrow to find out what happened after we left. I love you, Violet. Don't deprive me of the pleasure of having you in my arms."

She sighed and rested her head against his shoulder. "I won't, my love."

He kissed her again. "Bollocks, I'm going to miss you."

Violet did not think it was possible to already miss someone when that person was still beside her, but she did. "I'll miss you desperately, too."

She was going to miss young Innes as well. The boy absorbed affection like a sponge, but it twisted her heart to know how badly he'd been deprived of it. He could have done with a little more time in a loving home. Perhaps this would be one of her next projects, learning more about the Duke of Buchan and his feelings for his son.

However, she set aside thoughts of everyone but Romulus as her spectacularly gorgeous husband carried her upstairs to make scandalous love to her in the afternoon.

Good heavens, he was naughty!

But she supposed, when it came to Romulus, so was she.

CHAPTER TWENTY-TWO

London, England
September 1820

VIOLET WAS HOSTING a tea party at home when Romulus and Innes surprised everyone by tromping into the parlor to the cheers and greetings of the guests. They looked travel-worn and dusty, but Violet was too happy to see them to care about ruining her gown with their road dirt. She set down her teacup and ran into Romulus's outstretched arms. "Romulus!" she shouted for joy, her heart ready to burst with happiness.

"It's good to be home, love." He swept her into his arms and kissed her thoroughly, his rough growth of beard scratching her cheek as they embraced each other. He reluctantly released her, no doubt realizing friends and family were coughing and giggling at his show of affection.

Blushing, Violet turned to greet Innes.

"We didn't expect you until tomorrow," she said, giving the boy a heartfelt hug and ruffling his hair. "Look how big you've grown." The lad was as tall as she was now. "Did you enjoy your time at sea?"

Innes nodded. "Mostly it was quiet, but sometimes we fought pirates."

Violet studied both of them closely, relieved they appeared unharmed. She would learn more from Romulus later. "Innes, I'm glad you came a day early. There's someone here who would like to see you. I know you must be tired and hungry, but indulge me a moment and go wait for me in the study."

He nodded. "Is it Charles? Is he here?"

"Yes, he's here, and you shall see him in a moment. But there's someone else I'd like you to see first."

The boy obediently trotted off.

Romulus frowned. "What's going on, love?"

She sighed. "Don't be angry with me, but I've been meddling."

He arched an eyebrow, looking quite wickedly rugged and immensely appealing. "What? A Farthingale meddle? Unheard of."

She grinned. "The Duke of Buchan is here. I wrote to him."

Romulus groaned. "Violet, why?"

"I couldn't bear to see Innes so poorly treated…well, it's done. He paid a call on me when he arrived in town last week. He came alone, without wife number three. The woman is awful. I think the duke is regretting the marriage, but that's between the two of them. He wants to see his son. He loves the boy, and I cannot tell you how relieved he was to know Innes had been placed in your care. He was also most appreciative that we took the lad into our home. He's been waiting for your return, hoping Innes won't hate him for sending him off as brusquely as he did."

She eased out of Romulus's arms. "Let me introduce him to you, and then we must give him time alone with his son."

The duke had been standing beside Lady Dayne and Lady Withnall. He appeared eager to meet Romulus, so Violet left their side to allow the two men a moment of privacy. "Innes and I will await you in the study. Join us whenever you are ready, Your Grace."

Romulus and the duke strode in very soon afterward. Violet was just about to ask the boy if he was thirsty, but held off when the men walked in. She could feel his youthful excitement and apprehension. His little heart was surely beating wildly. "Father…"

"Innes." Tears formed in the duke's eyes as he opened his arms to his son. The boy ran to him. Soon, both father and son were hugging and crying.

Violet had tears in her eyes as she and Romulus slipped out of the room. When he remained silent a long moment, Violet took the opportunity to tell him of her exchange of letters with Sister Ursula and the plans for repair of the orphanage. "And I've also been giving weekly recitals at the war homes and local hospitals."

Romulus took her hand in his and gave it a light squeeze. "You've been quite busy."

"Never too busy to miss you. I'm so glad you're home. How long will I have you all to myself?"

"I don't know yet. But let's not think of it now. I missed you so very much. I went on deck every evening at sunset and watched the golden light fade over the water. I heard your song carried on the wind. It was as though you were standing beside me, smiling up at me." He grinned. "Singing to me. Yes, *singing*. Because even though you think I detest music, the truth is I love you."

He took a deep breath and caressed her check. "I'll love you forever, no matter where in this world fate and fortune take my ship. You will always be with me, my love. My sweet, beautiful Violet. How did I exist without you?"

"You managed quite well, I'm sure," she teased.

But his expression remained serious and achingly tender. "No, never. I still cannot believe my good fortune. You are so special to me. You are the sweet song of my heart."

"Does this mean you wish me to sing to you?"

He groaned.

"Because I know how much you love it, especially in the morning. Before you've had your morning coffee." She was still teasing him, wanting to coax a smile to his lips.

He shook his head and laughed. Then he bent his head and gave her an exquisitely bone-melting kiss. "How fast can we get rid of our guests? My low brain is in a spawning frenzy."

She blushed and eased away, putting a hand over her stomach. "Speaking of spawning…Romulus, my love. I have something quite wonderful to tell you."

Also by Meara Platt

FARTHINGALE SERIES
My Fair Lily
The Duke I'm Going To Marry
Rules For Reforming A Rake
A Midsummer's Kiss
The Viscount's Rose
Earl Of Hearts
If You Wished For Me
Never Dare A Duke
Capturing The Heart Of A
Cameron

THE BOOK OF LOVE SERIES
The Look of Love
The Touch of Love
The Taste of Love
The Song of Love
The Scent of Love
The Kiss of Love

THE BRAYDENS
A Match Made In Duty
Earl of Westcliff
Fortune's Dragon
Earl of Kinross
Pearls of Fire

DARK GARDENS SERIES
Garden of Shadows
Garden of Light
Garden of Dragons
Garden of Destiny

De WOLFE "ANGELS"
SERIES
Nobody's Angel
Kiss An Angel
Bhrodi's Angel

About the Author

Meara Platt is a USA Today bestselling author and an award winning, Amazon UK All-star. Her favorite place in all the world is England's Lake District, which may not come as a surprise since many of her stories are set in that idyllic landscape, including her award winning paranormal romance Dark Gardens series. If you'd like to learn more about the ancient Fae prophecy that is about to unfold in the Dark Gardens series, as well as Meara's lighthearted, international bestselling Regency romances in the Farthingale series, Book of Love series, and the Braydens series, please visit Meara's website at www.mearaplatt.com.

CPSIA information can be obtained
at www.ICGtesting.com
Printed in the USA
LVHW010939230821
695886LV00002B/150

9 781676 453574